CHRISTMAS
GRACE

CHRISTMAS GRACE

MINDY STEELE

Preview of *The Amish Cowboy's Homecoming*
Copyright © 2021 by Ophelia London

Entangled Publishing, LLC
10940 S Parker Road
Suite 327
Parker, CO 80134
Visit our website at www.entangledpublishing.com.

Amara is an imprint of Entangled Publishing, LLC.

Edited by Stacy Abrams
Cover design by Elizabeth Turner Stokes
Cover art by Photographer Tom Hallman
Alex Stemmer/shutterstock
robert_s/shutterstock
Delmas Lehman/shutterstock
Interior design by Toni Kerr

Print ISBN 978-1-68281-511-3
ebook ISBN 978-1-68281-512-0

Manufactured in the United States of America
First Edition November 2021

AMARA

AUTHOR NOTE

While I have lived near the Amish of Northern Kentucky, this novel and its characters are completely fictional. There is no intended resemblance between the characters in this book and any real members of the Amish community. Regardless of my research and hope to bring realism through the pages, each Amish community differs from another. Therefore, any inaccuracies of the Amish lifestyles in this book are completely my own.

GLOSSARY

ach: oh
aenti: aunt
all recht: all right
appeditlich: delicious
blut: blood
boppli: baby
bruders: brothers
bu: boy
buwe: boys
daed: dad
dawdi: granddad
danke: thank you
dochder: daughter
dummkopp: dunce
ehemann: husband
faul: lazy
fraa: wife, woman
freind: friend
freinden: friends
Englischer: English person, not Amish
Gott: God
gut: good
gut morgen: good morning
haus: house
hund: dog, hound

jah: yes

kaffi: coffee

kapp: cap, prayer covering worn by Amish women

kind: child

kinner: children

kumm: come

lieb: love

maedel: girl, or young woman

mamm: mom

mammi: grandmother

mann: man

mutter: mother

nacht: night

nee: no

onkle: uncle

Ordnung: Amish behavioral code: an unwritten set of rules and regulations that guide everyday Amish life.

rumschpringe: "run around time" a period of freedom for Amish youth before baptism

schee: pretty

sohn: son

stolze: prideful

verboden: forbidden

wunderbaar: wonderful

To Julie, who took a chance.
To Mom, who pushed me.
To Mike, you stepped up and let me dream.
You are all the givers of wings.

CHAPTER ONE

Grace Miller stepped cautiously across the lopsided porch of the old cabin, a deep sense of doom hanging over her small shoulders like a dark cloud. *Built on a tilt*, she thought to herself, eyeing the overhang of rotted wood and leaning post attached to the structure.

Her eldest sister, Charity, would have come to the same conclusion if she were here. Only Charity *wouldn't* be here. None of her four sisters would ever be where Grace was. Only Grace would be foolish enough to go against everything she had ever known to be right here.

She shook her head slowly, keeping a tight hold on unshed tears. She was not dreaming. This was very real.

She obediently followed her *aenti* up the untrusty step. Moving inside the doorway, she whispered a silent prayer for strength to endure this next trial as her eyes took in the room. Her home for the coming months was nothing like the one her *mutter* had described so kindly before she left. If a quaint little cabin had ever rested on this forgotten piece of dry earth, she wished it would present itself now.

The driveway itself, steep and perilous and certainly not maintained, had taken a herculean amount of effort for the poor horse to climb just to get here. Grace's shoulders slumped, suddenly realizing she would not again have such a luxury. If she was to ever travel beyond these four worn-out old walls, it would be on foot.

Being shunned in her community had been hard, but

she had endured it. Getting banned from her father's house
and the comforts it had given meant no horse and no buggy, which she had accepted. Living here for the months
ahead, would be the worst punishment of all. Her mistake
was a bitter taste on her tongue, and there was no washing
that down. The weight of everything she had brought upon
herself was too heavy to bear, but she had no choice.

Life wasn't all about her now.

And with that very thought, she pushed back her small
shoulders and lifted her chin. She had never been a quitter
before. She needed to think positively, just as Faith had
encouraged her. Think positively regardless of this gloom
and decay in front of her.

Walnut Ridge and its Kentucky hillsides and winding
roads was nothing like Indiana. She already missed
Havenlee and its sweet scents of open air and fresh mowed
hay, and here it had been only a few hours since she
boarded the bus and bid her home farewell. She would
miss the smells of her *mutter*'s kitchen, of water from the
nearby lake, the flat ground of her childhood, and the long
roads that one could see for a good distance.

Here everything was all up and down and left and right,
just plain curvy in every direction. And dry. Not a spit of
moisture anywhere, unless one counted what the overly
warm season was stripping from her pores. At least she was
on her own two feet. Rattled nerves and fear, they were
strong adversaries.

Dropping her blue bag, the few things her father permitted her to take, just inside on the dusty floor, she forced a
weak smile as her *aenti* scooted by her. After twenty-three
years living at home, a *haus* ten times bigger by measure to

this one, she reckoned the change would take every day she was here to get used to. Sucking in a deep breath of regret, ignoring *Aenti* Tess's rambling beside her, Grace snorted out the filth and untidiness that filled the dim little space.

"Grace!" Tessie barked, grabbing her sleeve. "Are you listening? There are rules here, too, ya know."

"*Jah, Aenti* Tess. I am." Rules. The always-present rules. She didn't mean to sound ungrateful, but what else could be said about sin or charity that her *aenti* hadn't mentioned already?

Her father's voice still rang in her ears, despite his being three hundred miles away, and Grace remembered every word he'd spouted about immorality and false promises. Sending Grace away from her home and family matched her offense, but the vinegary taste of his harshness was fresh as the morning milking she performed before leaving her family home.

"I do appreciate the charity, *Aenti*. I will make the best of it," Grace said in a surrendered tone. Though she barely remembered her *aenti*, Tessie Miller, for now, was the only tie binding her to family. She squared her shoulders again. She needed to be brave.

"You have no choice, that is for sure and certain," Tessie replied.

No, she had no choices left, thanks to making the wrong one. Falling in love with Jared Castle, an *Englischer*, was one thing. What he left behind for her to handle alone was another. And now, as far as Ben Miller was concerned, he had four *kinner*, no longer five.

How could a father's love be so quickly dissolve? She bit the inside of her cheek, just as she had done the day

Daed scolded her for bringing such shame upon him. If one were to look up "sin" in the Webster book, her name would be there. Of that Grace was certain.

Grace closed her eyes and swallowed back another sweep of shame. Telling her parents she had been seeing a man outside of the community nearly broke her *mutter*'s heart. Telling them the extent of her disobedience shattered their hearts into a million irreparable pieces. They would never forgive her, regardless of whether that was the way of Amish life, not with a *boppli* on the way to forever remind them of her weakness and of their failure as parents in the face of the community.

She was alone, tossed away like a dirty napkin and shipped off to face her consequences in this strange place, with people she didn't know.

Grace forced her eyes open again to keep from envisioning the look of pain that had been etched in her *mutter*'s eyes. Charity said she need not regret her yesterdays and should live with intent for today. However, Grace couldn't do anything except regret every single moment that had led her here, and there was no amount of begging for forgiveness that would soften it.

She recalled the snowy day, the warmth of Jared's hand in hers as he drove along the far end of town. The way he smiled at her that always made her tingle from head to toe. He was chivalrous, attentive over the few short months they had gotten to know each other. He was everything *Mutter* had said a *gut* man should be.

Jared asked so many questions about her life, her Amish upbringing, always with curiosity. Boys Grace's age rarely took time to listen to a girl's thoughts sprung out loud, and they never looked at her the way Jared did. It took him less than two weeks to be so bold as to hold her hand. Why hadn't she just ended it there? Had she not listened to her parents' warnings about the outside world enough to know how tempting it could be? Had her *mutter* not explained in detail the feelings that ran through young folks? She knew how *verboden* such friendships were. But Jared's smooth tongue had a way of convincing her they had something special.

He made promises, and so many of them. He promised to speak to her father and court her properly. He promised her his heart and that he wanted to make her his *fraa*. And she believed him.

She had cried the night that he'd promised to join the church and give her the life she had dreamed about since she was a girl. He'd wiped away her joyous tears and kissed her, a kiss that seemed to have no end to it. Jared had a way of turning her nos into yeses without her even realizing she had done so. Lovestruck, the *Englisch* called it, and she had a triple dose of it, blinding her to the obvious. Jared was a liar, a manipulator, and she was the naive girl who believed every honey-coated word he whispered.

Now here she stood, facing the consequences of her naivety.

The baby maneuvered around inside her, the reminder of her mistake catapulting her back to the present. She didn't dare cradle it, giving her *aenti* a chance to gift her with another one of those sharp, stony stares.

A baby was meant to be a blessing. She had heard that all her life, but this one was protruding evidence that she was a fallen women. She wanted to be happy, glad to know

Gott entrusted her to carry life inside her, but she didn't deserve sentiments of bliss or shadows of giddiness. Grace was a sinner—shamed her family, herself, and her unborn.

Still, in fragile little moments, Grace dared to let a smile tempt her sullen expressions when she felt the miracle inside her move about. No matter what wrongs she had done to put herself in this place of punishment, her child would not feel it equally if she could help it.

"Lay those in that room," Tessie ordered the men who had helped deliver Grace and her few belongings to the abandoned cabin. They complied without a word.

The heat was almost unbearable for the last days of October, and Grace found no relief in the shade of the cabin's sunken roof. She would miss her three-story home and the large basement that always provided a cool refuge on summer days. Grace stepped forward and took a short spin to see all the cabin had to offer her. And there was certainly no cellar. One couldn't really call it a cabin, could they?

To her left sat a small kitchen. A rusty cookstove, a shelf of dust and plates leaning against a far wall, a sink that had an old hand pump to work it. Grace cringed at the plainness or, for a better word, emptiness. The men began unloading her trunk, a bed her *aenti* had gifted her, and a small box with her Bible and other personal items. In the center of the open room was a square four-legged table that looked like something a child had rummaged together as a first attempt to create something useful. At closer inspection, Grace doubted it was even capable of holding her Bible for nightly reading without crumbling to the dirty floor.

A shack. Grace settled the debate in her mind. A broken-down, forgotten shack. The main room was half the size of her bedroom back home, and she stiffened when the man Tessie called Caleb opened the only other door to the next room. If this was what the front room looked like, who knew what lay behind the creaking narrow door?

A whiff of stale air was set free. Dust- and rodent-infused, it poured out and hit her like a punch. She was going to be sick.

Covering her face to protect what little she had eaten, which amounted to three hardened cookies her younger sister Hope had snuck into her bag before she boarded the bus, Grace managed to endure the rankness. For the life of her, she couldn't imagine such a place could ever be livable.

"I will *kumm* for you Sunday for church at the Glicks', unless you want to wait until the next gathering." She was surprised her *aenti* had even given her a choice. By the frown on her face and those sharp Miller eyes, Tess didn't seem the kind of person who gave options. Grace wasn't ready to be thrust into the community and stared at like a newcomer, even if she was one. Everything was coming at her a bit fast, and getting settled in seemed best.

She needed a moment to catch her breath, accept this new reality. "I would prefer to wait. I should get my *haus* in order first."

Tessie grumbled, ran a boney finger over the kitchen table, stared at the heavy roll of dirt collected there, and then grumbled again. "I have arranged work for you at the creamery until you are…well…for now, we shall say."

Her always frowning *aenti* grunted against the stench of the room but never attempted to cover the scowl on her face. *Aenti* Tess and *Daed* had this, too, in common—giving commands without an expression, like a general of some great army not willing to break rank with his men.

Turning on the heel of her thick black-soled shoe against the wooden floor, the same as Grace remembered her first school teacher doing while pacing the floors during reading time, *Aenti* Tess aimed for the door, and both men quietly followed behind her. Caleb tipped his hat, but his eyes, like the other man's, stayed forward. No way either would dare pass a pleasantry toward a sinner. Grace already endured weeks under the ban, shunned from her community until she kneeled and confessed her sins before the church in her district and was no longer disturbed by other's avoidances.

She bit the inside of her cheek, contemplating if she would ever again fit in when she returned to Havenlee. Nothing sprouted. Being an unwed mother justified avoidance, made you invisible or the subject of gossip.

"*Danke!*" Grace yelled behind them as the door slammed. And in that sound of wood slapping on wood, her future was set.

Grace was alone, shut away, and would be forgotten for the following months. This was her punishment for falling for worldly charms and sweet words. This was her punishment for letting Jared into her heart. This was her punishment for turning her back on *Gott*.

Dry autumn dust swirled above the floor. Sweeping her foot across the woodened planks, Grace found even the floor itself unlevel. The condition of the shack—*sinner's shack*, she settled on calling it—was in dire need of attention. She spied a cardboard box sitting near the sink and went to investigate. On the front, written in thick black lettering, was, "Grace, welcome to Walnut Ridge, Elli." Grace lifted the flaps and peered inside. There she found linens, crackers and cheese, and a new lamp already filled and ready for use. Digging deeper, she found a small box of matches and lit the lamp. In the glow of lamplight, she spotted a case of bottled water near the front door. Something she hadn't noticed or expected. Her parched lips were thankful, and she fetched a bottle from the plastic casing without hesitation. The warm liquid sent immediate relief down her scratchy throat and unsettled stomach.

As if first appearances weren't disappointment enough, adding light into this gloomy shack only awakened her to her current reality. The rusty water pump, the weak hanging cabinets, and the front door that, despite Tessie giving it a good slam, didn't shut entirely. In the silence of this nowhere, all her pent-up emotions exploded in a rush and Grace surrendered to her tears.

This far from anything resembling life, she could cry, wail, scream if she needed to, and no one would hear her. And so, in the solitude of her own making, she did.

A few moments later, Grace wiped her soaked face with her thin cobalt-blue dress sleeve and straightened her shoulders. First introductions were over, and it was time to live with intent and be glad *Gott* had seen to her most basic needs. It would be fully dark soon, she measured, and she took up the broken-handled broom in the corner and began making herself busy with the work.

"All things go better when one finds themselves in busy." She said aloud the words *Mutter* often sang on dreary rainy days. As the hours passed, Grace stopped only long enough to sip at her bottle of water and cram another slice of cheese on cracker into her mouth. Whoever Elli was, Grace was lucky the woman didn't know her cause for being here. The creamy flavors of the cheese and lavender-infused flavoring not only filled her aching belly but calmed her unsettling nerves. She had never spent a single night without her family, and now she was expected to spend at least sixty or more of them alone. She collected an old torn rag from one of the pantry shelves and began wiping down the remainder of the room.

The sinner's shack was the last place on the long stretch of valley road, and only two houses were close—if over steep hillsides was considered close. There was much to consider, now that she was here. Was there a midwife in the community? Back home, Edith Strolzfus would have delivered her child, her *mutter* at her side. "But *mutter* will not be with you," Grace murmured and brushed back another sob. Grace made a mental note to ask Tessie about a local midwife on her next visit, if there was one. Just because Father had sent her to live in her *aenti*'s community didn't mean she was Tessie's responsibility. She was an adult, after all, and very much responsible for her own mistakes—as well as her own survival.

When the late hour approached, Grace wrapped the cheese in the clear parchment it had come in and set it in a half-size refrigerator that was a mere few degrees cooler than the room itself. She stood back and admired how the place looked better already. But every good feeling that entered was quickly replaced by the sounds of her father. She envisioned herself and her sisters, still *kinner*, sitting at the kitchen table, *Daed* spouting stories, drilling obedience into their young girlish minds. Maybe if she had listened more intently, she would not be here. Now all those stories he had told about the shunned woman, a lesson for them to take in about the worldly sins around them, would be her story.

She took a deep breath, exhaled slowly. No one was going to come to her rescue, help carry her burdens. She was on her own. Grace would have to rely on her own fortitude to survive…and hopefully thrive.

CHAPTER TWO

Friday came with no shift in the current weather. Grace stepped outside, escaping a buzzing horsefly that had pestered her the whole morning. With what little money she had saved helping at her neighbor's produce stand and selling sweet rolls to the local bakery back home, she could at least not be so frugal and just purchase a good flyswatter.

She glanced over the valley below. Three horses grazed in her neighbor's pasture. A stream of gray smoke rose from a small structure, despite the warm weather, and followed the morning breeze toward a winding creek. The narrow gravel lane widened as her eyes followed it northwest. Houses dotted both sides of a road that ran as crooked as a snake. Then hills and dips played equal tricks to block out anything farther. *Not within walking distance.* A flyswatter would have to wait. Her feet had not swelled once, as *mutter*'s had when she was carrying Mercy, but if Grace had too far to walk, that would change rather quickly. Maybe *Aenti* Tess would be willing to take her, just for a few staples. Surely she didn't expect Grace to live on a half sleeve of crackers and a sliver of cheese for the next two months.

Maybe she should wander over the hill, meet her nearest neighbors. Grace squashed that idea immediately. The longer she stayed invisible, the better. The house below was three times the size of the sinner's shack and surrounded by acres of pasture and strong fencing. Surely a family lived there.

The sound of buggy wheels tangling with ruts and rocks, mingling with the heavy panting of horses alerted her, and she turned her attention to the barely visible drive leading to the sinner's shack. A buggy rattled and strained against the climb up the hill, and she raised an arm to shield the morning sun from her eyes and watched it approach.

"*Aenti* Tess," she breathed out with relief, desperate for company, until a second buggy came into view. Her joy was quickly stomped when she counted five white *kapps* in total cresting the hill. Brushing her hands down the length of her worn-out chore dress, she sucked in her concern at meeting the local women so soon and faked a warm, welcoming smile. When the buggies came to a stop in front of the shack, *Aenti* Tess slithered out of the buggy, giving her a disapproving frown. Did she object to bare feet, too?

A younger woman, close in age to Grace, climbed down from the driver's seat and tied off her *aenti*'s horse, a faded old mare that looked about as worn as a critter could get. Grace swallowed back her unease at this sudden bombardment, wishing she could hide her bulging middle, as she had for six months under her father's roof, but there was no hiding her shame now when it stuck out like a fly in butter.

One by one, a swarm of white *kapps* and gray-blue dresses of various sizes descended their high perches. They each gathered a basket or cardboard box into their arms, and as they walked toward the lopsided porch, Grace realized she would be hosting these women, here in her home of rotting sticks and leaning timbers, with only a handful of crackers and a smidgen of cheese to offer. Now she wished she hadn't eaten so much.

Her jaw was still open, and she closed it quickly as an array of smiling faces peered up at her. *Aenti Tess could have mentioned a local welcoming party was coming.* Grace mentally grumbled.

"Grace, this here is Elli Schwartz, Betty Glick, Hannah Glick, and Rachel Yoder. We have all *kumm* to help you get this *haus* in order." Tessie said with a hint of sarcasm.

Yep, much like *Daed*, her *aenti* was direct and wasted no time charging up the steps and into the sinner's shack. The women each tossed Grace a welcoming nod as they followed behind her *aenti* but thankfully didn't pounce on her with meddling questions or long-winded introductions.

Grace let out a held breath before turning on a bare heel and walking inside. A cleaning frolic was about to begin.

"It is so small," the girl named Hannah said, setting a box of canned goods on the unreliable table. Her quiet tone carried a pound of sorrow.

"*Ach, nee!*" Grace rushed forward, swooping up the box. "I fear that table is not worthy to hold a plate, let alone a box." Grace shifted the box to the counter.

"I can see you need many more things than just some dusting and paint." That was Betty, short, round, and smiling despite the look of surprise held in her soft brown eyes. "Well, don't you fret, my dear. We are a resourceful bunch." Betty winked.

Grace stifled a grin. She had no doubts, what with the way Betty planted two fists onto healthy hips and gave the shack a careful perusal.

"I am very pleased to meet you all, but you did not need to *kumm*. I can handle a place this small myself." Did they think because her morals were weak, the rest of her was, too?

Hopefully she didn't sound ungrateful. She *was* grateful. In fact, just having company had already perked up her downtrodden mood.

"Of course you can, but what good are we if we do not lend a hand to our newest Walnut Ridge neighbor? I'm Elli." The woman flashed an honest smile, and then went to removing items from her basket. "I brought more staples. Fresh corn my Abram picked just this morning and some ham and pickles. Tessie said you needed pots and whatnot, so we brought those, too."

Grace didn't know what whatnots were but her tongue dampened with eagerness, and her stomach was protesting her patience. She couldn't remember the last time she had ever been so hungry. Eating for two had her wanting, craving, and at all hours. Ice cream—did they have that? She quickly chided herself for the selfish thought.

If one of those boxes presented ice cream, any flavor, she would surely cry. Her emotions were a little unpredictable of late. "That is so kind of you, of each of you. *Danke.*"

"It smells horrible in here. I'm not sure I can stand it long," Rachel Yoder hissed, her pale face puckered as if she had just swallowed a whole lemon. The willowy *maedel* made no pretense that she was there willingly.

"Just open the windows and door," Elli said pumping a thin stream of water into a small bucket. "Step outside if need be. We have the whole day, and it is a little house."

Elli grinned, deepening the lines on her tanned face with age.

"Go fetch the cleaning supplies and get some air," Tess barked, pulling rags and trash bags from a yellow sack. Rachel turned up her nose and stomped out the door.

"It's been years since I've been up here," Elli said pulling plates from the leaning cabinet. Grace hadn't even explored the contents of the cabinet yet. The room quickly began to fill with chatter, but Grace secluded herself to the tiny bedroom, washing walls with Rachel. At seven months pregnant, her condition couldn't very well be hidden no matter where one landed, Amish didn't tend to spark up conversations with women like her.

Surely they didn't know she had once been shunned by her own bishop. If they asked, she would have to tell the truth, along with the fact that she had confessed and repented as required. It had been a hard obedience to muster, but Grace followed through, in hopes for total forgiveness. However, forgiveness had a long memory, and her father's, even longer.

• • •

After only a couple of hours, the sinner's shack smelled of lemons and possibility. Grace also felt more relaxed and grateful for even a small ounce of conversation that didn't involve her circumstances. These women where nothing like the women she grew up knowing.

Grace saw movement out of the corner of her eye. "Spiders! Gah! I hate spiders," she screamed, dropping the small gallon bucket of dirty water over the floor and clutching her chest. She'd caught a flash of brown scurrying down her chore dress and ran out the door in a panic, shaking the fabric wildly in her exit.

Once clear of the house, Grace stomped the dry earth around her, dust clouding up into a heavy plume. She expected some laughter after such a silly reaction to mere bugs, but not the kind the women were enjoying at her expense now.

It was a familiar scene. Each of her sisters always found amusement in her fear of spiders. Brushing away imaginary creepers from her dress, she righted herself, caught her breath, and straightened her *kapp*. She didn't like being the center of others' amusement. Nothing humbling about it, the way she saw it. And when was she ever going to get over this fear of spiders? If Mercy were here, she would have handled it for her. But her youngest sister was not here—she had to rely on herself now. Grace stomped some more to be certain the eight-legged monster didn't pester her again.

"You move fairly swiftly, considering," Rachel smarted off from the top step. In that shade of dark blue, she looked pale, except for the deep red of her warm cheeks. Rachel was making no secret of the fact that she had no intention of being a friend to Grace. That was fine by Grace. It was part of the punishment she deserved. She was not blind to the fact that she would be met with judgments similar to those she'd received back home once the rumor mill started.

"Here, let me give you a look-over," Elli quickly interrupted and joined her in the yard. With one hand, she brushed Grace's shoulder and trailed the length of her for any further crawling pest. "Tessie tells me you are a good hand in the kitchen. Have you ever made cheese?" Elli's brows rose and stayed there, looking quizzical.

This was the woman Grace would be working for, and also the one who had gifted Grace the box filled with linens, a lamp, and food when she first arrived. Something told Grace she had a hand in this cleaning frolic as well, sensing her *aenti* was not so freely willing to volunteer.

Elli was only inches taller, but twenty years or better separated them in age. She was also different, Grace noted, as she had listened to the women chat for the past hours as they made a shack into a home. Elli dressed with the same plainness as each of them, but something about her stood out, catching the eye. She held a strange confidence that made her, well, interesting. Even more so the longer she spoke.

Grace finally grasped the disparity: Elli had no accent. Her English was spoken far too well to ignore, and Grace quickly made a mental note to herself to know more about the woman. Confidence was one of the many things Grace was lacking, but would need for the road ahead of her.

"*Nee*, I have never made cheese before, but I will do my best to not disappoint you." Grace nodded humbly. She did love learning new things, and if working at the creamery helped her save enough to support herself, she would master any skill Elli was willing to teach her.

"I am sure you will do fine, my dear." Elli smiled, and the blue of her eyes almost twinkled. A mix between cloudless sky and a picture Grace once saw of the ocean.

"What do you enjoy doing with your time?" It was an odd question, but Elli was a bit odd for an Amish *fraa* now, wasn't she? One could not overlook the small hole in her left ear, an indication she wore, or once wore, earrings, like *Englischers* did.

"I don't rightly know how to answer that," she replied. "My sisters and I were taught to seek out our separate talents, not dawdle, so each day ran as smooth as butter." And it did, just as her *daed* said good planning and order would. Only Grace had dared to disturb the order of things, and for that *daed* washed his hands of her. Elli led her back to the porch steps. "My sister Charity loves sewing, which I know enough, but nothing like her. Faith makes the finest quilts in all Havenlee. *Englischers* pay well for them, too."

She flicked a stinkbug from the railing as Betty stepped out onto the porch with six cups of something steaming nestled in a skillet made to serve as a tray. It smelled heavenly, a blend of minty freshness and coziness. Betty *was* resourceful.

"So you have two sisters," Hannah asked, taking a cup from Betty's tray and breathing in the aroma.

"I have four," Grace replied too quickly. Just mentioning them made her stomach ache. "My younger sister Hope grows the most beautiful gardens, and Mercy, well, she is fifteen. Her talent for now is finding hers before *daed* gives her one." She snickered, and the women snickered, too. This was nice, almost normal, despite missing her sisters terribly. Grace was glad they had come, and she sipped at her cup and let the minty taste revive her parched tongue.

"I have all *bruders*. Five of them." Hannah rolled her eyes above a thin-lipped smirk. "I would trade any one of them for a sister. I even have a *sohn*. Seems it is *Gott*'s will I be surrounded by men." It was nice to hear laughter once again from the group. With the exception of her *aenti*, who was bending a chipped sliver of paint from the side of a porch post.

"And what was your talent?" Rachel asked with a hint of sarcasm peppering her tone.

"Mine was next to *mutter* in the kitchen," she said with confidence, well-known back home for her baking talents. Pride, another sin she needed to work on. She was becoming a regular chatterbox as well. Grace fidgeted with her cream-colored teacup to stop her rambling.

"Charity, Faith, Hope, Mercy, and Grace. Your *mamm* and *daed* chose wisely. Do ya have *bruders* ?" Betty asked. Betty had introduced herself when the women arrived this morning as the *aenti* of Caleb and Elis, the men who had delivered her here. Her hair was as black as nightfall under her *kapp* and she went on all morning about the upcoming weddings of both her nephews. It had been so long since Grace had attended a wedding, but in her condition, she was certain it would be longer still. She had no plans of venturing out into the community more than was expected. It was one thing to slip from the faith; it was another to walk about for everyone to see that you had done so.

"*Nee*, no *bruders*." The baby moved—well, more like stretched—and Grace turned away from prying eyes to cradle her growing girth until the uncomfortable feeling had passed. Hopefully no one noticed.

She could never tell a soul how she really felt—the joy that welled up inside her each time she was reminded she would soon bring life into the world. No, she was meant to act shamed, which she *was* for allowing her condition to be present in the first place, but *not* for the innocent life that would result from it.

"When are you expecting?" Elli asked boldly, stepping up alongside her. Elli picked at a spider web between two wooden rails that had long lost whatever held them tight. Grace swallowed hard. Looking heavenward, she eyed the dull blue of the sky, seeking a darkened cloud to relieve her overly warm flesh. This would not be the first person in Walnut Ridge to ask the question, and she knew she would have to simply get used to such forwardness.

"Last week of December," she muttered, wishing for a hole to tuck into. In her community, such things were rarely spoken about, and never in her case. Each of these women had to see her for what she was—a fallen woman, wayward in the faith. She was fortunate *Mutter* had taken her to the clinic for a checkup before packing her blue duffle bag and whispering a goodbye.

"A Christmas *boppli*. Wouldn't that be just *wunderbaar*?" Hannah said it with such wistfulness. Grace hadn't considered that. Worse, she hadn't thought past the next day and now was reminded that she was spending Christmas alone, without her family.

"That makes you over seven months. You are so tiny. I was that size with Noah at only two," Hannah said, adding to the conversation Grace wished had never started. Hannah had a quiet nature about her that made her the epitome of a plain woman. Much like her sister Faith, in truth, and Grace believed the two were about the same age as well. Her delicate way and tender smile made Grace miss Faith even more than she had already. Despite her father's orders, each of her sisters had spoken to her until the day she left. In whispers in the night or in the barn during morning milking, but they took every opportunity given to them to do so. Maybe she should write to them. It wasn't ideal, but it was something.

"I was never that size," Betty jested. "You are too small. We need to fatten you up."

Grace cocked her head to the side, studying the lot of them. It was apparent that things in this community were nothing like the Old Order community she was raised in. In Havenlee, women worked all day without need of frivolous conversations. And speaking of pregnancy in public, much less an unwed one, would not be permitted in whispers, or any tone.

The women were offering her friendship. Grace had not expected that. Not at all.

She didn't deserve it, either. Before a few days ago, she had endured five whole weeks of the opposite within her family home. Her bad decision had forced a lot of changes in her life. Like eating meals alone in a dark sitting room while her family gathered around the table, having her father look through her every time he entered a room, and worse, not sitting with her sisters at church and enduring the judgmental glares aimed her way in the far corners where sinners sat.

She could beg forgiveness until the sky fell, but it mattered none in her father's eyes. If Grace had not agreed to her *daed*'s plan to leave home until her child was born, she was certain he would have paraded her around daily to set an example to all the young girls on the cusp of womanhood. Yet, she didn't get the feeling these women did a lot of parading.

"*Danke* for the box you left for me." She looked to Elli.

"The linens and lamp were much appreciated my first night." Changing the topic was her only defense from these women pulling more out of her. "I cannot tell each of you how grateful I am that you came to help me today."

"Kindness given keeps coming back," Elli added.

"Someone must be coming," Betty said as the sound of another buggy rattled up the hill. Was all of Walnut Ridge coming to see her this day?

"We never told anyone else we were coming," Rachel added, as if their coming was meant to be kept secret. Grace bristled at the comment. Would all the members of Walnut Ridge welcome her this way, or like Rachel, would they treat her accordingly?

A man's voice, urging his horse through the climb, sounded among the trees. She recalled the small home the night she had arrived, its lamplight in the wee hours of early mornings, and the sound of banging that echoed along the deep valley long into the night hours. She had a feeling she was about to meet another member of the Walnut Ridge welcoming committee—this time, her neighbor.

CHAPTER THREE

Cullen Graber wiped the sweat pouring from his face with the tail of his untucked shirt. This had to be the hottest autumn he could remember ever to hit Walnut Ridge. He was ready for winter already. At least in the chill of a frosty morn, the forge was more welcoming.

Gripping the hammer again, he pounded the steel locked securely in the vise, willing a slight angle into the thick metal. Behind as he was, finishing all the rails ordered for the local buggy shop, he needed to simply muster through to catch up. No stranger to enduring heat, he continued on just as he always had.

If there was one thing Cullen Graber did well, it was to keep on keeping on.

Humming an old familiar tune, he maneuvered the steel in the vise, the sound made him miss his mother's humming, the sweet lull of her voice and rich accent. He missed a lot of things, none of which could be returned. But settling to be nothing more than the local smithy was safe. This world was peaceful, respectful of a working man, and there was nothing that could be taken from him any longer that he couldn't easily replace. If a thing broke, he fixed it, or simply bought a replacement. It was as simple as that.

It wasn't like that with people. So he kept them at arm's length. A hard task for one born Amish, when everything screamed *family*, but after this many years, no one thought to remind him he should be married by now. They simply stopped pestering on that account, since he had stood his ground so long. Only downside to that was no more young *maedels* trying to catch his eye with their baking skills as they once had. Good thing Elli and Betty pitied him or he would have starved relying on his own.

Still, there were moments. Days when loneliness crept in and reminded him how life once was, what was lost. He liked the solitude of the farm, but there were only so many conversations a man could have with himself before it wavered on crazy. That was why he never missed a church Sunday, never missed a wedding, and even made a point to ride into town each Monday for supplies and to say hello to a few friends. Balance, he liked to call it.

But sometimes, he wasn't so sure this lonely contentment was good enough to carry a man all his days. Lucas never missed a chance to remind him *Gott* did not intend for us to live alone, that it was time to move beyond the losses he had endured. Cullen would offer that same advice to another who faced loss, but for him, it was different. Marty was gone. His parents were gone. And grief could not be measured by clocks and suns and moons. It sure couldn't be measured by others' opinions.

Besides, he had nothing left to offer a woman anyway. Any love he had been born with was gone. He had given away all he had. Yes, alone was safe.

Being the only blacksmith in Pleasants was good for the pocket—not so for humid days. Surely a good rain would pronounce itself soon enough. Loosening the vise, he released his creation, dunked it into the quenching bucket, and reached for the next piece to bend to his will. Both had to be a perfect mirror of the other for the buggy shop to

buy them, and the Hiltys were his best customers. The
sizzle of hot steel and water colliding ceased, just as
laughter rang over the valley. He stepped out of the forge
and glanced up the hill.

A couple of days ago he spotted Elis and Caleb
Schwartz and two women driving up the lane toward his
humble home. A brilliant red and orange horizon framed
the work wagon into a pictorial scene of late day. Neither
woman riding in the back with bedding and a trunk looked
anything like Emma or Mirim, the two women who were to
wed the Schwartz cousins next month, but Cullen tended
to mind his own business.

His small parcel of only eight acres was secluded
enough, but as the wagon passed by his drive, he couldn't
help but wonder where they could possibly be heading so
late. His was the last house on Walnut Ridge. There was
really nowhere else to go from there.

Elmo Hilty owned a bit of land up the hill, but that old
road wasn't even visible any longer. Caleb had urged the
horse up the long hill that led to the old cabin. It was an
old *Englisch* getaway that rested on an open flat, midway
up the mountain. Elmo had bought it when he was young.
For what reason, Cullen hadn't a clue.

It had no value, no tillable land worth working, and no
fences for animals. Cullen had watched the cabin's decline
since he and his best friend Lucas's *rumschpringe* days of
reading books they weren't supposed to and smoking
cigarettes they weren't supposed to, either, all the way up
to recently, when quail or rabbit season gave him a reason
to walk the hill.

The trunk and bed Caleb was hauling implied that

someone was spending a few days in a run-down cabin not fit for mouse or bird and now that two more buggies had traveled up there again this morning, Cullen suspected that might be true.

Minding his own was a noble habit he'd learned early on by his father's instruction, but the old structure wasn't safe. He growled, hating to be disturbed, and set his tools aside. It was time to see what all the fuss was about.

• • •

The large shadow burst into color once the man came into full light. Betty quickly waved the stranger over. *Now why did she have to do that?* Grace wondered.

A large hand waved back and the man aimed the buggy straight for Grace's door. A pearly smile that could be seen at a distance caught her attention. The dark gelding had already built up a heavy lather on his coat and muzzle, and Grace pitied the poor animal for being made to pull a wagon with a full-grown man up the steep hill. The driver tugged on the reins effortlessly. His rolled-up sleeves displayed arms chiseled and strong—capable, Grace imagined, for all the early morning and late night banging.

"Cullen. Good to see ya today." Elli patted the horse, frothing from his work, and stepped to the side of the buggy. Grace sneaked a glance from the safety of the only steady post she had.

Cullen was quite tall—even sitting down, one could see that. Under the brim of his straw hat, dark hair peeked out, but the length was fairly acceptable. He swiped away a bit of perspiration trickling down the side of his face with the sleeve of his shirt.

"A lot of comings and goings of late, had to see for myself what would bring anyone up here to the middle of nowhere." Grace nearly nodded, agreeing with his point. Up here was nowhere. He stepped down from the buggy with the ease of a much smaller, limber man and peered at the cabin. "By the looks of it, I see you all have been tidying up the place. I should warn you that it is not safe. Even that roof looks to be untrustworthy."

Adjusting his hat, Cullen turned his attention to the group of women perched on Grace's lopsided porch.

"If you all are eager to clean something, I will never turn you away." He winked at Betty, and she shook her head at his playfulness. Was he hoping those handsome looks would get him free labor?

Grace growled inwardly. If the man was unwed—which she couldn't fathom he was by his clean-shaven face and surprising good looks—then he was most certainly one of those who liked having no family to take care of but would grin for a free meal and clean laundry. Charity had told her about such men, the forever bachelors, even before Grace had gained firsthand experience herself.

"You want a tidy *haus*, then I reckon you get to picking out a *gut maedel* and get married," Betty bantered, her tone equally as teasing. The banter here was strange, unlike any Grace had heard at home, women teasing men and everyone laughing about it.

"And yet I found a chicken casserole and corn pudding in my oven two nights ago." Grace appreciated a man with humor and stifled a grin. Cullen apparently had the upper hand, and Betty waved him off. *So he's not married, and a smile does earn him free meals.* Grace mused.

Scanning the lot, he nodded to Hannah and Rachel but stopped short when his eyes rested on *Aenti* Tess. Tessie had a way about her that could peel a smile away from the happiest of hearts, and his gathered expression was proof of it.

"I guess it was you with Caleb and Elis who came to see the condition of the old place." She nodded, and his dark eyes took in the delicate state of the place. A strange look washed over his strong features, like he was trying to find a missing piece to a puzzle, and Grace felt her account for being here would be aired out like the morning's laundry. Must all strangers be wise to her sins? Faith told her living so far from home would be a clean slate, a new start. But Grace was old enough to know one couldn't outrun their sins; they followed you everywhere and rarely died a full death. Her stomach tightened knowing that smile he was flaunting so freely would soon drop into a scowl.

"Well, I don't seem to recall a thank-you given for my venison stew or that full plate of peanut butter cookies," Elli quickly added.

"Best I ever tasted." Suddenly, his eyes locked onto hers, and Grace wanted to retreat inside, no matter that the bleach was pungent and the doors didn't close properly. How could one look see so deeply, beyond the outer shell?

"Cullen Graber, this here is Grace Miller. She is from Indiana, where I was born," Betty announced.

"Hello Grace Miller," his voice grew deep, causing her already frayed nerves to unravel.

"She is Tessie's *bruder* Ben Miller's daughter and will be staying a spell in our community."

That was putting it mildly. She was *forced* to live here. His frowning expression came as expected and she immediately missed the playful smile. Grace lifted her chin. She shouldn't care what this handsome stranger thought. Had she not learned already that a nice smile was a dangerous thing.

"Here?" Cullen's voice hitched an octave. His eyes traveled to the cabin again before settling back on her. Couldn't he have just said *nice to meet ya* and gone on his way? Grace tightened her grip on her teacup.

"Cullen is your neighbor, just over the hill there," Tessie added.

"Tess, this is not the most livable place for a woman." His brows gathered just as *Daed*'s did before delivering a lecture.

"For a woman?" Grace hadn't meant to say the words out loud, but she obviously had by his taken-aback expression.

"I...I didn't mean it like that." He removed his hat displaying a wide ring where it fit snuggly on his damp head. He ran his long fingers through the thick shock of dark hair, his first sign of any nervousness. He wasn't smiling all willy-nilly now, was he? It somehow made him even more handsome. Drat the man. "I meant, the place hasn't been fit to live in for quite some time. For anyone."

"I will make do," she said, scrunching her lips to one side defiantly.

"Just being neighborly," he added, a hint of surrender in his tone.

"It's nice to have *gut* neighbors, *jah*? You will feel right at home in no time," Betty added. She clearly meant well, but Grace certainly didn't like thinking of the sinner's shack as a real home.

When he looked to her again, the depths of his gaze caught her off guard. Those dark eyes matched the deep walnut color that had stained her and her sisters' hands each fall when they gathered walnuts for hulling. Without the shield of his straw hat, she had missed that brilliant detail. His head tilted, taking her in, then snapped back into place. "I hope your *mann* is handy with a hammer. If he could use the help, I am glad to offer it."

She clenched her teeth at the comment, biting a little bit of her tongue as she did so. Her *mann* was more than five hundred miles away in Missouri and had not replied to one letter she had written him so far, but she appreciated the assuming observation. In truth, Jared had made it clear he was *not* her *mann* and not concerning himself with her current state. Defending his country was his calling, not raising his child and wedding its *mutter*.

Grace half expected her *aenti* to speak up at this point, revealing her reason for being here and without a *mann* to accompany her, but surprisingly, Tess remained quiet. None of the woman spoke, not even Rachel.

"When will you have Abram's sign finished?" Elli interrupted, saving Grace from any further attention. The woman had a gift, and Grace was glad to be a recipient.

She stepped closer toward Betty to continue hiding her ever-growing midsection, but Cullen's hawklike eyes searched out her slightest movements. She could tell his suspicious gawking had been rewarded when his eyes widened slowly in realization of her sin. Maybe if she had taken the time to let out her dresses before coming, she could have spared herself for a few more weeks.

There was no hiding her middle now. Her petite frame only enhanced the seven months she had conquered so far.

"I just finished my last order for Ben Hilty, so it will be my first duty *kumm morgen*," he assured Elli, but those suspicious dark eyes never left Grace.

A heavy bead of perspiration slid from the base of her hair line and disappeared under her dress. She fought the urge to smash it or wiggle at the sensation tingling between her shoulder blades. He had questions, she was sure of it. Good thing such questions weren't proper.

Rachel snickered, drawing his attention away long enough for Grace to catch a breath she had not even realized she was holding. She had done this a dozen times back home, practiced even more for what she expected to face here. Why was this one man making her so uncomfortable?

"Tess, I really feel you should consider this. Your *haus* has plenty of room for a couple until something more suitable can be found. One good storm and this old cabin might cave in on their heads. That would not be right." Cullen's warnings were kind, but Jared used to pretend he cared about her well-being, too. And who was this man to talk about her as if she wasn't standing right here? Well, back between a post and Betty, but that wasn't the point. He needed to keep his thoughts to himself.

"Grace will stay here as she has been told. It is not of your concern, Cullen Graber." Grace wanted to float her *aenti* a smile until one thick brow arched on Cullen's face. Surely that big head of his had a brain in it.

Cullen shook his head. She lifted her chin, along with a

knowing brow, to send him a firm message. Do not judge, less ye be judged.

"I will leave ya to do your cleaning, ladies. Please be mindful." Cullen placed his straw hat back on his head with a little more force than needed and gave Grace a curt nod. "It was nice to meet you, Grace. You may tell your *ehemann* I have a few leftover things in my barn he is welcome to for repairs. And if you need anything, just ask. I always have plenty." There wasn't a husband to tell, but his offer was kind enough.

Grace watched him climb back into the buggy and gather the reins in his hands. With a firm click of his tongue, the horse responded, taking them back over the hill where they belonged.

"Are you all right, dear?" Betty rested her hand on Grace's arm. It was a foreign comfort, but she needed it.

"I don't think I will ever get used to the stares, even if I earned them." The teacup in her hand felt as heavy as her heart. And suddenly going back into the gloom of the sinner's shack didn't seem like such a bad idea. She could close the door, close out the world, and no one could ever again look at her.

Cullen Graber may have tried to look concerned, but once he knew there was no *mann* living here, she was certain that would be the last she would be seeing of him.

"Oh dear, you are not being judged. That is only for *Gott* to do. What kind of community would we be if we only helped the perfect? It is our duty to support one another. You are not the first to ever make a mistake in this world. We all have sinned in one way or another," Elli said, but Grace didn't think any of these women capable of sinning as she had. "I tend to gossip and still cannot embrace speaking your German words like the bishop or Tess over here likes." Elli grinned. So Elli wasn't born Amish? That made more sense now.

"I let my *mamm* keep Noah anytime I go anywhere," Hannah added. Grace had been curious about that, since it seemed all Hannah could talk about was her *sohn*.

"*Ach*, Hannah, everyone knows you do it because Marie is lonely after raising so many *kinner*," Rachel interrupted. All eyes trained on her. After a very impressive eye roll, Rachel let out a very unladylike sigh and said, "Fine. I tend to try too hard to make things perfect."

Hannah snickered and quickly covered her mouth with her hand.

"She does," Elli said with two raised brows and a shake of her head. Grace looked to her in utter surprise, then turned to each woman one by one, seeing them with fresh eyes. These women were nothing like any Grace had ever known. No matter how many times she had the thought, they would go further and shock her simpleminded self once more.

"And no sin is greater than another, you remember that. We all fall short at some time. None is perfect but *Gott*. It is what we learn from our mistakes, what we do to right our wrongs, that matters." Betty squeezed her shoulder. If they were referring to repentance and confession, Grace had done both—the whole heartfelt and painful ritual that all sinners went through to get back into the good graces of the church and community. And yet, Grace had still been pushed away from the community and family she loved to be abandoned in the middle of nowhere.

These women were being too kind, offering compassion to Grace so freely. Amish were taught to have a forgiving heart above all, and here in Walnut Ridge, it appeared they took it very seriously. Even her best friend, Claire, who had known her since their first days of school, had refused to acknowledge her once her condition was made known.

At least she wouldn't need to worry what her neighbor thought once the rumor mill began. Grace was certain that even in communities as different as Walnut Ridge, gossip still pumped endlessly.

"It still hurts when strangers stare at you like that," she muttered. "I have asked forgiveness and confessed, but that has not freed me from others' judgments."

"Nothing frees us from others' judgments. All are human," Tessie added.

Elli nudged her. "No judgment would ever come from our handsome Cullen on your condition, just so you know. Of that I can assure you," she added with a warm confidence.

Another tear threatened. Grace squared her shoulders, faked a smile, and went back inside her sinner's shack, where only she belonged.

CHAPTER FOUR

Sunday night Cullen finished the last verses of Psalms 25, and the words seemed to jump off the pages to stab him. His heart had been troubled; today he felt desolate and afflicted just as David had. He shook off old memories and old hurts threatening. One thing about the past, it couldn't be changed. Surely loneliness was spawning this downtrodden mood. He closed the book, whispered a thankful prayer, and readied for bed.

Under a thin sheet and the sounds of an owl giving away its position, Cullen revisited the strange encounter with his newest neighbor. He had known Betty and Elli all his life, and he knew when the women were hiding something. It wasn't like he hadn't seen a woman in her condition before. And where was her husband anyway? Why was he not there to help tend to that fallen porch before someone got themselves hurt? Before Grace Miller got hurt? And what kind of man ordered his *fraa* to live in such conditions when she clearly had family with room to spare? It was all a mystery, one that made his blood warm. It would be the right thing to do, riding up there again in a couple of days and lending a hand, the neighborly thing to do.

Some men didn't like unexpected visitors, but it was clear some needed a little help whether they wanted it or not. He closed his eyes but couldn't get those wide blue eyes out of his mind. The details his memory was capable of absorbing astonished even him. When he first locked eyes on her, Grace looked completely stricken, like she had just witnessed her first hog butchering.

She was awfully frail for a woman in her condition, too, despite how she tried to look stronger than he thought her to be.

He flipped to his left, shoved the feather pillow under the crook of his neck, and tried finding sleep. The lone howl of a coyote echoed through the valley, as it did most nights.

Grace's dark hair complemented her delicate features. And those little bare feet... He shook off the improper thought, tried again to put the *fraa* up the hill out of his head, and rolled left. Blue eyes awaited him there, too. Yep, he was lonely all right.

Since when did he toss and turn over a woman? He often dreamed of Marty, but ten years had a way of blurring those visions. Maybe it was time to heed Lucas's advice. Perhaps float a smile Beth Zook's way? She made some mighty tasty cabbage rolls. They did have a few things in common. Beth was close to his age, and she did have *wunderbaar* patience with *kinner*.

He shook his head. Beth also had a lazy eye that sometimes confused him if she paid him much attention, and he heard she wasn't much for anything outdoors. If Cullen was to ever consider flirting with such a thought as courting again, surely a woman who enjoyed the outdoors was as important as one who was handy in the kitchen. Sara Shrock was pretty, kind of. If tall and stick-thin was your aim. He moaned. *Looks don't matter*, he reminded himself. *It's what's on the inside that counts*. Did either Beth or Sara have blue eyes? He hadn't a clue, but maybe he should find out. Letting his thoughts linger on the newcomer was not acceptable. Except, when she tried on an angry look, Cullen had seen only fear. Did she fear the roof would fall in as he mentioned, or being new to the area?

"Stop it," he chided himself. He had to ignore the attraction he felt. Grace was married, pregnant, and *verboden*. Still, a girl with eyes like that would be hard to ignore.

• • •

Night fell, bringing with it an eerie solitude. Being raised with four other siblings, Grace soon found she didn't like being alone one bit and quickly took out the little box of matches and lit one. Lifting the handle on the lamp Elli had gifted her, Grace slid the match inside and the wick caught, fending off a parade of unnatural shivers that climbed up her arms.

She made a full circle of the room before settling to shut all the windows. It was November, normally a time of cooler weather, leaves going dry and brown and crumbling under the slightest of footfalls, yet this evening was stubbornly humid. Who would believe in such weather that Christmas was a mere two months away?

Grace blinked, hoping to clear her blurring vision. How would *mutter* prepare a Christmas meal without her, and who would help Faith make ginger cookies for the *kinner* for the Christmas recital? Hope would be busy making colorful baskets of canned goods like jelly, pickled vegetables, and bright red tomato sauces, from her garden, as gifts. And none of her sisters could share a kitchen without a quarrel, stirring *mutter* into a conniption. Mercy would be cutting pine boughs for decorating the windows and kitchen table without her. They had always shared the duty since Mercy was old enough to follow in her shadow. The scents of *mutter*'s pies cooling on the table in the back room would now be replaced with wood smoke and rotten timber. Grace's shoulders slumped and she bit her bottom lip. Who would help Charity deliver gifts if Grace was here, instead of there? Christmas would go on without her.

She gave her hand a slap. The hot air was unbearable, but the gnats were worse. Attracted to her lamp, the buzzing bloodsuckers already had her suffering three bites. "Go away." She swatted at her ear, the hum of another pest searching out a free meal. "Don't you know it's November?" she barked, as if insects had ears and could speak her language. Nothing in this strange community was normal, she quipped.

Putting on her gown, she grumbled at the look of her slightly swollen ankles and settled onto her bed. She inhaled a deep breath, let it out slowly to invite a sense of calm in, and kicked away the covers, unneeded on such a night. She cradled her belly and began humming a lullaby her *mutter* had sung before Mercy was born.

"I *lieb* you with all my heart. You are mine and I am yours and we will be our own family," she whispered to her growing middle. "Please forgive me for leaving you without a *daed*, without a *dawdi* and *mammi* and *aentis* who would *lieb* you. I will do all I can to replace what I have taken from you."

Guilt wrapped around her like a warm blanket, but as the little one inside her edged closer to the hand she pressed firmly on her stomach, the feeling faded like the last shadows of night when the sun awoke to welcome a new day. How did one expect her to wallow in shame and regret with such love living within her? As happened every night around this hour, the baby stretched, kicked a couple of thrusts under her left rib, and practiced a routine of maneuvering about. Strong like its father, but Grace would teach her child of kindness, of love that endures beyond all, and to never walk away from family. She would always love her child, even when mistakes were made. She watched her gown rise and fall and let her smile roam freely, with only God as a witness to her happiness.

Jared was no good, unworthy of even knowing such love as she was overcome with. She had been blind, letting him close to her heart, but that would never happen again. No man would ever have her heart again. Not a single part, chamber, or vein, unless God blessed her with a *sohn*. Never again would she make snap decisions, no matter what she thought she felt at the time. It was clear she couldn't trust her own heart for making important decisions. No, Grace would think and pray every step from this day forth, as many as God would gift her.

The baby settled back into a comfortable place, and Grace took the opportunity to tuck the blanket between both knees, for her own bit of comfort, and shifted to one side. She slowed her busy thoughts of missed Christmas traditions, midwives, and preparing for a winter that seemed to have no interest in arriving, and searched for her own rest.

• • •

Laying on the edge between awake and dreaming, Grace stirred to the sound of a low hum on the other side of her bedroom wall. The night often held things that the day kept hidden, just as dreams hid themselves in the light of day. Something nocturnal, most likely a harmless rodent or coon, lurked outside. In the silence that followed, she sank deeper into her pillow, vigilant but searching for the slumber she'd been pulled from. A deeper vibration rattled her fully awake. It was solid, throaty, and very audible. She was not dreaming, and each of the tiny hairs on her arms and neck were awake, too.

She looked over for Charity sleeping in the bed next to hers, a habit that had fended off many a restless dream before, but Charity wasn't there, and she snapped back to her current surroundings. A rustling outside in the dry grass that she had not yet chopped down followed. She tensed and cradled her belly instinctively. Footsteps thudded against the earth, menacing and sly.

Someone was lurking outside.

With panic driving her heart into an uncontrolled pounding, Grace rose slowly from her pillow and positioned herself on her knees. Time stilled while she bent an ear to gather any further evidence as to who could be out there. She moved closer to the pane of glass just above her bed. The late hour revealed nothing but darkness in the moonless night. If someone was out there, she couldn't tell in the shadowless void. What she did know was that she was no longer alone on this hillside, and the very thought of that sent a wave of fear coursing through her veins.

Sliding to the edge of the bed, Grace moved cautiously and quietly until her bare feet rested firmly on the wooden floor. Stepping tenderly on old boards that creaked in spots she had not yet memorized, she took up the lamp and with trembling fingers quickly lit it. The glow gave an immediate sense of security, and she relaxed her breathing.

Through the bedroom door, she searched the shadows dancing about thanks to her shaky hands. The footsteps rounded the left side of the shack. Sounds of brittle leaves crushing underfoot sent her heart pounding wildly all over again. Standing as silent as a mouse in an open field, Grace listened, her eyes traveling with the sounds of the steps to the front of the cabin and to her only door. The false sense of security that light gifted hit her unsteadily. The broken front door suddenly became more concerning now than why she was sent to live here in the first place. It seldom closed properly, even after putting a lot of effort into it. The door also swung inward just as easy as it did outward, which gave cause for more alarm. If someone was out there, it would take little effort on their part to come in here.

Fear for her life and that of her unborn overwhelmed her, and she launched herself into action to secure the only way in or out of the little run-down sinner's shack. Setting the lamp on the feeble table, she fetched the only chair she had and crammed its back up under the door's loosely made handle. Stepping away slowly, Grace heard the footsteps outside cease, and she held her breath. Maybe she was overreacting. A dream that may have convinced her of danger where there was none.

To her right more movement, confirming her original

thoughts. This was no nightmare come to life; this was real. Her heart, fully aware of her mind's thinking, raced faster than a four-horse team, its pounding ringing in her ears, pulsating in her neck, and causing her limbs to shake uncontrollably under a crowd of goose bumps. The need for her family, her community, someone, had never been so great. Whatever was out there, Grace was in its natural habitat, this shanty forgotten in the wild.

Was she about to be fed to the wolves? Fearful tears slipped down her cheeks in droves, but thankfully tears rarely made a sound.

Just beyond the front door, a growl began, slow and raspy, lingering and torturing her before shifting into a wicked howl. The call was so piercing that Grace had to cover her ears. Light flickered and danced in the eerie cast of the lamp, making an already scary situation worse. Tears of terror ran rapid.

"Go away!" she cried out. As if a four-legged beast in the wild took orders.

Backing away slowly, Grace bumped into the far wall, preventing motion and any hope of putting more space between her and the dysfunctional front door. This was not a time for freezing up and letting fear win over her limbs and head. Holding her chest, securing the thuds of her heart, Grace considered her options. Did coyotes fear people? An urge to cry out for her *daed*, for anyone, filled her lungs, but reality forbade it. No one would hear her this far away from any other home. No one would come to help her against the beast at her door.

"*Gott* give me strength and safety. You are all we've got."

More footfalls, more growls, and the door rattled. The chair proved just as dependable as the door and the kitchen table and scooted against the force, scrapping over the floor with a heart-stopping screech. Scanning the room in a wild panic for something, anything, to defend herself against the creatures scratching to come in, Grace took up the broken-handled broom nearby. Even at barely five feet, she found the broom had made simple sweeping a chore, but currently it would be her best defense against the beast threatening the life of her unborn child.

Face pouring with sweat and tears, she wiped away the fear and flipped her head, taking a failing braid of black hair with it to one shoulder, and steadied herself. Prepared herself.

When the chair fell to the floor, her life flashed before her. It was a real thing: a vision of laundry flapping in the breeze and *kinner* running about. Whatever strange force allowed for it, Grace strengthened in it. A wave of protectiveness ran through her to stand firm against what was coming through that door. Every wrong decision she had made no longer mattered—only this moment and the future she would have to fight for.

The dog stepped into the doorway, his long brown and black coat matted in burrs and debris. His teeth were the visions of nightmares. Wild, hungry eyes told her she could not simply raise her voice and have him follow her command. Feral as a starved cat but bigger, so much bigger. And he was more equipped to cause harm than one small woman with a broken broom.

Two more dogs, not coyotes at all, slithered in behind him. The white one looked like the same dog Claire's *daed* used to have guard sheep, only thinner, hungrier, his tail showing no signs of wagging. The thinnest one was a mix between lab and devil. Silver haloed a muzzle that bore teeth just as threatening as the other two.

Grace may not have ever seen coyotes up close before, but these wicked allies couldn't be that. Had they escaped some cruel owner only to find her here, alone and vulnerable?

With a prayer in her heart and a weapon in her hand, she waited for them to lunge. The broom would be her only defender, and she gripped it tightly, hoping her trembling hands could continue to hold it. For tonight, she could not call out to her *mutter* as she did as a child with a sore belly, nor scream for her *daed* as she had when the rooster found fun in toying with her.

Tonight, Grace would have to stand alone, or fall alone, with only the Lord invisibly beside her. "*Gott* be with us."

CHAPTER FIVE

"Nice to s-s-see ya away from the f-f-forge," Whitey stuttered, reaching out to shake Cullen's hand. Cullen came every Monday like clockwork to the old junk yard for scrap metal, just as his father had before him. Already behind schedule, he hoped to make quick work today of sifting through old cars and ancient tractors for useful pieces before delivering Abram Schwartz's new wooden shop sign he'd finished late last night.

"Nice to step away from it for at least a spell," Cullen replied. Truth was, he loved his work. It was satisfying and didn't require anything from him but some muscle and years of expertise as a blacksmith. Two things Cullen had plenty of.

Clifton Pennington was the man's birth name, but these days *Whitey* had become the name he answered to. The local mechanic was a thin and jolly man, but after being struck by lightning years back, not only did the color of his hair change overnight, but his sound as well. Cullen recalled Whitey being quite the talker when Cullen had accompanied his *daed* on trips to sift through the rummage as a boy. Now the man's winded stories had become no more than stuttered, simple replies. And though Whitey preferred to settle in silence now, Cullen had heard his singing on more than one occasion when Whitey thought himself to be alone. And how that man could sing, Cullen marveled. Time spent here with Whitey was as much a pleasure as it was business.

Once the buggy was loaded with a few useful pieces of metal, Cullen wiped his brow and climbed up into his seat. He released the brake. "I need to get this sign to Abram's and head back to work. *Danke* again, Whitey. See ya next week?"

Whitey nodded and quickly disappeared back into a sea of debris, a tune already whistling on his lips.

Driving back toward Walnut Ridge, Cullen passed by the old house where Marty had once lived. Like every Monday, he looked toward the empty and hollow shell abandoned all these years and let in a string of melancholy that would carry him for another week until he passed by it again. A yellowed curtain blowing in the warm breeze was his reminder that that part of his life was gone. Marty had sewn the curtains herself, *mamm* taught her how, and yellow had always been her favorite. He was partial to it himself, considering her blonde mane was what had first attracted him to her.

They'd wanted a life together, *kinner* filling their home. She would have made a *wunderbaar fraa* and *mutter*, he thought. Ten years was a long time to mourn, his friends Lucas and Caleb reminded him on days when gloom shadowed his face. Ten years was a long time to miss someone, but who put limits on such a thing? Oddly, for a week now, Cullen realized he hadn't thought of Marty. He had been busy, orders piling up daily. Then there was jumping up at every little sound floating through the holler, wondering if Grace's *ehemann* had gotten to her.

He pulled his attention away to concentrate on the road ahead. This weekly routine had become common, a routine that only brought forth ache. Yet, he couldn't imagine not driving by Marty's old *haus*, keeping her to memory, even if that *haus* represented the worst of them. The words of the bishop sprang into his mind again. "Do the same thing day in and day out, receive the same results." Bishop Mast was preaching encouragement, sticking to the path *Gott* laid before us and never wavering, but Cullen took the words in with fresh ears and let their meaning sink in to his current humdrum existence.

If he continued along this path, nothing in his life would ever change. Well, he had smiled at Sara on Sunday, so there was that. Cullen just wasn't sure he was glad it appeared to make her so pleased after he did it.

Cloud-filled skies tore his attention away from the brown and dying season. He missed the colors of autumn, its vibrant reds, oranges, and brilliant birch yellows absent in the drought that had laid claim over the valley. But heavenward, everything looked as it should be. As he had as a boy, Cullen made out faces in the clouds. There was a dog with one ear and one cloud that resembled what he figured mermaids might look like. In the orbs of various blue hues, an eye looked down on him. Oddly, it brought a measure of comfort.

Dry, lifeless air filled his lungs as the buggy went from blacktop to gravel, and for some reason he couldn't explain, his new neighbor entered his thoughts again. Since meeting her, Cullen couldn't stop poking at their encounter. Her sly and bashful attempt to hide her belly was unsuccessful, but why the woman felt the need to do so was a bit puzzling. It wasn't proper to talk about such things, or parade around boasting with pride like the *Englisch* did when one was pregnant, but Grace wore a look of fear, maybe a hint of embarrassment, too. He'd recognized it quickly—Marty had worn those same disturbing expressions often. But Grace was nothing like Marty, who had plenty of call to look sorrowful and embarrassed. Grace was Amish. She had family, community, an *ehemann*. Marty had the results of her father's anger left boldly on display for others to see and no *mutter* to comfort her.

Why Grace had darted him those same looks was beyond him. Babies were miracles, promises from *Gott*, and Grace should be glad her family was about to add to the fold as He intended things to be. Cullen grinned. Grace Miller was such a small thing tucking into the shadow of Betty Glick. Pretty, too. Those eyes, even at a distance, he thought to be as blue as the water of Twin Fork Lake, as blue as a big bold sky.

Shaking his head, clearing it of any improper thoughts, Cullen tried to put the newcomer out of his mind.

Come to think of it, he realized that since the day he went to investigate the cause for all the recent interest in the old cabin, he'd seen no one come in or out on the cabin road. Why would a *mann* leave his beautiful *fraa* alone in such a place? Times had changed. He shook his head again. Many Amish men found themselves seeking work outside the life of farming, but three days was not normal by any standards he'd heard of. She was young, too, maybe nineteen or twenty. Would she not be afraid with her *mann* nowhere in sight? "Alone" was not a word considered in the Amish world. There was family, community, and friends. "Alone" was a word only he preferred, or at least he thought he did.

And there was the local wildlife to consider. He'd heard the coyotes on the hill night before last, startling him from some much-needed sleep. He should have been used to the sounds of the hillsides surrounding him, but they were closer than before. Close as they were just days before clearing out his *mutter*'s chicken coop. Thankfully they silenced after a spell and he fell back to sleep knowing whatever game they had been chasing had lost its fight for survival, and this time not one new hen in his coop suffered.

He hoped Grace hadn't been frightened by them. Tessie Miller should have never insisted on a woman in that condition living in such a place when she had plenty of room for Grace and her *ehemann* in her own home. Tess liked to be all hard sticks and as bitter as the late afternoon *kaffi* she always offered him on days he stopped in on his *mutter*'s dearest friend. But Cullen knew Tess's heart, as few did, and it was wide and giving—when she wanted to use it, that was.

Pulling into Abram and Elli's drive, Cullen again had to set aside all thoughts of the pretty blue-eyed newcomer. Why couldn't he just shake these thoughts of her? Elli emerged from the creamery barn wiping her hands on her apron front. She went to the back side of the wagon and inspected his work.

"It looks *wunderbaar*, Cullen," Elli praised following the curve of the upper arc with her hands. She had always been a fan of his talents, even going so far as to advertise word of mouth and hang a flyer on the front wall of her creamery. The number of customers that frequented Abram's woodshop and Elli's creamery had abetted his prosperity further than he could have imagined. It didn't hurt that she had *Englisch* family who liked his products, too. If work ever slowed, he could hang a flyer up in other places, but for now that was the last thing he needed, as behind as he was. Business was good.

His *daed* would have been proud of him. *Mutter* too, if they were still here. Oh, how he wished they were still here. At least he had told them goodbye that morning before they left for town. If he had known it would be the last farewell he would ever give his parents, he would have hugged them, told them he loved them, too. One always thought they had more time to do such things, but he should've known better.

Of all people, Cullen knew better. Learning that lesson as a young man, to never forget to leave someone knowing they are in your heart, in case *Gott* called them away and in your heart was the only place they would ever be any longer. He shrugged off the despairing thoughts of his parents and began unloading the sign he had made for Abram.

"You can say 'wonderful.'" Cullen teased. Elli was always trying to practice her German on him, but the way he saw it, she was Amish no matter her stumbling tongue.

"I promised Abram I would try harder, *all recht*." She lifted a stubborn brow.

"All right." He chuckled and got down from the buggy seat.

"Have you seen anything of your neighbor of late?" Elli asked, stretching her neck to look at him.

"*Nee*. Why?" With both arms extended fully, Cullen lifted the sign and rested it on the ground.

"Grace assured me she would be here at first light, but she never came. I hope the poor thing isn't unwell. I gave her a number for a driver but never gave thought to see she had the means to afford one." The worry etched on the two lines of Elli's forehead told Cullen the always-positive woman was sincerely concerned.

"You told her there was a phone at the end of my place, didn't you?" Cullen's wasn't the only Amish business that had a phone somewhere nearby. Amish weren't permitted to have them in their homes, but a phone shanty far from one's house had never caused concern and helped a great deal when dealing with customers. He should have thought to have offered that information himself when he met Grace. Somehow the surprise of her condition and the fact she was going to live in a shack fleeted it from his thoughts.

"Tess told her in case she wanted to call home and leave a message for her parents or her sisters."

"Well, she didn't attend church, either. Maybe she is waiting for her *ehemann*," he shrugged. "New place all alone, maybe she is shy." He hoped Elli didn't think he had looked for Grace on Sunday. That wouldn't be proper.

Elli laughed, causing his ears to warm. "She will attend the next one. She needs time to adjust to her new surroundings first. But she is not shy. Not really. And Grace has no husband."

Cullen froze at that last bit of information. Slowly, as the words replayed, he felt his hands roll into fists. Tess had made it clear Grace would do as ordered, meaning Grace did not choose to be here. Cullen understood some husbands tended to be harsher than others, but now it seemed Grace was suffering a different fate. A newcomer, pregnant, unwed, it didn't take a genius to figure out that Grace was sent here as an act of punishment for jumping the fence and veering off the Amish path.

"Unwed," he muttered. "Does the bishop know?"

"He does. Tess made sure of it," Elli rolled her eyes. "Grace faced her community elders, accepted her punishment. As I understood it from Betty, she confessed before her church."

"Then why is she not with her family, people who can care for her, help her?" His knuckles were going numb and he loosened his grip.

The repercussions of shunning, the hard lesson of love behind its purpose, brought the sinner face to face with the sin. Cullen understood and upheld the century-old method, seeing many a young wanderer slip into a worldly place of exploration after taking his baptism promising he would be of sound heart and surrendering will. But Grace was alone, in an unstable cabin not worthy for rats. Where was the other guilty party? It was best he kept some questions to himself.

"I don't know, Cullen. I don't know what makes one family be one way and the next, another. But she is here now."

Grace had a cautious way about her, but when she locked gazes with him and those blue eyes turned icy over his unintentional insult, he knew better. "Is it normal for her to say she will do something and not?" Elli shrugged, and a small prick of concern crept into his gut. Cullen had just assumed that as a new member of the community, Grace would have had many who would have looked in on her.

"I just met her, so I don't know her habits. She didn't strike me as one who would forget her first day of work. She needs the wages too badly." Of course she would under the circumstances.

Cullen's heart sank inside itself. He had always been blessed with a warm home and a good meal and he, too, knew just how tempting the outside world could be. He had never thought to cross lines after his baptism, but lines had wavered in his youth. He had to give high marks to a sinner who faced her community, confessed her immoralities, and accepted her fate. There was something to be said about that alone.

"I'm heading back now and I will go look in on her," Cullen said a bit more sternly than he meant to.

"We both will," Elli said firmly. "Let me tell Hannah and Rachel where I am going."

CHAPTER SIX

The more Elli rambled worriedly, the more Cullen felt it was necessary to push his horse a little harder. Grace Miller was not only expecting in a couple of short months—which he still couldn't fathom, given the size of her—but she was alone in that cabin. Every scenario imaginable surfaced, and he slapped the reins once more.

Cullen wouldn't judge her or her situation. Judging others was a sin, too, one he had never courted with before. But her well-being and that of an innocent couldn't be ignored as easily as it seemed to be for others.

"We shouldn't worry. Grace will be fine." Elli stiffened, looking ahead as she always did. "I shouldn't have shared her business with you." Her hands wrung inside each other, her features pinched as if she were scolding herself for gossiping. "It's not right to give you a bad impression when no one really knows her whole story. I for one know what it is like to be judged before people got to know me."

"You were seeking. That's different," he said flatly. Seekers were *Englischers* who wanted to become Amish. Elli practically lived the life already, but when she fell in love with Abram, her commitments took full form. "But I am glad you did tell me. If I knew she was alone, without a soul to look in on her and far from family, I would have seen to it that she was okay. The bishop would not scold looking in on another's well-being."

"I still shouldn't have told you, it was wrong of me, but I

think Tessie hasn't been checking on her like she should have. Her *bruder* sent word to do little for her, but not let her starve." Elli groaned. "I should have taken it upon myself to see to her, but I have been so busy at the creamery." She shook her head. "It's no excuse. If that were my daughter…"

Cullen reached over and patted Elli's hand. It was no one's fault.

"It's been days since we were up there cleaning and stocking her pantry. What kind of neighbors have we been?" Elli's voice cracked, no longer sounding convincing but shaky, emotional. What kind of neighbor had he been? Cullen appreciated Elli's honesty. Many would not be so quick to help one who had fallen.

The closer they got to the little cabin, the more guilt found a hole to wallow inside his gut. Even if he hadn't known she had been sent here to hide her pregnancy, Cullen still should have seen about her and the husband he thought she had. They were newcomers who deserved help getting settled. It was the Amish way.

God did not say to forsake the fallen. Bishop Mast had said nothing of shunning a newcomer during services yesterday, but Cullen was fairly certain the bishop wouldn't have. John Mast was a kind shepherd.

The sound of clacking scrap metal in the back played an unpracticed tune. He veered more to the left to avoid another string of dips in the gravel road. He couldn't help but wonder if Grace had been afraid all these days alone, if she felt as if her community had just left her to the wolves, hoping to erase whatever stain she placed on her family name.

"If her *daed* sent her here to hide her shame from their community and Tessie agreed to help her, then she should have done so. I shall have a word with her on this." Cullen spoke between clenched teeth.

It unnerved him, the cruelty of others. Worse was how some fathers tended to treat their offspring with hardness instead of love. Marty's *daed* had been the hardest of them all. Cullen should not have waited so long to take her from that house. Marty was going to join the church, just as he had. If she just would have had more time, if he would have just moved things a little faster, life could have been different.

He shook his head clear. *Not right now.* He wasn't going to do that to himself again, dig up ten-year-old hurts. He needed to focus on the day, the present.

"What kind of people are we that we don't tend to our own?" The reprimand was for him as much as it was for his community. And if *Gott* had seen to it that the expecting woman was safe and well, he would share his thoughts with Bishop Mast in hopes that such encouragement would be placed upon listening ears during the next preaching. "He who is without sin, cast the first stone." Had their minister, David Zook, not preached that into the hearts and ears of the community regularly?

"I'm glad to know you care about others, about our little Grace enough to help. I think sometimes being a friend to someone who needs one can be a healing balm to much of what breaks us."

He was always helpful. Lent a hand whenever an extra was needed, but Elli's tone suggested more. Was Elli referring to Grace needing a friend, or him?

Reaching the cabin, Cullen stopped the charcoal gelding inches from the porch, or what was supposed to be a porch. It had been more than six summers ago when the porch sank under the strain of a heavy winter storm. The front door lay open, but he suspected the warm weather might be the cause of that. Upon closer inspection they noted the linens scattered from the inside of the cabin, out, and white sprinkled across the threshold. Something terrible had gone wrong, and he sprang over the side of the buggy, not taking the time to help Elli down, and in one step reached the rickety porch. Sliding a boot over the porch planks, he felt the coarse texture of sugar underneath.

"Did something get in here?" Elli asked, standing right behind him. How the forty-five-year-old woman got down and near him so quickly was a mystery, but not the biggest one right now.

"I don't know." But he did. The frosted floor revealed nothing, but something had been spilled on the ground to his right, and the footprints there were as loud as his own adrenaline-fueled heartbeat. "Elli, stay here," he ordered in a firm tone. Cullen hoped, for once, she listened. Elli tended to beat her own rhythm more often than not. She had spent far too many years in the world to simply listen to the likes of him.

Sunlight leaked in a stream over the heart of the room. He searched the shadowy corners, the floor, but Grace was nowhere in the small space that made up a home. He peered ahead at the only other door in the cabin and rushed through it with haste.

"Grace! Grace Miller!" Fear for what he might find was

smothered by the need to know what had occurred here and how he was going to fix it. Busting through the bedroom door took no effort with its rusty hinges. He had put enough heft into it that the whole thing came down in a slow-moving crash to the floor. Dust swirled upward, and he tasted the flavors of years of rot and earth in the air. Fanning the cloud, he coughed out the debris threatening his lungs.

"Oh, Grace!" Elli cried out, shoving past him. Feet glued to the floor, Cullen let Elli approach the half-dressed woman hunkered down in the shadows behind a fortress made out of a small bed. A thick string of crimson streaked the bedding and crossed the room. Fear for Grace, for what injuries she might have sustained, sent his heart hammering against his chest. A strange wave of protectiveness washed over him. His eyes narrowed, following the trail of blood covering the wooden floor and into the far corner. There in a dark corner next to a worn-out old black trunk lay the source of the lost liquids. A *coyote*. "She killed it," he muttered, momentarily relieved and shocked that the little woman had managed such a deed, especially one this size.

Turning back to face her, Cullen watched Grace's head rise slowly upward. Bloodshot eyes rimmed with swollen flesh immediately began pouring everything she had left down her cheeks. And he was certain by the looks of her, she had little left. It was all he could do not to rush to her as well, scoop her up and deliver her straight to her *aenti's* door. Let Tess see the results of her neglect. No one deserved to left to fend for themselves.

He removed his straw hat to keep from clenching his

fist so hard. Maybe he should write her family back home, too. Describe this scene. Surely it would bring them to their senses and break their hearts. She needed to be home, with family, cared for. Not dumped off and forgotten.

Grace's long dark hair hung in a tangled braid over one shoulder. She looked a mess. Taking a slow, cautious step toward the bed, he noted the broken broom handle gripped tightly in her hand, dark crimson dried on the splintered end. It would not have been his weapon of choice, but he was learning that she had very few choices now, didn't she? A surge of pity washed over him.

Elli gently pried the broom from her grasp. "Shh now, dear. All is okay."

Grace's knuckles remained white from gripping the broom handle for dear life. Insight clasped Cullen by the heart. Grace had indeed fought off the menacing coyote he had heard last night. He couldn't believe himself. Why hadn't he thought to check on her? Was this who he still was? The man who was always too late to make a difference?

"I prayed *Gott* would tell someone I was here. Are they all gone?" Grace looked about wildly, as if anticipating another beast to pounce out of the darkened shadows of the dim room.

"*Jah*, the coyotes are gone, Grace," he answered, still lost in the look of her. Her expression matched that of defeat, mingled with determination. It was an ironic mixture. She kept her frazzled gaze on Elli while her lower lip trembled, sending a rippling effect over the rest of her until even her shoulders trembled uncontrollably. Cullen figured she was experiencing a stage of shock, though he wasn't an expert on such things.

He had read about it once, after finding Marty that night her father kicked her out. She, too, had trembled like that. Martha, the local midwife and only person with knowledge of such things, had said shock did that to a person after an accident or a terrible event. Fluids, warm blankets, that's what Grace needed, best as he could remember. That's what history was screaming into his ear.

"I only got one of them *gut*. I hurt the other before he took off with a third. They were not afraid," she said, her voice quivering. "They were not coyotes," her whisper added before lowering her head again.

Elli closed in and offered a gentle hand around her shoulders. Cullen watched Grace lean into that comfort as if she had been starved of such attention. Not too many women would have done what Grace had, and certainly not gone unscathed. He flinched. He hoped she was unscathed.

Elli looked to him with a long face, and he motioned his hand for her to look Grace over.

"Check her for injuries." Cullen turned his back to them, not leaving entirely, and focused on the dog in the corner. Grace was right. At first glance the tan coat resembled his wildlife neighbors, but now that Cullen's eyes had adjusted to the dimness of the room, the critter was double in size, and the black saddle along its back revealed a dog, a dangerous pet loosed from its restraints. He made a mental note to inquire, seek its owner, and let them know what had occurred here. Maybe even contact the local sheriff. He was good for handling such things.

"They are gone, Grace." Elli assured her once more.

"Are you hurt?" Sliding the bed from the wall, Elli began searching Grace from head to toe.

"Please call me Gracie. You came to find me when no one else cared. You are my *freind*." Her weak, raspy tone melted Cullen's heart.

"Can you move, Gracie?" Elli asked in slow, drawn out words.

"I am afraid I have been down here since they chased me into the room last *nacht*. I am not certain I can get up myself." *All night and all morning?* Cullen mentally slapped his forehead, hard. It was official; he was the worst neighbor.

When he heard them stirring, Cullen turned as Elli helped Grace to her feet. Her gown was stained with dirt and splatters of blood, her legs certainly too weak to hold her, and that shaky arm was not capable of cradling her center as she was trying so hard to do. Despite the need to offer compassion, help, Cullen hesitated. He had never touched another woman besides Marty or his *mutter* before. *Special circumstances*, he told himself.

Stepping around the angled bed, Cullen bent, and picked Grace up from the floor. Her body was thin, too thin for a woman in her condition, and he was careful not to break her like a dry stick in his healthy arms. The scent of sweat and blood and lavender wafted from her. He didn't care much for the smell of blood, never had much stomach for it, but the soft hint of lavender had a way of drowning it.

When he aimed for the door, Grace squirmed with resistance. "Where are you taking me?" She pushed against him in a panic he was unprepared for. She sure could make something so easy become difficult.

"You cannot stay here alone, Grace Miller. It is not safe for you in your condition. I am taking you to be seen by a doctor, then delivering you to your *aenti*."

"Let go of me!"

Cullen suddenly found out just how strong the exhausted newcomer was after fighting off dogs with a broken-handled broom from behind her bed.

In one surprising motion, she leaped from his cautious hold and hit the sugar-covered floor. Her bare feet slid, pushing away from his kindness. Cullen reached out to steady her, but the look of horror on her face stopped him dead, and he raised his arms in surrender, hoping she would still herself before she fell. "I am no *hund* you need to order about." Was that what she thought he was doing? *Shock*. She was surely not thinking clearly.

"Grace, Cullen is only trying to help you, and he is right. You cannot stay here. Your arm is bleeding and needs tended." Cullen knew by the worry in Elli Schwartz's eyes that she was thinking rabies, as was he once he noticed the amount of blood covering her sleeve.

"They only scratched me, and they were not mad. They were hungry." Her stubbornness yanked her away from Elli's touch and she quickly covered the wound with her other hand. Hiding it, she winced. "I am not to go elsewhere. This is where my *daed* ordered me to stay and I cannot disobey him." She took a deep breath. "*Danke* for coming to see about me, but I will be fine."

She planted her feet firmly and righted herself as if ready to defend against him.

Cullen took a step back, throwing up both hands once

more to calm her. Was she not seeing the concern here?

Studying her and her heated determination that she needed no help, he considered grinning. With her messy hair, filthy nightgown, and those brilliant, raging blue eyes, she was a sight, and she had a bit more spunk than the woman he had seen cowed behind Betty days ago.

"You have been through a horrible ordeal," he tried to reason with her in his calmest voice. "You have to trust we only want to get help for you. You could get an infection. You need to be seen to."

He awaited her reply, an audible answer over that silent glare. It didn't come. He lifted a brow to encourage her further. Nothing, just proud defiance, or was it trust she was having a hard time with? She made him want to pull his hair out.

"Cullen, please excuse us for a bit while I help Grace get cleaned up," Elli said. Cullen gave her a nod. Maybe Elli could talk some sense into her. Because against her wants or not, she would be tended to. Stomping out the door, for the life of him, Cullen would never understand the female species. If there were a front door that worked like front doors should, he would have given it a gruff slam in his exit.

CHAPTER SEVEN

After two full weeks of resting, as Martha Shrock insisted, in the sinner's shack with nothing but her own voice to listen to, Grace couldn't believe how lovely her *Aenti* Tess's poor struggling gelding sounded rattling up the hill. Betty had come by once, but it was clear she didn't like climbing that hill one bit. Or maybe it was the descent that made her all jittery. Abram had delivered her a box of fresh goods Elli insisted she needed, along with fresh gauze and ointment for her freshly removed stitches. There was also the invisible visitor. The one she was sure she had frightened off well and good two weeks ago. He had left over three dozen eggs in the passing days on her porch, but had waited under the veil of darkness to do so. It was sweet, regardless of the fact that he clearly wanted no cause to face her after the fit she'd thrown.

Dressed in her nicest robin-egg-blue dress, just recently loosened of a few threads that made it a bit more well-fitting than she felt comfortable in, she climbed into the buggy and drew in a ragged breath. Her nerves had only begun to calm after her horrible night, but facing another line of fresh faces sent them stirring again. This would be her first time attending a Sunday church that was not in her own community.

Touching the place on her arm where fresh white cotton gauze covered itchy flesh no longer holding six stitches, she suddenly felt that if she had contracted rabies, it would have been easier to have dealt with than being the new face walking into the unknown. Where was her bravery now?

"You healin'?" Tess asked in a dry voice.

Grace nodded, but neither of them broached the topic of the horrible night the stray dogs had found their way inside the shack. She rubbed at a stain of dust that had fallen onto her apron front, then licked her thumb to help remove its blemish from the white. Like everything about her, it was a mistake, and the little speck spread like spilled *kaffi* and took hold of the fabric. *Stained*, she chastised herself. Now her Sunday best was as stained as she was. She let out a heavy sigh.

The bishop's home was over the next incline ahead, according to her *aenti*. The overly warm weather had ceased its tormenting of the valley and now presented itself like a proper autumn morning with cooler temps. Grace was glad for the silence that rode between them. It gave her another opportunity to chide herself for the way she had treated Cullen and Elli. They had only meant well, seeing about her as they did, even forcing her to be stitched up by a local midwife slash Amish nurse, though Martha was well-equipped and educated, surprisingly. Amish didn't attend school after the eighth grade, but Martha had taken advantage of her *rumschpringe* years to take nursing classes and returned to not only be baptized, but to help all the Amish communities that made up Pleasants County.

Grace wished she had used her run around years more wisely. Though a family of her own had always been her hope, she would have preferred opening her own bakery, starting a family the traditional way, but those were no longer possibilities.

Despite feeling as big as a barn crammed with critters, Grace couldn't help but recall how effortlessly Cullen had swept her from the floor, his muscular arms with a light-as-a-feather touch. He had to understand her rejection of his help, spawned by too many mistakes trusting people to be sincere in their feelings toward her.

But Cullen didn't know. He could never know how just his presence made her nervous. He was just too handsome for his own good, and that wouldn't do now that she was resigned to a life without a man in it. Still, she couldn't help but notice how his suspenders drew taut when he had lifted her or that he'd smelled of smoke, earth, and man. It didn't go unnoticed the way his dark *kaffi* eyes winced at the first sight of her kneeling behind her bed. And what man would let her talk to him as she had and simply bite his tongue and step outside? It just didn't happen.

"Bishop Mast and our ministers know you are coming. He is aware of your situation. I should hope you conduct yourself properly if he speaks with you," Tessie said as if in warning.

Grace wrung her hands together, nodded obediently, and tried to ignore the humming of her irregular heartbeat. The thought of facing another group of elders had her stomach in knots. *Ordnung*, or the traditional rules and practices of the Amish faith, was generally the same from community to community. Some had more liberal allowances, like pastel colors, cell phones for business use, and even divorce, if the circumstances were dire. Havenlee had no such liberties. Surely her condition was evidence enough that she hadn't forgotten her lost morals.

She could still remember her first Sunday church gathering after her secret was no longer a secret. It was directly after the bishop had made her invisible to the community, invoking the banning that was spawned "out of love," as he called it.

Entering her *onkle*'s home that morning, a home she had played in and run through all her childhood, she found it as foreign as her shack. Eyes darted past her, and bodies slid away when she went to take a seat on the lonely bench in the corner. Her friends and family avoided her as if she were poison ivy and her sins catching.

She would never understand shunning. After all the years she had been preached to about forgiveness, grace, and *Gott*'s mercies, it seemed so contradictory, despite all the assurances of its need as a gift of love to help the sinner repent and turn away from their sinful behaviors and find their way back into the fold.

At first, being invisible was the hardest thing Grace had ever endured. Now, as her girth grew and her emotions regularly became unhinged, invisibility was a gift. As Tess drove up to the massive black barn with fifty or so other buggies, a knot inside her tightened. The image of lambs being led to the slaughter came to mind.

She carefully lowered herself to the ground, without assistance from one of the three young boys handling the horses today. Staring at the ground, for she could no longer see her feet no matter how small Hannah thought her to be, she obediently followed her *aenti* toward the house. For such a small woman of age, Tessie's stride soon left Grace to her own grave peril. Yep, she was a lamb all right.

"Gracie!" Grace looked up, and Hannah was the first to

greet her on the front porch. She looked like sunshine after the storm, her bold green dress matching that of the shirt on the little towheaded boy straddled comfortably on her hip.

"He is adorable Hannah," Grace said.

"He is a handful, I assure you," Hannah jested, handing Noah over to a man standing nearby Grace could only assume was Hannah's *ehemann*.

Hannah grabbed hold of Grace's hand as if they had been dear friends since childhood and immediately escorted Grace into the huge white farmhouse. "It is *gut* you made it today. I hope you are feeling well. We have all worried about what happened to you."

Grace didn't know what to say. Why would people she didn't know worry about her?

"The bishop's *haus* has many rooms, but we shall all gather in the sitting area," Hannah informed her, looping her arm into Grace's as if she were fearful Grace would run. She would need to be more careful of how her face looked to others. It did no good to be so easily readable. "Small features still make big impressions," her *mutter* always reminded her when her thoughts read like a book on her face.

Inside, a cool breeze wisped through hallways and rooms, and it did wonders to calm her frazzled nerves. As they drifted from one room to another, Hannah shared the history of the old house. Grace found the home to be mazelike and more than once wondered just how fast she could find her way back out to the main door if need be. The narrowing hallways were close-fitting and dense with strangers moving here and there. "I will show you around a bit, *jah*?" Hannah said pulling her farther still.

Grace nodded, regardless of how badly she wished to sit in some lonely corner and fade into the background instead.

The house had been an old orphanage, Hannah revealed, when that was still a thing, from the 1800s. And that explained a lot about the way rooms were scattered in an oddly chaotic fashion. Grace could envision classrooms and sleeping quarters filled with children who had been abandoned or had lost those who brought them into the world.

She thought of all the fearful and thankful faces brought here. She had not yet decided which she felt in her own abandonment. *Raw*, that's what she still felt. Not just abandoned by the one who promised her a future, but by her own father who shared her same blood. Here, in a place where emotions were likely scattered as wildly as leaves on a stormy autumn day, she felt a strange calm she hadn't expected. She, too, was like a forgotten child, perhaps. Would her *boppli* feel the same way some day?

Bodies flowed in and out of rooms and doorways. Grace stiffened with every brush of an arm. A narrow white door opened abruptly and brought her to a startling halt, separating her from Hannah.

"*Ach.* Sorry," an older woman said in equal surprise, descending a staircase to enter the hallway, not taking into account traffic flowing on the other side of the door. "You are with child." Grace cradled her middle and took a step back, bumping right into another body close behind her and stepping on their right shoe. She let out a timid huff, but heard nothing from behind her. Two hands instinctually steadied her shoulders so as not to let her topple and quickly let go once the threat was gone. Grace didn't dare turn and face her victim, another set of eyes penetrating her. It was unnerving how narrow these halls were and how fast a heart could race and not burst.

"I shall be more mindful not to hurry. Forgive me, Grace Miller." The woman smiled solemnly, but Grace only stilled at the mentioning of her name. Suddenly the warmth of the narrow hall reached a few degrees higher and she cupped a hand over her wounded arm.

"Nothing to forgive. I am *gut*," Grace replied respectfully. When the woman who knew her name—though Grace did not know the woman's—closed the door, Hannah came back into sight.

"That was Jane Mast, the bishop's eldest," Hannah informed. "Never married, and teaches at the school. Oh, hi, Cullen, how did I miss seeing ya behind our little Grace here?"

Hannah smiled just over her head, and Grace suddenly felt his towering presence. Cullen must have been who she had bumped into. Grace swallowed a lump that had formed and quickly stepped in line, following Hannah into the large sitting room. She refused to turn and greet him. So far nothing about this first gathering with the community was going as she had hoped.

Stepping into the sitting room, a sea of beards stopped midconversation to look at her. At their stony expressions, Grace lowered her head, playing invisible. Brushing past, Cullen uttered, "Excuse me, little Grace," a playful grin spread across his wide lips that only teased at her, and suddenly Cullen's presence behind her didn't feel so unnerving. She rolled her eyes, but kept her lips tightly shut. She knew better than to speak to him here, and glancing up again at the gray beards, she knew she was right. Cullen joined the men to one side of the room, and conversation once again wheeled the community leaders back together.

Grace lowered onto the stiff bench just behind Hannah. Casually, she scanned the room before settling her sights on the only clean-shaven man, to her right. Cullen was quite a bit taller than any of the older men laughing at something he said. Yet why was she taking the time to notice that? He was clearly not the only beardless man in the room now that she pulled her gaze away and took in the gathering room. Her *daed* was right; she was a sinner of weak morals.

When hats started being hung on the walls by a few late arrivals, Grace knew the time had arrived and forced herself into attention. Cullen took a seat to the left and glanced her way with a half-hearted smile. Would he do that for the next three hours? Grace hoped not. She had been rude to him, and she was never rude. But she was tired of being treated like a woman who didn't deserve forgiveness. Wasn't forgiveness essential to their way of life? With that thought to herself, she lowered her head for the minister's prayer.

• • •

Cullen sneaked another glance at Grace sitting next to Beth Zook and Walnut Ridge's most recently baptized members. Grace looked like she was going to throw up, and hopefully a smile from a familiar face, even if it was his, might rein that nausea in before she made a spectacle of herself. She locked eyes with him, stared blankly, and then directed those big blue eyes to the center of the room. Was she not even going to at least try to be civil? He *had* been supplying her eggs, after all. Not that she knew it was him, or did she? Surely no one other than the women who found themselves concerned for her would be leaving her eggs. The thought ran through him surprisingly fast.

With so few *maedels* in Walnut Ridge, he hoped her condition at least allowed her peace from the unwed men of the community. Nothing was worse than a few desperate boys fearing they would never be family men or lonely widowers needing help to raise a family, making quick pests of themselves.

In truth, she was unwed, baptized, and having a baby. Certainly not how things were done. But at least she was safe. Grace was safe from pestering boys, and after installing hook-and-eye latches until he could build a better front door, she was safe from wild dogs.

Every time Cullen thought of her, the temperature rose a few degrees higher. He hadn't expected that, not from someone such as her. He turned his attention back to David Zook, the minister preaching today, and put Grace and her blue eyes and dark hair out of mind.

"For it is by grace that ye be saved…" David began. Cullen's eyes lifted and shot across the room where God's Grace sat, head down, hands folded primly around the miracle inside her. Even the fallen deserved grace. Even they deserved second chances.

I hear ya Lord.

CHAPTER EIGHT

Elli and Abram Schwartz's large two-story home sat on the top of the longest hill Grace had ever ridden up. Looming gray clouds gathering under a dull morning sky didn't subdue the mood inside the massive house filled with chattering women. The white walls carried the echoes of laughter down long hallways, just the same as her family's cellar had carried her voice as she told her sister Hope her most precious secret.

Those words had traveled, too, all the way to the kitchen where her family had gathered for breakfast. That day had been equally ominous; it was the beginning of everything that had forced *Daed*'s hand in sending her here. Grace pushed the horrid memory out of her mind before it could ruin the current one in the making.

Canning bees with all the right people had a way of lifting spirits. Aside from baking for large gatherings, it was a favorite of Grace's. She'd experienced so few canning frolics, as *mutter* preferred to avoid nonessential gatherings. So Elli inviting her today was a rare and delightful treat. Sweet smells of sugar and berries flooded the rooms, bringing to mind similar days with her family. Only back home, jelly making took place in season, before the berries spoiled. All canning was done when the bounty was freshly picked, but Grace was learning once again, Elli tended to do many things differently. Like having *Englisch* relatives with electric freezers, allowing one to save a season for a day when her full-time creamery needed less from her.

"Does the bishop not mind that you use electric freez-ers?" Grace asked timidly, knowing full well such a thing in Havenlee would draw a visit from the local ministers. Taking the damp rag and wiping the warm jars of jelly and jam clean, Grace eyed the full table of various bold colors and textures before screwing on a freshly heated set of caps and rings. Though their house in Havenlee was large enough to handle a room full of women, it was her moth-er's anxiousness that had prevented such activities as much as *daed*'s rule that each had their own place. Mercy was like her *mutter* in that way. Maybe that was why her young-est sister preferred the outdoors. Giving her a chance to breathe more freely and not let close quarters suffocate her youthfulness.

Goodness, she missed her sisters terribly.

"The bishop likes my elderberry jelly far too much to make a fuss over such a thing, and anyway, it is not my freezer." Elli hiked a grin, the sharp blue of her eyes danc-ing like a cat with a mouthful of bird. The kitchen buzzed with activity. Each woman scurried about, preparing the blackberries and elderberries for jams and jelly.

"Much of this will be sold in the creamery or Sadie's store, but we also hold back a fair part to fill baskets for Christmas," Betty added from behind her.

"Some in Walnut Ridge have so little, and it is expected that we to share what *Gott* has blessed us with," Tessie said. Grace suspected she herself might be one of the receivers of such gift giving, and her *aenti* was letting her know it.

"Tess here makes little hats for the hospital, for the babies," Elli said. Grace didn't know that. "She crochets mittens and hats for our baskets this time of year."

"You crochet?" Grace said with a hitch of surprise. Tess nodded, but her lips were tighter than a sealed jelly jar.

"*Mammi* knew how, but her fingers were too tired for teaching my sisters and me. I have always wanted to learn." Grace lowered her head again when Tessie said nothing to this.

The women thawed and drained and cooked the berries down, adding the measured amount of sugar, pectin, and lemon juice, all while carrying full conversations. Certainly nothing like the quiet kitchen Grace was accustomed to. And no one person was steady to one duty, either. They all seemingly knew the process by heart and stepped in where it was required.

Maybe that was why so many things had failed in her father's *haus*. If one slipped, or simply was not present, the whole process of the day was spoiled. Such days could spur *daed*'s temper. It would take a bit of getting used to, but Grace longed for the closeness of community, inclusion that the room around her was offering.

"We are glad you came today. More hands, more hearts," Betty said with a bubbly smile. "How is your arm?" Betty pinned her with a motherly look.

"*Gut*. Martha says it will barely scar. She says the *boppli* is *gut*, too."

Mentioning the baby was probably not acceptable, but the words had slipped out before she considered them. Grace simply yearned to tell someone, and calling home would not be permitted. Grace used the tongs to lift another three caps and rings from the steaming water on the stove as Elli poured another three jars with deep purple liquid beside her. A hiss sounded as water dripped on the stove.

"That is *wunderbarr*. It will be a blessing to have a wee one at Christmas. They are calling for a cold front this week and much rain. Have you gotten all you need to stay warm? Is your pantry full enough to keep you both fed?" Betty's concern wore in her eyes. There was no hiding it. To her right, Elli assured Rachel that adding more lemon juice to the jelly mixture would take that frown off her face and set the jelly firmer. Grace suppressed a grin when she noted multiple splatters on Rachel's apron front. Rachel didn't have to be perfect, and Grace wished she wouldn't try at it so hard.

"Oh, don't fuss over her. Grace is not the first woman to ever be with child," Tessie barked, pouring another clear freezer bag of limp blackberries into a colander sitting in the sink. Freezing might have its perks, but fresh were better in Grace's way of thinking. And what did her *Aenti* Tess know about such things? She was a spinster, unwed, having no *kinner* of her own.

Peering across the table as she finished sealing the jars, Grace studied her *aenti*. Her small frame bent slightly, salt and pepper hair pulled tightly under a perfectly starched *kapp* and with shoes Grace thought too big for her feet, giving her a few extra inches in height. Her always-present frown never offered a welcoming. Like a bitter tea crying to be sweetened, but Grace wasn't sugaring her just for a spoonful of kindness. How did a person stay so hard, all the time? Even in her current situation, Grace could find little pockets in her day that made her smile or feel some sense of joy.

Grabbing a pen, she began filling out the labels Elli had given her and wrote the appropriate flavor on each jar.

"We can fuss if we wish. It's not every day that a *maedel* takes on a pack of stray *hunds* and wins," Elli shot back, and Betty agreed.

"Well, I can't imagine living all alone in the woods like that. Why would anyone want to live in such conditions?" Rachel lifted her chin as if wading through high waters.

"I didn't choose to," Grace muttered between clenched teeth, tired of letting words just fly past her as if they didn't hurt.

"Did you not? Our choices lead us to our destinations, do they not?" Rachel rolled her eyes again. It seemed her most favorable gesture. Grace reached for another jar before sliding back into the chair Elli had given her. *Aenti* Tess and Rachel were right, she grasped. If Grace hadn't fallen for Jared, for his charms, she wouldn't be here. She put herself here, and here she was. Making a choice between what she knew to be wrong and what was right in the sight of God.

"Ladies, I think it is time to schedule the cookie exchange. Thanksgiving is next week, so after that, of course. And we need to plan the next quilting bee. We must finish both quilts before the auction first of the year," Betty chimed in, shifting all the talk from Grace to something else.

While the women scheduled days and which house would be host for a quilting bee, Grace added the labeled jars of jelly into boxes and began stacking them in the corner by the screen door.

"Let me help you," Elli said, coming to her side. Smiling

at Elli's need to always make her feel included, Grace warmed to her. Elli was a friend, and that was something she could use now.

"You are being too kind to me. *Aenti* Tess might not like you doing so." Grace whispered softly toward Elli's holey ear.

"I have taken a hit or two from Tessie Miller myself. Don't you worry, dear. God tends to all his children, despite her opinion." Grace hoped Elli was right. No amount of praying for forgiveness had eased her hope for His mercy for her mistake, but she at least didn't feel so alone now.

"Have you still got plenty of flour, eggs, milk? You know I have more than enough," Elli was too kind. "I have plenty of apples, too, from Troyer's orchard." Grace was about to open her mouth, to say just how wonderful a fresh apple pie or apple spiced cake sounded, when Betty interrupted.

"She has eggs aplenty, that's for sure and certain," Betty jested under a throaty breath. Did she know about her egg benefactor? Grace's face grew hot.

"Well, then I will send you home with milk and flour. He is such a good fellow," Elli winked, and quickly stood.

"We shall have the cookie exchange a week after Thanksgiving," Elli announced to the room then turned to Grace again. "I expect you to come. To Thanksgiving here *and* the cookie exchange."

Grace wiped her hands on a nearby cloth, and carefully considered her answer.

"I would like that, but only if you tell me what to bring for the Thanksgiving meal. At home I made all the desserts and rolls. I make a cranberry dessert, too." Grace didn't dare mention her well-known custard. Too many eggs in that recipe and she didn't need another remark about her neighbor, nor to give anyone the wrong idea.

"That sounds delicious. Whatever you want to bring, I'm sure it will be eaten up," Elli said.

• • •

Aenti Tess's buggy came to a stop in front of the shack. For the life of her, Grace would never get used to riding up that steep, treacherous hillside. Surely that was the cause for her terrible backache. "*Danke Aenti* for allowing me to *kumm* today. I hope to get to join in more such days."

"Not sure how many such days you will be permitted," Tessie was quick to reply.

"But Bishop Mast has not said anything against it." Grace defended. The women didn't mind her presence and *Daed* was a whole state away. Grace bit the inside of her lip.

When Cullen and Elli had brought her back from receiving stitches at Martha's, Bishop Mast was waiting outside the shack for her. He seemed more concerned about her well-being than her reason for being discarded in his community. He was firm but empathetic. Why was her *aenti* being so unreasonable? Grace tossed her an angry frown.

"That is not a *gut* look on you." Tessie glared. "You should not be riding in a buggy for much longer. It is not *gut* for the *boppli*." She almost sounded sincere.

Taken aback, Grace climbed down from the buggy,

careful not to disturb the fresh wrapping on her arm Betty had insisted on. Speechless over her *aenti*'s sudden concern, Grace said nothing to the remark as she lifted a small bag of food staples from the buggy floor. Tessie reached over, gripped Grace's free hand, and slipped a thin envelope into it.

"What is this?" Grace asked, perplexed.

"A gift. It is not much. I have so little to share"—Grace knew that to be true—"but it will get you a few staples to eat and such." Tessie eyed her intently. "If I know my *bruder* you have little saved to support yourself for the days ahead." The kindness was so unlike her *aenti* that Grace froze, unable to respond to the generosity. "There is a loose board just under the pump sink. Use a can to secure it and hide your important things there. And close your mouth. You look foolish."

With that last firm order, her stiffly posed *aenti* clicked her tongue, leaving Grace standing with the small envelope clenched in her hand and a lot of questions dancing in her head.

It took Grace a few seconds to come to her senses with her *aenti*'s change of heart and her surprising wit. Who would have imagined Tessie Miller had a sense of humor? After a day of only backhanded compliments, the compassion was unexpected. She pondered whether she should have even accepted the envelope. Tessie, too, was alone. Was it selfish to take from someone who had little as well?

The changing weather was less miserable today. Grace felt a surge of energy that she hadn't expected after a full morning at Elli's. It would be a good time to get a few things tended to around the cabin. Stepping onto the lopsided porch, she felt her eyes go straight to the place where her laundry had hung just this morning. It was nothing but two leaning posts and air. Her laundry, including the line itself, had vanished.

"Who would steal laundry?" she queried. Pondering the thief, she slipped the envelope into her dress pocket and maneuvered around the small cabin in search of her clothing. The day quickly turned woeful with a thick overcast of threatening weather. Not even a bird took to the skies. A few stray darkened clouds, the same color as Hope's darker blue eyes, moved in, hanging low along the hilltop, while the rest moved as if running for their life. Nature was a fickle creature, always arguing with itself.

Her eyes widened as Grace came to a stop when she found where her clothes had gone. Each dress, her undergarments, and the few kitchen linens were now hanging from new posts with new string, and facing southwest to get the full effects of the day's gathering winds. Her face flushed knowing someone had handled her unmentionables. "Who?" She could only hope it wasn't her local egg supplier.

The sound of banging metal echoing along the valley made her wince.

CHAPTER NINE

The curve of the metal was perfect, despite the bellows not regulating heat properly. Cullen dunked the metal, shaped with an arc at only one end, into the large wooden tub of water. Two days was all he had to finish the sign for the Country Kitchen store belonging to Matthew and Sadie Miller, and for two days he couldn't keep his mind on anything he should. Cullen was too old for daydreaming and too young to be letting his attentions wander about aimlessly. His neighbor was none of his concern, but she had seeped in and taken root, holding his thoughts hostage.

Despite the bellows smoke, a cool breeze carried with it a hint of some much-needed rain. Cullen inhaled the scent of a fast changing season. Pulling the metal out of the water, he heard a loud *pop* sound and quickly tossed the piece to the ground and moved back, avoiding any sprays of hot metal that might escape the core and onto him.

"Well, that's a fine job, Cullen," he bit back at the ruined mess sizzling in the dust and claimed himself no better suited than a mere amateur today.

If he had gotten his head into what he was doing instead of filling it with nonsense, he would have waited for the metal to have cooled properly before removing it from the quench. He shed the gloves and stepped outside for some air. November was placid compared to the long summer that seemed to run over fall with all four hooves, but at least the cooler temps offered some relief from the forge. The trees following along Crooked Creek and those forming the perfect mountain dome across the fields had resorted to a brown brittleness instead of being painted with the vibrant colors of autumn that the glorious Kentucky mountains generally offered this time of year. Leaves were easily ripped from the limbs and rained down as if nature only now realized she had skipped that part of the process. Everything was lifeless and thirsty for even a few drops of what the heavens held above him.

Nature was wicked like that, withholding its capabilities only to dump them over your head later. He peered up at the darkening sky—she was indeed going to be dumping buckets sooner rather than later. It was no secret that a dry season this prolonged would not only come to an end at some point but would overwhelm you when it did.

A banging sound bounced from one hillside to another. Peering up the hill, just as he did every night before he turned in after a long day, Cullen listened more closely for the source of the echo. Having heard the howls of coyotes the previous night, he took it upon himself to walk up the hill with his shotgun. There was no way Grace was going to endure another encounter like the one she had already.

He was careful to not alarm her with his presence; she was skittish enough and seemingly not so content in his company. Sneaking around, he felt like a watcher, an intruder, sitting on the bank overlooking the run-down cabin. But he had to be honest with himself—the blue-eyed beauty's singing from inside the little cabin's thin walls not only charmed whatever menacing wild things lurked around her, but him as well.

Out of nowhere, something crashed, its hard descent

reverberating over the hill and lingering far into the valley.
Without a second thought of his earlier reminder to keep
his distance, Cullen hurried around the hill to investigate.

· · ·

"Are you all right?" The voice came from behind her.
Spinning around, hammer in hand, Grace found Cullen
standing just ten feet away. His face poured with sweat and
wore a panic she had seen once before in those large
brown eyes. He was working to catch his breath, and failing
at it rather badly, truth be told. His eyes darted from her to
the porch, now with one less post holding up a slanted tin
roof, then back to her again.

"*Jah*. I am fine." She quipped, pretending that his being
up here didn't surprise her.

"But I heard…" Both hands on his knees, he was still
fighting for air, the snug fit of his light blue shirt rising and
falling at lightning pace. A chuckle welled up inside her,
but she shoved it back into place. He was a sight, all
worried and frantic looking. Which he had no cause to be,
matter of fact.

"Well, I aim to finish what I started, so you might hear
more," she snapped confidently. Turning toward the porch
again, she swung, and the hammer banged against the next
stubborn post. Worse than not having a porch to sit on in a
late-day sunset, was having one that might just fall on your
head. "I almost fell last night. This porch is a death trap. I
am tearing it down before it becomes the death of me," she
stated in a louder-than-usual voice.

And she would have already succeeded if he hadn't

shown up, distracting her like he was. He shouldn't be here, especially not looking at her like she was off in the head, like he was right now. It took all afternoon loosening nails and nudging the porch, and she wanted to see it through. She swung again, not caring how ridiculous she might look at eight months pregnant swinging a hammer. This would give the rumor mill something more to talk about.

"What's wrong with you?" he blurted out.

"Some might say plenty," she said, then took another swing. A bigger hammer, that's what she needed.

"And some might be right," he shot back, straightened. "Not only should you not be doing this, but a storm looks to be coming in. You should go inside, let someone—" He hesitated, calculating his words. "Let someone bigger handle this."

Was he growling at her? Grace shot him a glare. Who did this man think he was, ordering her around?

"I feel big enough today," she quipped. "I'm plenty capable. And the day is still young," Grace said exuberantly, ignoring his prodding for her to abandon the task at hand.

"This day feels old to me," he shot back with an equal pluck, running his hands through his damp dark hair. She hadn't meant to frighten him, but was rather flattered the longer he stood there gathering himself.

Grace sneaked a peek at his long frame, his befuddled expression, and a pair of dark eyes that looked as capable of reading one's secrets as smothering out a flame. She pulled her gaze away and took another swing. Her arms were starting to feel like noodles, but quitting now would only make her look weak.

One side of the tin roof and worn rafters groaned, and Grace stepped back to watch all her labor finally pay off. It was good the handsome, nosy neighbor was here to see that she could handle herself, she thought. If he witnessed her independence firsthand, he would not be so quick to run up here every time the slightest noise penetrated the valley below. Time stilled, she took a breath, waiting for the death trap to tumble to the ground, but the porch only lowered with a slow-moving moan and rested again, mocking her.

Grace let out an unladylike sigh. Turning to Cullen, a smug look of amusement on his chiseled face, she hiked one brow. He must think himself some hero, always showing up when he thought he was needed. She didn't need a hero—she needed bigger muscles.

Cullen's rich molasses hair was matted to his head, a ring embedded where his hat normally sat. Those lips that seemed to want to say something stayed tightly together, forming a line between them. He was strong. Blacksmith strong. Half-raised sleeves couldn't hide the bulk produced by his trade. The day he'd barged into her home, she hadn't noticed a lot about Cullen Graber, but his willingness to talk about her living arrangements with her *aenti* while she stood there, invisible, still left her with mixed feelings. Now she was noticing a lot more about him, and for the life of her, she couldn't figure out why.

Hadn't she learned her lesson already? A handsome man hanging about was the last thing she needed in her life.

In three strides, he was beside her. The same teasing grin draped his lips as it had at the bishop's home when he called her "little Grace." "My turn." Cullen reached out, gesturing toward the hammer gripped in her smaller hand.

"I can fix this," he said with confidence. His voice was deep, gritty, like that of an older, much wiser man. Which he wasn't—old, that was. Cullen carefully removed the hammer from her hand as she stood, disoriented for the moment. Why was she being awkward? And why did she let him have her only hammer?

A play of amusement danced on his lips as he strolled past her. Grace inhaled the scent of smoke and iron and man and found the combination pleasing to the senses. Jared often smelled freshly bathed, often perfumed, nothing like a working man at all. Was she comparing him? Her conscience reared up and gave her another mental slap. What was wrong with her?

"I don't need help." She quickly added. Paying no mind to her, he walked away, hammer in hand, but his low chuckle lingered. Didn't he have his own work to tend to? *Daed* would call him idle-brained, leaving one chore, unfinished, to tend to another. Grace was still undecided.

"*Stolze*," he muttered, shaking his head.

"I am not prideful, and that is my hammer!" Grace yelled after him. Truth be told, Grace had found it in the old outhouse, but still—it wasn't *his*. "And I am plenty capable of destroying things myself." Like her life, she bit back.

"Is it common for a woman to pack a hammer when she moves to a whole other state?"

She didn't have to see his expression to know that strong brow over his left eye was raised.

"How would I know what is common?" She growled

inwardly and gave her best Rachel Yoder eye roll. In front of the stubborn post, Cullen squared, planting two big feet firmly apart. He lifted the puny hammer as if it was more than just a mere stick and took one hard swing. In a loud smack of metal on wood, the post surrendered. Everything swayed right and came crashing to the ground in a glorious second.

He grinned, and Grace found herself grinning, too.

When he crossed two large arms over his broad chest, wearing that king-of-the-mountain smile, she dropped her grin and swallowed whatever the thing was stuck in her throat. Despite that handsome grin, she wanted to argue that she could have accomplished getting it to fall herself. But who was she kidding? She couldn't dispute his presence any longer.

The man had perks, useful ones. Maybe she couldn't count on his help all the time, but for today, whatever he offered she would accept. If she could endure judgmental glares, she could manage Cullen Graber's astute smirks.

They weren't so bad after all.

Without being asked, Cullen began pulling boards apart and stacking them in a pile a good twenty feet from the sinner's shack. Why he insisted on being here, she hadn't a clue. Biting her tongue, so as not to anger him into stopping, she went to the mess, picked up a splintered and broken board, and carried it to the pile.

"You know if *Aenti* Tess sees ya helping me, she will make a fuss." His laugh was infectious, but she refused to let it rattle more than just a few hairs on the back of her neck. "What I mean to say is *danke*, but I do not think it would be proper for you to be here. I wouldn't want someone to get the wrong idea."

"To help another as *Gott* instructs?" Cullen said. "Do not be concerned for my reputation," he chuckled. She tugged on a sheet of rusted metal, forming her own pile of debris that wouldn't burn.

"I didn't mean—" Why was she making such a mess of words?

Cullen paused, shook his head. "I know what you meant. Tess and my *mutter* were *freinden*. She would have my skin if I didn't offer help." He floated her a friendly smile. That made her relax just a little more. Back home if a boy helped you, gave you flirty grins, he was interested in you. Cullen was just being friendly. A good neighbor.

Cullen lifted a section of porch that would have taken her hours to dismantle and, with a grunt, added it to the growing pile. The way his body strained and twisted sent another surge of heat over her. The man was *strong*. When she caught herself staring at him for a third time, Grace figured it had to be those pregnancy hormones she read about. They were certainly messing with her thoughts. She should read over that chapter in the pregnancy book again to be sure.

She straightened her *kapp* and did an awkward knee bend to retrieve another splintered board. Bending over so frequent already had her back aching, but she didn't dare stop.

Within an hour, they had the whole porch detached from the shack and discarded into two massive piles. It would have taken her days to complete this chore alone in her condition.

"We can burn this later. It won't be long before those

clouds make good on their teasing," Cullen warned. Grace followed his gaze, peering upward at a dreary array of blue hues. No clouds of cotton dipping into the treetops. A snap of the laundry hanging broke her stare and she realized Cullen was studying her, not the pending weather he had been talking about. She felt her face flush just hoping he wasn't thinking of her laundry, too.

"I'm grateful for your help today," she quickly admitted.

"I was happy to lend it. *I* would be grateful if you wouldn't try your hand at building a new porch."

"That's not for you to concern yourself with," she said calmly. "I know I am the rumor of the community, why I'm here, and so on. I am thankful for the eggs, the help, and even for you rushing up here when you thought the roof fell on my head," she grinned, then collected herself quickly. It was just hard to get the picture of him rushing up here out of her head. "You should tend to your work, and let me tend to mine." Surely he could see how helping her might come across as wrong in the eyes of his community. Grace was only thinking about his reputation, after all. A man like this one didn't deserve such idle talk. And what if he had a girlfriend? Gossip had a way of turning a simple gesture into suspicion. Grace didn't want that on her conscience.

"I have no doubts you *can* handle this, but you shouldn't *have* to." Did he really believe that? *Daed* insisted she should have to face life alone, considering she alone made the choices she had. Did Cullen truly see past her sin?

"And even a smithy can drive a nail and dig a couple post holes."

Tugging the end of his shirt, he found a clean spot and

raised it, wiping the sweat from his face. *Now why did he have to do that?* Her breath held as his middle, firm and toned, was exposed. She turned away quickly, shamed to have seen, and did all she could to will her breaths into a steady rhythm again. She was glad his focus was on the shack and not on her for the moment.

"There is much to do here before the weather moves in. I will have the lumber to replace the porch come end of week."

Grace turned to face him again, but his gaze was set on the naked house. "I cannot pay for such a luxury," she reminded him. Large stones and wooden blocks that had supported the porch foundation were scattered where the structure had once stood. Cullen handled a few until he found whatever it was he was looking for. He was ignoring her. "Did you not hear me, Cullen Graber?"

Was that a growl? Was he bear or man? She tapped her foot repeatedly on the dusty earth.

"Such a man," she muttered under her breath.

Bending and stretching, he began stacking the stones next to one another, and she realized he was making her a safe way to enter the sinner's shack. Grace hadn't thought about how she would get back inside. Her crossed arms lowered, as did her temper. She watched as he put one stone into place, then removed it for another. When he was satisfied with the placement of the stones, Cullen climbed the wide steps, bouncing and rocking his weight to see them secure. He was pleased with himself, and it was written all over his face.

He was even better-looking with a genuine smile of accomplishment instead of a teasing smirk.

Opening the front door, he paused, looked back to her, and frowned. Shrugging, she said nothing. He opened and shut the front door, examining its capability. Was he considering the door his next charitable project? Was that what she was, some project? A charitable thing that would bring him favor in the eyes of the bishop or some doe-eyed girl?

"I appreciate your help today, but you don't need to worry about that door. You have work to tend to and, to be honest, we don't even know each other—"

When their gazes locked again, Grace could see him wrestling for a comment. He was a thinker, someone who didn't act spontaneously, but rather considered his words, his actions, carefully. Faith would call him boring, but Grace rather liked to know a man who considered his actions before testing them. If only she had been more inclined to such habits, she would be home right now arguing with Faith about what was boring and what wasn't.

Cullen walked to her and offered a hand. "I am Cullen Graber, your neighbor. It is nice to meet you, Grace Miller from Indiana." Why was she smiling? "I live alone. My parents are no longer with us and I never had siblings. I am the only blacksmith in two counties. I have many friends and family members here and I can even introduce you to them if you would like." His smooth, dark eyes grew more serious. "But your condition will not allow my conscience to rest if I were to let you tackle such work alone. We all help one another here, as community should." She was realizing that fact the longer she lived in Walnut Ridge. "My *mutter* would be ashamed if I didn't offer." And her *mutter* would be ashamed if she accepted his kindness. "And that door is just another reason I worry about you up here alone."

Grace hated that she made him worry. She was not his concern, but it was clear he was determined to help despite her trying to urge him not to. Letting out one long, exasperated breath, Grace surrendered and shook his hand. She couldn't ignore the shiver that ran up her arm, down her back, and refused to stop until reaching her toes. Cullen was nice-looking, kind-hearted, and any girl would have the same tingling reaction, she told herself. She needed help before winter came, and another friend while she counted the days before she could return home would make the days go smoother. After being raised in such a large family, it couldn't be ignored how quickly loneliness got to her. Yes, they would be friends.

Grace took a deep breath. "Hello, Cullen, I'm Grace. I have four sisters, no *bruders*, and will soon be a *mutter*. I will accept your help on one condition." Looking down at her, Cullen tilted his head, waiting. Grace realized they were still holding hands and pulled away quickly. "You let me cook for you, for all your help. I heard Elli and Betty Schwartz make mention of bringing you food on occasion, and that way I will also be doing something for them for all the kindness they have shown me." Any man living alone would agree to such an offer.

"Agreed." The singular word came out in a rush. He studied her, looking as if something else wanted to come out, but his lips stayed closed. She didn't urge his thoughts into the open. She couldn't let him get the wrong impression of her, as he most probably already did. She needed help to ready for winter and there was no way she was ruining that. And there was no way she would let anything lure her astray ever again, even tall, dark, and handsome neighbors.

"I will return to burn this mess. Until then." He nodded and walked over the hill. Looking down into the hand that had fit into his so easily, Grace ignored the warmth that still remained there.

Cullen was help. His hand in hers was a partnership, nothing more.

. . .

Cullen treaded down the hill, replaying the whole afternoon he had spent with Grace Miller. When he'd heard the crash and went running, he was revisited by that same sickening feeling in his gut that he felt when he and Elli reached the cabin, fearing that Grace had been hurt. It was normal to care for the well-being of a neighbor, wasn't it? Maybe he was being selfish. He couldn't help Marty, a fact that took him years to accept, but Grace, he could.

He shouldn't have smiled, teased her as he had, but when she stood there with that little hammer in her hand looking so confident she could destroy a whole house, he couldn't help it. He imagined she tackled everything in front of her that way. It was kitten cute. *Kitten cute?* He shook his mother's words free from his thoughts. Men didn't talk or even think like that.

"What are you thinking Cullen?" he chided his thoughts. "She's carrying another man's child. She isn't even staying here after…" He picked up his pace, his footfalls landing harder on the ground. "She is outspoken, stubborn, and…" And what? Beautiful. She was beautiful.

And not *just* beautiful but strong and determined and, at times, when she let her guard down, nice to talk to in a snappy, sarcastic kind of way. She was getting under his skin. Had he been too quick to agree to help her? What would others think?

Suddenly, his own words came back to hit him like a hammer. God said, "do not pass a man in need," but what did He say if it was a woman? Not to mention a pretty one?

CHAPTER TEN

"I can't help in the creamery. You won't let me make the soaps. What can I do?" Grace leaned on the outside wall, hoping that was the last of her breakfast finding its way back. She would have cried harder if her sickened state would allow for it. Her only chance to make an income was to work for Elli in the Schwartz Creamery, and that was no longer an option. She thought her nauseous state had passed months ago, but just a whiff of milk curding had told her just how wrong she was.

"You are not the first who couldn't handle the smells here, and I won't be exposing you to lye," Elli said more sharply. "Plus, not everyone likes working around goats. My Abram says they stink worse than cheese making." Elli chuckled. "We will find something better for you, so don't you go and feel disheartened."

Elli's comfort did little to help. The Schwartz family was being kind as it was to offer her steady work, and there was no place for her in the store with Hannah and Rachel already working there. Maybe it was for the best, she considered. Between the scents of burned milk, molding cheese, and Rachel Yoder's harsh comments all morning, which were far more difficult to deal with than Nubian bucks in rutting season, she would be better off anywhere but here.

"I bake. Any need of that?"

"There is always need, Gracie. Someone can always use

what we have." She doubted that statement was entirely true. "I used to sell my homemade goods to the Country Kitchen before opening the creamery and store. Let's start there." Elli was such an optimist. The woman never settled for a no, always had an answer for everything, and never turned anyone away.

Before Grace could consider Elli's idea of selling her baked goods, they were standing at the counter of the Country Kitchen speaking with Sadie Miller. "Ya *daed* and I are *blut*. A wee bit distant and we never see him at family get-togethers, but we are family the same. His *dawdi* and Matthew's were *bruders*." Grace hadn't known that. She thought her only connection to this community was the stern *aenti* who kept mostly to herself. "I would love it if you brought homemade goods to sell for the bakery. You can work from here until you need to be closer to home, then I will supply you with what you need and you can work from there."

It sounded perfect. Grace felt a tinge of hope for the first time since April, when Jared had laughed in her face.

She had never known women like the ones who lived here. They spoke their minds, were bold, and did what needed done despite the roadblocks. With any luck, the next few weeks might not only give her time to bring her *boppli* into the world, but she might learn a little of what she was lacking in the wait. Speaking one's mind, especially a woman's mind, was not something so easily overlooked. If her *daed* were here, she was certain his head would spin right off his shoulders.

"Do you do cookies or specialty breads? I could use baking skills most of all. What about muffins? They sell rather well here," Sadie said. Unlike Elli's creamery, the Country Kitchen sat on a busy roadway where customers, both Amish and *Englisch*, could easily come and go as they wished.

"*Jah*, I have many recipes my *mutter* passed to me. I can make tarts and fried pies as well." The sparkle that filled Sadie Miller's eyes told Grace she had the job.

• • •

Matthew Miller and Cullen were using every muscle God gave them, attempting to unload Matthew's new sign for the Country Kitchen. How Cullen had managed to load the thing alone was beyond him, especially now that he was handling the bulk for a second time.

"Freeman, get over here," Matthew barked over a strained grunt the moment Freeman's buggy came to a rest in front of the store. As usual, Freeman took his time, but he did offer assistance. With six hands and some further grunting, the three managed to get the sign unloaded and placed into the already-dug holes next to the main road.

"Looks *gut*, Cullen. You have a gift, son," Matthew said, stretching out the bend in his back after carrying all that weight such a distance.

"*Daed* says much the same of your parts for our buggies. He still can't figure out how you matched pieces so perfectly without a pattern or something to go by." Freeman Hilty was only two years younger than Cullen, a short-tempered fellow always set on his next big thing, always planning for his future, without putting God or anyone before it. Maybe that was why courting had been

such a waste of time for the man. He was so pushy for a
bride that the fellow had scared away every single woman
in the valley.

Laughter broke their attention, and all eyes shifted toward the storefront. Cullen set his gaze on Elli and Grace
waving goodbye to Sadie Miller smiling on the front step.
Grace looked happy today, and she wasn't trying her best
to hide her rounded middle as he noticed she often did
when attending gatherings. He took in the shape of her.
Grace was a small woman, and the bulge of her circum-
stance looked like a scrawny kid hiding a kickball
underneath her apron. For the first time, he wondered what
kind of man would leave a woman in her condition, abandon his *Gott*-given child.

Grace laughed again, and this time something flickered
in her face that bordered on silliness. Unaware she was
being watched so closely, Grace was different, comfortable,
herself.

He imagined her childhood was spent teasing her sisters
and whispering shared secrets. Having no siblings of his
own, he could only imagine how five girls growing up in
one place spent their time. Watching her keep step with
Elli across the gravel lot, though, she was not a girl anymore—that was certain. Grace was beautiful, fragile as
metal heated to bend to his will, yet she could be strong,
once cooled. He wondered if she had any idea how she
confused him.

He shifted from one boot to the other, pondering what
her story was. She didn't like attention, and maybe that was
his answer. Every tiny feature that shied when attention
was given, every angry scowl he seemed to bring so easily

out of her, glowed with an energy he wished he could bottle and keep for himself. He had long ago put away his boyish tendencies, but when she was near, he remembered them. What would *Gott* think of him now, daydreaming about a woman like Grace Miller?

Her head lowered so often, he thought maybe she simply had a fear of stumbling. But nothing about Grace Miller appeared clumsy; her graceful movements said just that. She had slipped, how far was obvious. But she faced that sin, confessed. If she had earned her forgiveness, then why did she act as if none had been given? This was a question he was curious to find answers to.

"Is that Tess Miller's niece everyone's been talking about?" Freeman interrupted Cullen's thoughts, and when Freeman moved forward for a better look, he was inter-rupting Cullen's view, too. "Kinda *schee*, don't ya think?" Freeman was ogling, but hadn't he just been doing the same thing?

Before Cullen could respond, Freeman was off and quickly reaching the women's side. Matthew and Cullen passed a knowing smile of amusement at Freeman's well-known eagerness and walked over to greet them as well.

"Here, let me help you." Freeman took Grace by the arm and helped her into the buggy.

"*Danke*." Grace dipped her head and gave him a smile for his attempt at being chivalrous. How did Freeman Hilty get a thank you so quickly? She wouldn't even look at him now. He knew, because he waited.

"I am Freeman. Freeman Hilty." Freeman swelled as if he were a balloon and the extra air would somehow make him larger in the newcomer's eyes. Cullen passed a smile to

Elli; they were both thinking the same thought, he concluded. Everyone in Walnut Ridge had fallen witness to Freeman's charming attempts at one time or another. He should really start breathing and stop puffing his chest like that. If Freeman turned purple, neither he nor Elli, and he was pretty sure Matthew as well, would intervene.

"Grace Miller." Her tender voice was just as tempting as her smile. The smile Cullen had hoped to bring out of her was finally there, in the open, and aimed...directly at Freeman Hilty.

"Well, Matthew, looks like Cullen has done a fine job with your sign," Elli quickly added.

"*Jah*. He never disappoints," Matthew chimed in.

If they were trying to distract Freeman from gawking, it wasn't working.

"We should go. Grace here and I have cookie planning to do." So Grace would be helping with this year's cookie exchange. Cullen was glad. It was good everyone was taking to her so well. Well, not everyone.

"I will let you two be on your way now, Grace Miller. Maybe I will see you again soon?" The big cheesy grin, the gleam of hope in Freeman's eyes... Cullen was certain the man had just set his sights on Grace Miller, and his stomach twisted with the realization of it.

The last thing Grace needed was Freeman Hilty pestering her.

When the buggy pulled out of the gravel parking area, Grace glanced back. It would have been better if she hadn't, but Cullen couldn't deny a sense of triumph when their eyes locked for even that quick second. "She going to be living here?" Freeman tore open Cullen's feel-good moment.

Cullen couldn't hold back his tongue any longer. "Grace doesn't need you shooting her attention." Grace didn't need *his* attention, either. It was a good thing Matthew had wandered off while Cullen was daydreaming. The older man would have seen straight through Cullen's contempt and picked up on his out-of-character need to protect a newcomer who was of no relation to him.

Freeman narrowed his dark eyes greedily. "She has no *mann*. Her *daed* dumped her off here and left her for Tessie to deal with. What concern is it of yours what she needs?" Freeman's brow rose challengingly. He had a way about him that was set between pouting over not receiving his way and looking a lot of the time like he wanted to start a fight. Neither was acceptable of an Amish man. "I find her *schee…*" His words trailed off as he watched the buggy ride along the stretch of county road before disappearing over the next rise. "And the kind of *maedel* who would be grateful that a man would take an interest in her, considering her situation. You should mind your own business." Freeman marked his territory before stomping off like a banty rooster fluffed before a fight.

"What was that all about?" Elisha Schwartz had appeared from behind, most likely picking up a few sweets for his family, but Cullen's eyes were still set on Freeman walking away.

"Freeman being Freeman," Cullen scoffed. There was no way Cullen could allow Freeman to take advantage of Grace because of her circumstances. Marriages of convenience happened from time to time, but not this time. In Freeman Hilty's beady brown eyes, Grace was a sure thing. He was a man who wanted nothing but a *fraa* but didn't have the wits about him to get one the proper way. "What are your plans tomorrow?" Scratching his chin, Cullen let an idea take root.

"Not much. My regular chores in the morning and I got to be moving calves to feeder lots by Friday. Why?" Elisha was Lucas's little brother, Cullen's oldest friend who now lived outside the community, but his family carpentry skills might just come in handy. Elisha moved a toothpick from one side of his mouth to the other.

Cullen turned to him. "How good are you with porches and roofs?"

CHAPTER ELEVEN

Three days later, Grace found out that letting Freeman Hilty drive her home from baking all day at the Country Kitchen was not the worst idea, considering her aching feet. Adding the extra spoonful of baking soda, by Sadie's request, to the morning biscuits, however, was. She was certain not one single customer all morning believed in her ability in the kitchen, and this after the days of success she'd had, too. One *Englisch* woman even made a point to spit a bite of her bacon biscuit back into a napkin and return it to Grace with a huff. The whole matter was unsettling.

"I wouldn't let it trouble me if I were you. It was a simple mistake," Freeman said, trying to cheer her up. Freeman had frequented the Country Kitchen all three days, always offering a kind word or compliment. So when he mentioned his love for anything made with cinnamon, Grace took the subtle hint and made fresh cinnamon rolls this morning. He was nice, a little odd the way he spoke with a false authority that made others cringe, but Freeman didn't seem to mind speaking to her with others around. She missed her sisters, her friends, and was making the best with what she had. One thing she was learning under the wings of the Walnut Ridge women was to always be kind to others, offer charity when you can, and never judge another.

The Hilty family built Amish buggies and grew corn

over many separate parcels scattered across the county. Freeman worked in the buggy shop with the other men in his father's hire. Grace suspected he had few friends by the way most would seemingly avoid making small talk with him while they awaited their orders. Maybe it was the way he carried himself. It put Grace in mind of a puffed-up rooster. Maybe it was his fast-moving tongue, not everyone liked yappers like her sister Mercy was. Grace didn't mind, either. Freeman was nice, Sadie thought him harmless enough to drive her home, and the fact that he stood just a few inches taller than she made her less uncomfortable sitting next to him in the buggy seat. And not once did he look at her like her nosey neighbor did.

A cool wind blew, threatening more rain. "It was nice of you to offer me a ride in case it rains again," Grace said.

"You should not be walking all the way to town in your condition." Her condition? She was pregnant, not handi-capped.

"*Danke* for the concern, but the walking is *gut* for me. It is barely more than a mile now that I know I can cross the Glicks' field." In truth, her feet were so swollen every afternoon after work, she had to soak them all night in warm water for any bit of relief. Matthew drove her home her first day when the threat of rain teased the area, and though rain never came that evening, she was glad to receive his kindness, too.

"I can give you a ride in the morning, if you would like, and pick you up after your day as well."

Grace gasped at the offer. Was Freeman only being neighborly, like Cullen and Elli and Betty, or was he flirt-ing? She quickly shook off the thought. She was a pregnant castaway from another state, only here for a time. She was safe from such thinking.

Seeming to sense her concern with his offer, Freeman hurriedly added, "Listen, Grace. I only want to help. We can be *freinden*. Everyone can use *freinden*, *jah*?"

"I am not sure how to keep accepting everyone's kindness." Maybe it was trust she was having such difficulty with. Freeman was only being kind, and yet her gut felt all twisted and unsettled. And if he drove her to work and drove her home, wouldn't there be talk?

"You should accept all kindness. Kindness can change your way of life," Freeman smiled, baring a white line of crooked teeth. Maybe he was right. She would have a friend, and a ride tomorrow. But what would her *daed* think of her, if she accepted yet another man's help? It was the Amish way, to offer and accept help, but fear of further judgment disturbed the balance of her thoughts.

"I don't think I can accept your offer, but *danke*." No, she would never again be the center of someone's gossips.

"It is not proper for me to be riding with you."

"We are riding now." He lifted a thick brushy brow.

"More than the occasional, it might rain, ride with you, then. *Daed* said I should not ask for help. I should do things on my own. My *daed* feels I have not paid enough."

"Paid enough?" Maybe not the best choice of words, but the correct ones, in truth. "You think you must pay for making a mistake. That is for *Gott*. Not man. I have made a few mistakes myself." He chuckled. "I hope you know you can trust me."

His crooked smile, starting with his lips, continued until it covered his whole face. Something told her she should try trusting folks again, but trusting herself was another matter. *Daed* was right; she couldn't make a good decision if her life counted on it. She would accept help when it was necessary, but stay vigilant. God wouldn't scold her for that.

"Then as a *freind*," she enunciated the word, "I accept your offer, Mr. Hilty. I would be glad for a ride into town tomorrow. I have only a few days left at the store, then I will be cooking from home. Sadie feels standing all day is too hard for the…" She stopped short of stating the obvious.

"The *boppli*. *Kinner* are a blessing. A gift. I believe you will make a fine *mutter*, Grace Miller." Freeman Hilty might need to learn how to talk less, walk softer, but one day he was going to make some *maedel* happy. His heart was too sweet not to.

"Call me Gracie."

Freeman's horse began the hard pull up the steep drive. Grace didn't mind the rough terrain, her cheeks sore from smiling. She had a job, a few friends, and possible transportation for her next working days. Life was strangely getting better. It was like she blinked and the sky was beautiful, the day perfect. She even felt a little happy to be returning to her run-down sinner's shack. It might not be much, but it was home.

Gasping, Grace braced herself at the sight of her little sinner's shack. "Cullen," she whispered in a tone meant only for small creatures. Another one of Betty's many nephews, this one Grace believed was called Elisha, was working on the roof. Cullen and another man she had not met yet were nailing flooring onto a quaint little porch.

Cullen's head rose, and when his dark gaze met hers, she couldn't help but return his smile. What had he done? Despite her giving him such coldness, he was here doing what he said he would and then some. Keeping his word.

"Well, looks like I am not the only one who is offering kindness." Freeman said, and pulled back the brake. He was right. Cullen, too, was kind.

Freeman rounded the buggy and came to her side. Taking hold of her elbow, he carefully helped her to the ground. Stepping into the open, Grace marveled at the change a sturdy porch and new roof made to the run-down shack. Elisha lifted a hammer in greeting, and so did the other man, still with no name.

"I know it's not the best, but it is sound enough, Elisha assures me, to get ya through winter," Cullen said, closing the distance between them until they were both side by side and gazing at the same view. She barely reached his shoulders and peered up, way up, to catch a glimpse of his features. He was proud of himself—she could see it written in his dark eyes and smug grin. Today a light fleck of green sparkled over the deep brown in his left eye.

"Do you need another hand?" Freeman's voice pulled her away. The men eyed one another without a word for a stretched-out minute. The glare passing between them was oddly uncomfortable. Instead of friends, Cullen and Freeman looked like two angry dogs ready to prove who was eating supper leftovers first. Having a bit of knowledge about angry dogs herself, Grace considered going inside and retrieving the broken broom handle she had used once before to handle that behavior.

"We got it. There is little left that she needs now." Had

Cullen just marked a line in the dirt between them? Grace took a cautious step back. Cullen towered over Freeman, but the smaller man held his stance against it. She couldn't decide which man's actions upset her more. They were acting like *kinner*.

"Well, I pray Grace won't be here long enough to be in need of such quick fixes," Freeman added, waving an arm toward all the hard work Cullen and the men had achieved so far. That wasn't nice, she thought.

Turning to face her, he took her hand and gave it a gentle squeeze. "I will see you first thing *kumm morgen*, Gracie." Climbing back into the buggy, Freeman drove away.

"Freeman offered to take you somewhere?" His eyes followed the buggy disappearing over the hill.

"Sadie had him drive me home in case it rained," she answered quickly. "He offered to drive me tomorrow, so Matthew won't be troubled."

Cullen didn't respond with words, but that ever nerving growl couldn't be ignored as he walked away and returned to his nailing.

CHAPTER TWELVE

Thanksgiving had come and gone and in came the chill of the season. The heat from the forge mingled with cold air, casting a perfect mix of two opposites colliding. Cullen loved winter, considering his trade. Hot summer days made smithing more like work than something he truly loved. But this year, everything felt different and he couldn't quite put his finger on why. The need to be someone else, do something besides hammering steel and iron was challenging him. Maybe he was restless, or maybe...

He knew it was Grace. It was her predicament, her presence. It was her. He simply could not get Grace Miller out of his every waking thought. Even in the deepest slumbers, she was there. It was utterly out of character for him, but the attraction held firm. He could no longer deny it.

His heart did little flips every time she quirked those kissable lips to one corner. *But she is carrying another man's child*, he again reminded himself. He needed to simply put her out of his mind, his thoughts. But how could he when every time he stepped away from the house, he returned to a new dish awaiting him, taunting him? Grace was an excellent cook, and he was becoming a big fan of fried pies and oversized muffins.

Something about her got to him in a way he couldn't explain. Did feelings really need explanations? He thought not. He could explore them. Let them take him somewhere he hadn't gone in years, or he could walk away, save himself a whole heap of troubles.

How long were they going to keep this up? Him helping her, her helping him, but neither meeting on the way. Freeman had been making his routine trips in the mornings and evenings, taking Grace to work all week, and that had given Cullen plenty of time during the hours she was away to see that wood was chopped, chairs mended, and the stove was nice and warm when she got home. Things a man would do for someone he cared for.

Maybe he could get her flowers. Women liked that sort of thing. He shook his head, clearing that last revelation. He had work to do and flowers and feelings weren't a part of it.

He hung the meat hooks for the local slaughterhouse on long nails driven into the back wall. "One less thing," he told himself. Every corner of his *daed*'s workshop was crowded. Scratching his head, he figured it was about time to make a delivery or two and collect what was owed him.

Unlike his *daed* before him, Cullen had learned the skill of welding as well as blacksmithing, and the bishop had seen no issue with his doing so, as long as he only used battery power, that was. What one skill lacked, the other offered, and he could always make enough to provide for himself, and maybe one day, a family. Now that making signs was becoming a trend in the surrounding area, he was glad he had disputed his *daed*'s feelings on the matter. They seldom disagreed.

Like that first time he brought Marty home to meet his parents. Sometimes a thought took a bit of adjusting for others to accept it. And it took a bit of adjusting for his *daed* to understand how much he truly loved Marty Daily. Everyone thought it was a boyish crush, a teenager tramping between two worlds. Once they got to know her, *Daed* and *Mutter* loved her, too. Who couldn't love her? Marty's charms were infectious. If only he hadn't gone about it all wrong, maybe that love would have come sooner. Then everything would have been so very different.

He could never make that mistake again. Grace deserved someone reliable. Someone who would be there for her when she needed him.

The first drops of rain were soft and welcomed. It had been over a week since a few late-day showers quenched the dusty valley. Stepping out from under the roof, he opened his wide hand and caught a few drops in his palm. Breathing in the scent, its hopeful smell refreshing, he realized how badly he had missed rain. Just about as much as he missed his mother's cherry pie fresh from the oven. Did Grace bake cherry pies? The woman's kitchen talents were going to be the ruin of him.

She had delivered the apple pie when he wasn't home yesterday. She did the same with a pot of stew Sunday when he lingered after church with Elisha and Caleb, talking weather and horse flesh. She didn't once glance his way during the service. He knew because he waited. But he did note that she rode home with Tess, not Freeman.

She was avoiding him. Why? Maybe for the same reason he visited the cabin and had seen to her needs while she was off baking for Sadie or attending one of her frolics with the women.

Elli, not so cunningly, had told him Grace was going to be baking from home from now on. He agreed. The weather was changing and Grace had no business riding around every day in that condition.

Images of her standing with two fists on her hips and darting him that death glare when he arrived to find her destroying the porch flashed in his mind's eye. Something had sparked between them that day. It hadn't been subtle or sneaky, like a small lie meant for good that only grew until pain was caused. It was fast and earthmoving, and he did feel pain from it. He'd had his love of a lifetime, thought he was content in being blessed to have received, even if only for a short youthful while. But now his thoughts were scattered and out of his control. All he kept seeing was that smile. Catching her off guard, making her blush and scatter her words, and those wide blue eyes full of surprise, pleased him, would always please him.

The wind picked up, bringing larger beads of rain with it. He pushed his hat more firmly on his head and peered under the brim up the hill. Hopefully the new roof was doing its job.

By early afternoon, darkness swallowed everything in the area and drenched it without any thoughts of slowing. A northern wind brought with it a colder chill, a second prayer on many lips he thought had been answered in one day. A sure sign that winter may have well have arrived once and for all.

Sifting the coals remaining in the forge, urging each one to die, Cullen listened to the roar of the tin roof and thought about nothing but Grace. He put away all his tools, the hammer, his bending fork, his clamps, and apron. All of which had their own place. With his shirt already soaked to the flesh, he eyed the coals once more—they were obeying—and he made a dash for the house.

For the first time in over three years, his home felt quiet. Too quiet. Thunder crashed nearby and everything brightened for two full blinks, only to disappear into the void again. The thunderstorm was growing, not weakening one bit. Abandoning his better judgment, he took his heavy raincoat and flashlight from the hooks by the door, slipped into the coat, and took up his hat, pushing it down snugly on his head. He had to be certain she was safe, the need to offer protection overwhelming—whether she liked it or not.

He rubbed his forehead, nervous his tongue would tie into a knot, or maybe it was the tight fit of his hat, he wasn't certain. Thoughts of his younger days when making his own mistakes invaded. He'd always had his family and his community to help guide him back to what was right, to ground him in a sturdy, reliable faith. No one liked the time he had spent with the *Englischers*, but when Marty had decided she wanted what his community had to offer, even the bishop tried to help her.

Hiking up the steep hill, he scolded himself for getting involved with another damsel in distress. Like Marty, Grace had no one. Only, Grace didn't come with bruises and a history of a life lived hard, she came with baggage. And whatever filled it was all she had.

Images of Marty flashed with each streak of lightning that arrived in the long valley. Meeting her when they were only eleven, he supposed he even loved her then. It was blonde hair and blue eyes that first caught his eye, but the way she could sit and talk for hours and hours lured him in. Once a week he got to see her when *Daed* rode into town, and some weeks he was lucky to see her twice. Slowly those Thursdays his *daed* drove to town became their day, since she wandered about without a soul watching over her as she did. When they were sixteen, she missed her first Thursday meeting him. He thought she had grown tired of the Amish boy with big ears and simple thoughts, but he later found out she had been in the hospital with three broken ribs and a concussion.

Marty Dailey's life had been hard from the beginning. Her mother had left home shortly after her eighth birthday, and her father just as soon she stayed out of his way as opposed to in it. The drunkard lost more than he won gambling and became the root of many whispers in the area. Even among the Amish community he was well known.

It was only when Marty became the target for his frustrations that an eighteen-year-old Cullen found his size had a use better than simply reaching the top shelf of his *mutter*'s pantry to retrieve what she could not. That day not only reminded a grown Cullen that he was no longer a child to be beat on for simply taking Marty fishing like her father did years earlier, but that he was a man not willing to stand by and watch another be hurt. Cullen would never regret presenting himself to Steve Dailey. Declaring his love for the man's daughter and daring him to lay a hand on her again. It was only that he never swept her away from her father's house that very night that he regretted now. It was strange how quickly a day could change the whole course of one's life. How one decision had a way of affecting so many.

The storm grew into a living, breathing thing and drew him back to the present. Cullen stepped onto the little cabin porch, glad to be out of the weather, if only this much. He shouldn't have come here. Had he not learned his lesson on the limitations of his charity? Grace may not be the battered girl Marty was, but she was still in need of protection.

"Oh, make up your mind already, Cullen," he mumbled to himself. It was time. Cling to the past, ponder it and dissect it, or knock on this door.

Lamplight flickered inside. Peering through the pane, Cullen could see Grace safely tucked inside. Her open Bible sat on that poor excuse of a table, green material scattered by her Bible's side. Her back was to him while she sat in the only chair in the cabin. Hopefully he would soon remedy that issue as well.

She was sewing, probably for the *boppli*, and he watched until her hands came to a pause. He realized she was crying, and he instinctually scoured the room for what might threaten her peace, ready to intervene. Seeing no cause for alarm, his heart sank and settled in the pit of his stomach. She was lonely.

Loneliness had a strange effect on a person raised in a large household. He never had such luxury, being his parents' only child and all. But Grace, he had learned from talking to her, had four sisters. Four other females to work side by side with, share stories and secrets and hopes with. With her head in her hands, she must be feeling the lost connection. He knew what that felt like in his own way.

A howl in the distance pulled him away from spying. Through dark and rain and rumbles, the menacing calls grew, and others joined in from one hillside to the next. Cullen took a deep breath, lifted his hand, and knocked.

CHAPTER THIRTEEN

Grace startled when the knock came at the door and jumped to her feet. She gathered her shawl around her shoulders and wiped the earlier sadness from her eyes. It would do no good to be seen unhappy when she had so much to be thankful for. She had a roof over her head, money hidden in a jar, and wood to keep her from freezing. Just the thought of Cullen leaving wood on her porch made her smile. She needed to bake him something worthier than pie for all he was sneaking around and doing for her. She would never admit it aloud, but Cullen Graber was the kindest man Grace had ever known.

With one hand she unlatched the door and opened it. Under a stiff hat, strong chin tucked tightly into his coat, the cold, wet visitor was none other than the man who was consuming too many of her thoughts of late.

"Cullen Graber? What in the world are you doing out in this weather?" Cold air nipped at her bare feet and warm cheeks and she began to shiver. Grace didn't care if she looked a mess. She didn't care that Cullen had shown up again unannounced. She was just so relieved he was there. She wasn't alone. When she looked up at him, she was met with sorrowful eyes. Eyes like that should never look sorrowful, she thought.

Cullen just stared at her. Her wide eyes glistened with evidence of her earlier tears and he immediately wished he hadn't seen her crying, however, those tears had given him the courage to knock, disturb whatever saddened her. He should say something, but was trapped in her beauty. The curve of her chin, the way a few wandering threads of her hair curled around her delicate neck. He was wet, the temperatures were dropping at a rapid pace, and yet, Cullen was sure he was sweating.

Cullen wasn't a talker like Mercy or Freeman Hilty, but if he didn't say something soon Grace might have to shake him. He was silent but present. How had a man like that never been swept up by one of the local *maedels.*

She tried again. "Cullen, I asked you what you're doing here?" He flinched and greeted her with a broad smile. That smile had some strong effects and Grace did well to control her breathing. He really should smile more often.

"Storm is growing a bit." His voice was scratchy. He cleared it and removed his hat. Water poured onto the porch floor and splattered her feet.

"*Jah*, it is. But that is not an answer." Arms crossed, Grace tapped her foot against the new wood just like her *mutter* would when waiting for answers. His eyes went from her drumming foot and slowly trailed the height of her.

"*Kumm* in and warm up. Maybe it will pass soon," she opened the door wide enough that he could slip through. Stepping back, she felt the rough wood brush against her bare feet and gathered her shawl more snuggly, clasping it at her neck.

"I came to see you were okay. If you needed anything." His long fingers twisted the hat in his hand. It was sweet and not the kind of sweet Jared would have offered.

"I need nothing, *danke*. Have you eaten? I have

breakfast about done." She wobbled toward the stove, not daring to look back and see if he would follow. She could hear him remove his coat. This would be the first meal she shared with another person here. Something about that lifted her earlier woes. She would never get used to eating alone.

"Breakfast?" He walked over beside her.

"I have a craving for breakfast," she quirked a grin. "I take bacon very seriously."

"I have the same such cravings, often." He chuckled. "Let me help. I might not know how to make a pie, but this I *can* do." The storm outside didn't seem to want to let up and neither cared.

They both worked in silence. Every step on old boards, every poke of the fire, made Grace nervous. Did he know what she had done? Surely he hadn't walked all the way up here in a storm because he wanted to check on her. That would be crazy.

She had kept her end of the deal, cooking for Cullen on occasion, but sneaking around his home and yard, seeing what made the man, was overstepping a bit. His small two-story house was perfectly plain, and surprisingly clean for a bachelor. Did all men without a *fraa* to tend to their daily needs do that? She figured not. Jared wouldn't even toss out old pop bottles or fast-food wrappers from his truck.

Each trip she made over the hill, she wandered further, past a respectable point of simply dropping off a pie or stew or leftover cold chicken. And little by little she had seen all he had in full. *Mutter* had always said she was too curious for her own good. Cullen washed and cleaned any dishes she had brought into his home, always setting them on the table for her to retrieve. He knew she had been in his home, and yet said nothing of her boldness, and she was glad of it. Was he going to now? She bit her bottom lip as she cracked eggs into a bowl.

She liked the little touches he made his own. The old quilt, in much need of repair, draped on the back of his couch, the cherry cabinet in the corner, a book of hand-written recipes Grace could only assume belonged to his mother, laying open as if he used them or simply refused to touch her last creation on display. He wasn't much for sweeping, that was for sure and certain, cobwebs in many hidden corners. If she revealed her fear of the eight-legged monsters, she had a feeling he would tend to that as well. As Cullen collected bacon from the pan and plated it onto a dish nearby, Grace couldn't help but sneak a glance at him. Who wouldn't admire a man who worked daylight until dusk, and still made time for the things that were important in this world?

While she set the table, Cullen removed the last slice of bacon sizzling on the stove with a fork and gave her a smile. She would do well to not look at it so often. Wasn't it a similar handsome smile, an act of chivalry, that caused her downward spiral? Cullen could have her respect, her politeness for all he was doing for her, but he couldn't have her heart.

Nope, never that.

"Biscuits should be done." She stepped to the stove, but he refused to budge and give her the space she needed to pull the biscuits from the oven. Had he not heard her while staring into the empty pan of bacon grease? "I need you to step away from my stove, Cullen Graber." He did as she asked and without a grumble. Where had his mind gone just then? Grace didn't suspect him to be the kind of man who daydreamed. Curiously, she sneaked a peek at the skillet. No answers there. She pulled the biscuits from the oven and set them on top of the stove. "I wasn't expecting company. Hope this is enough." Surely a man this size could eat his weight in her biscuits.

He was staring again. Why did he always have that strange look on his face with her? "It is plenty. *Danke* for sharing your supper, breakfast with me." He winked playfully.

"Will you be helping Sadie anymore this week?"

"I will be baking here until the *boppli kumms*. Freeman volunteered to *kumm* in the *morgen* to take my baked goods to Sadie, and I will be joining him for dinner tomorrow night." Was Cullen going to offer to drive her? Would she let him if he offered?

Placing a biscuit, an egg, and three slices of bacon on a plate, she set it down in front of him, then retrieved her own. "Francis Hilty invited me for dinner after church Sunday," she added. She really wanted Cullen's thoughts on the matter. It was nice of Francis, like Elli, to invite her, but she didn't want to give anyone the wrong impression. She was tired of eating alone, too.

Cullen lifted his plate from the table and placed hers in the spot. She had only one chair to offer and yet he wouldn't take it. "You need to sit. I will stand, Grace."

"But you're the… And this is my…" He lifted a stern brow and she did as he asked, though it felt uncomfortable to do so. One thing she'd learned about Cullen Graber, unless she was up for a quarrel, it was better to just accept his politeness. Plate in hand, Cullen bowed his head and Grace followed. *Daed* always led prayer, and nowadays she prayed alone. It was nice to feel something almost normal in the sinner's shack. After five very long minutes, Cullen cleared his throat and she raised her head. The Walnut Ridge ministers would have been pleased by that long prayer. Grace just wished she knew what all a man like Cullen prayed about.

"Are things feeling more at home now?" he asked, smothering jelly that Elli had given her over his warm biscuit.

"If one could call a sinner's shack a home," she muttered. She needed to get ahold of her sarcasm when he was near.

"Sinner's shack, huh?" She hadn't expected a laugh. Maybe a disapproving brow or pinched lips, but never a chuckle. It was a happy sound. One that his whole face participated in.

"It will do for now. After the *boppli* comes, I will return to Havenlee, and to my *daed's haus*."

His look of surprise caught her off guard, and she pushed the bacon biscuit into her mouth to keep from saying more. Truth be told, Grace dreaded returning to Havenlee. If not for her sisters she would disappear, find some small Amish community far from Indiana, maybe Montana, or even Idaho, where no one would know her. Sadly the Amish had long connections and no such place existed. Living a normal life in Havenlee was out of the question. People would always see her sin, but she would have her family. Hopefully those discerning looks and disapproving whispers that made her weep into the night, wouldn't spread over onto her innocent child. She swallowed hard against the lump of barely chewed food. Surely no one would ever treat a child differently just because they had no father.

"Maybe you will find our little community has much to offer," Cullen said, and watched her reaction over the rim of his *kaffi* cup.

"I must admit, Walnut Ridge has surprised me. I was so afraid coming here, but Elli and Betty have been so kind." She forked up another bite of eggs. "Your bishop is nothing like mine."

- "He is your bishop, too." That was true, at least for now. "Freeman has been kind to you as well." Was that a question or a statement, she couldn't tell.

"We are *freinden*."

"*Freinden*?"

"*Jah*." she quickly added. "That is all, since you're asking." She lifted a brow. If Grace wasn't mistaken, Cullen didn't like her friendship with Freeman. She didn't like not knowing why. "He knows this. He thinks I should stay in Walnut Ridge and start new and fresh."

"Does he?"

The question was simple, but for the life of her she couldn't figure Cullen Graber out.

"Freeman has been kind enough to drive me to work and even deliver my cookies and sweet rolls so I can still have an income." Cullen looked over his *kaffi* cup as he sipped and pinned her with a look that asked for more. "I am of age to decide myself whether I stay or go, but this shack is no place for a *boppli*." She looked around the room and tried to look disappointed, yet part of her was proud how much she had warmed to the small space.

He agreed with an understanding nod but didn't voice it. Did she dare mention that every inch of her dreaded returning home? The fear of how her son or daughter would be received in her *daed*'s eyes?

"Why not stay with Tess? She has room." Did he want her to stay? That was a silly thought.

"I have disregarded my *daed*'s wishes once. I do not wish to do so again." Squirming in her chair she found Cullen was not shocked by her words, but rather, pleased by them. They were like two mules that argued against the same opinion.

"We are all human. *Gott* shows mercy to all. He offers grace to all," Cullen said.

"Mercy is for those who sneak into town to watch movies or smoke cigarettes. Not for this. Not for foolish girls who fall for the wrong people. I took the wrong path and cannot undo that mistake. I should have chosen the path of no mistakes." She let out a sigh.

She had never spoken so freely with another concerning the shame of her heart. But Cullen was a good listener.

"You would be surprised how easy such can be for some, but in reality, a flawless path does not exist. We fail. We get lost. We all make mistakes. There is no place so far away that *Gott* cannot find us and offer His mercy and grace to us."

Cramming the rest of a biscuit into her mouth, she pondered those words. Silence filled the room, birthing an unease between them. She had asked for the church leaders' mercies, and though they had given it, here she was. She had asked for *Gott*'s, and here she was.

"I am sorry this person hurt you. That was his failure and you should not let that discourage you from moving ahead. Life can only be lived in one direction, Grace."

As he lowered his empty plate into the sink, she felt he understood, though she knew he could not. What could a man like Cullen Graber know about *verboden* love and unforgiveable sin? "I hope you would take my word when I say be wise when it comes to Freeman Hilty. He is not what he seems, either. Freeman has a way of planning ahead without thinking."

"You are saying trust your words but not Freeman's? I am human, as you say, but I am no fool who has learned nothing from my past mistakes. Besides, we are only *freinden*. I am with Elli, Betty, and Hannah, too. Should I be cautious of them as well?"

"*Nee.* You will never find better than those three. They are the most caring women I know, but I have known Freeman all his life. He means well, but looks to the morrow, forgetting *Gott* asked us to live in the today. He is like a child given too much. A man only takes a girl home to meet his parents if he has an interest."

His generous description was unnecessary and his overly calm manner unnerving. He had no right to say such. The chair dug across the floor as she came to her feet.

"Freeman is not the kind of man who speaks of others so carelessly. His intentions are to be my friend. He spoke it plain and up front. His *mutter* invited me. She wanted to welcome me to Walnut Ridge as she does anyone new to the community." How dare he presume the worst. Freeman all but told her that Francis invited all newcomers for a welcome meal.

"I assure you I have no *interest* here in Walnut Ridge, nor do I plan to ever have one. I am not some desperate *maedel* seeking a father for my *boppli*." The warmth of her cheeks was a sign of her rising temper. Her *daed*'s final words came back in a fiery flood. *"Once a fallen woman, always a fallen woman, unworthy of knowing what's best for her."*

Stomping to the door, Grace yanked hard and opened it. Despite his kindness and confusing need to look in on her so often, Cullen had just revealed his quiet opinion, loudly.

Elli was wrong. Cullen *did* judge her.

"Is that what your last friend did? Run away from his"— his eyes targeted her growing middle—"commitments?"

Gasping at his forwardness, she let her eyes meet his with fury. This man pushed every button, crossed every line, and all the while offered her a false security that she wasn't so alone up here.

"Why do you keep showing up here?" Grace found that inner Elli she had hoped was somewhere inside her.

"Just being neighborly," he said, his tone calm, always calm, and she hated it.

"You do that for all the *maedels* in Walnut Ridge?" She raked the cutting words across him like a hay mower.

"*Nee*," he replied between gritted teeth and stepped out the door. Grace followed. She needed to rid herself of this man and his need to derail her faith in others. She didn't even feel the rain hitting her arms, her bare feet.

"Why aren't you married, Cullen Graber? You help when it is clear you have much work and chores of your own. I know you're older than I. Why is a man your age not married?"

"Not by much. I'm twenty-eight." He tilted his head and held her gaze.

"I'm twenty-three. Now answer the question. Why is a twenty-eight-year-old with steady work and a home not married?"

"Why aren't *you*?" There was no winning with this man. Blood rushed to her head, her fingertips, her knees. How could he be so calm right now?

She exhaled a raw burn, admitting defeat. "He left, okay?"

Unshed tears threatened, but she willed them to wait.

"She's gone." Cullen let out a staggered breath. Why had that been so hard for both of them to say? A long stretch of silence replaced the cold, damp air between them.

Standing there, staring at each other as rain pounded them in a sidelong fury, Grace opened her mouth to say something, anything, but not a worthy word was within reach. As Cullen placed the hat on his head, she could see his expression had not changed during her heated rant, or the truths that poured out with it. Cullen Graber was as calm as when he'd walked through the door.

"Some men take, and some give way more than they can afford." Tipping his hat and stepping down from the porch, Cullen left without looking back.

She knew because she watched him until he disappeared over the hill.

• • •

"Stubborn, stubborn woman." He could have held his tongue in respect, but wrestling to see her perspective, her fresh view of a man he knew was not seeing her as friend material, Cullen couldn't. Kicking a clump of mud, it stuck to his boot instead of sailing into the air like he wanted. Cullen came to terms with the fact that this was how his whole day was going to be, one big sloppy, sticky mess.

Closing his eyes against another invasion of grief, he tried to focus. Marty had all but consumed his heart for as long as he could remember. Letting Grace Miller into what was left of it was a mistake that he couldn't seem to stop making. Why was *Gott* toying with him? Had he not kept to himself, followed his faith? Did he not always offer help to those who needed it?

He did, and in that little argument with himself, his answers presented themselves.

Grace was the opposite of Marty, he brooded. Marty died trying to save her drunken *daed*, while Grace needed saving—and not just from Freeman Hilty but from all the people who should have never let her down. Ten years from now, would she be as bitter as Tess? Would he?

He mentally traced over the last ten years of his quiet life. They were lonely years, but safe, his heart guarded against any further mistreatment. Grace had out of nowhere barged in and ripped the shield from his armor, awakening a protective need to shelter her, to care for her.

Everyone deserved to be cared for. Did he?

CHAPTER FOURTEEN

Cradling a plate of assorted cookies in her hands and trying not to think about Cullen's warnings, Grace passed a weak smile to Freeman in the buggy seat beside her.

"Don't be nervous, Gracie." He smiled to assure her. "My parents are excited to get to know you better. *Mamm* is kind to all who *kumm* to live in our community. That is why she invites them all to dinner. It is what she does. It will be *gut*, I promise."

She hated that word. "Promise," a loosely given thing like the last crumb of one's favorite dessert left on a plate, only after everyone else had their fill. But still, hoping he was correct, she let the damp of the day fill her dry lungs. November had been unseasonably warm but December was making up for it. It was utterly dreary. The cold wet penetrating bones buried under wool socks and what her *daed* called "thick skin." She wasn't certain she was ready for snow, for colder weather, or becoming a mother in the midst of it. At least Cullen had seen to it that she had wood to burn. So there was that. She would just need to figure the rest out herself.

The closed-in buggy offered little warmth, and she shivered against the chill. Freeman turned down a long lane, one she had only passed by exiting the valley but had never been on.

"That is *schee*." Eyeing the dark, damp soil of turned fields that Freeman said grew pumpkins as they drove along the gravely lane, Grace thought of home. "You must raise a lot of pumpkins."

"More than anyone else around," Freeman replied. She and her sisters bought all their pumpkins from Sara and Joe Zimmerman, her lifelong neighbors. A fleeting thought of what her family was doing washed over her. Faith would probably be finishing her Stars At Night quilt to sell, and Hope would be canning venison and possibly helping Mercy in collecting pine cones and boughs to dress up the family table and mantle for the Christmas holiday. To see her sisters again, help prepare for a Second Christmas, work alongside her *mutter* again...she missed that. She missed them.

"You look sad for someone who finds beauty in empty pumpkin fields." Freeman looked at her with a thick puzzled brow. A shiver ran over her. Grace hoped she wasn't coming down with a cold. She tightened her shawl around her for added warmth.

"I bet you are missing home."

"*Jah*. I miss my sisters. When I left they weren't permitted to say goodbye. I wrote letters, but it is not the same." He reached over, patted her hand and offered a crooked smile.

"Maybe they will *kumm* visit." Grace appreciated his positive words, but *Daed* would never allow for such a hope. "You are no longer under your *daed*'s rule, Grace. You should try to enjoy yourself, and *Mamm* has worked hard to ready a meal for your coming."

Grace came to attention. "And it was kind of her to do so," she quickly replied. She hadn't meant to sound selfish. What kind of *freind* was she, talking about her own sorry state when Freeman and his family were offering a warm meal with fellowship? She straightened her shoulders and set aside any thoughts of her family. Freeman was right. Francis was going through a lot of trouble, entertaining a guest, and she should appreciate it.

They pulled up the wide driveway and Freeman quickly got out, dealing with his horse. Grace opened her side door and he was there, offering her help down from the buggy. For a small, stout man he was rather quick on his feet. The Hilty home was a two-story white *haus* with bold red roof and shutters. Morning bacon had gone down easy with the craving she needed to fill at the time, but now the greasy taste had risen from her upset stomach and she had to force it back to where it came. Why was she so nervous?

"That is the buggy shop." Freeman pointed to the large, open metal building to the left of the house. Puffing up again, he was clearly proud of his family's place and sharing it with her. "Let me show it to you before we go inside." Grace wanted to protest, considering how cold the evening was becoming, but he was just so eager to show her. What kind of *freind* would she be if she ignored his wishes?

Trying her best to walk normally was getting harder, but she managed to rein in the ability and keep her waddle to a minimum.

"It is a *gut* life we have here," Freeman said, another hint of pride in his tone as they stepped into a small office. A long metal desk sat facing the door, papers strewn over its top in a messy pool. On the wall hung drawings that Grace could see were designs for buggies. Who would have guessed so many existed? She hadn't thought one much different from the next.

Freeman was acting strange today. She had noted it when he picked her up—less talkative, more rigid—but she tossed the concern aside. She, too, was still a bit scatter-brained after her quarrel with Cullen. She shouldn't have spoken to him the way she had, and now she might have lost his friendship for it. Grace studied the scribbled drawings of buggy boxes and carriage tops on the wall, wishing she had the luxury of her own buggy. Wishing she knew who Cullen lost. He'd said, "She's gone." Who was she? And where did she go?

"You and your family have been blessed." She needed to stop thinking about Cullen.

"*Jah*. We work hard. There are things still lacking, though." His voice behind her was barely audible as she closed in on a drawing with a side step that would be right handy for a woman of a certain height.

"Lacking?" She narrowed in on one design. The buggy looked to have something like rain wipers on the front. Or was that the back? All those lines and angles were too confusing.

"No one to share it with." He cleared his throat and added, "I was hoping you could change that for me."

Grace pivoted to face him, the words heard but their meaning eluding her. He had caught her so off guard, the sudden movement caused her head to swim.

She liked Freeman just as she had told Cullen she did, but as a *freind*. Like Hannah, Elli, and Betty. Cullen had warned her, and yet, she didn't heed his warning. Proof again she was not a good judge of character when it came to trusting others.

Grace suddenly felt her head would spin right off her shoulders like one of those topsy spinning gadgets Mercy had toyed with as a child.

"I care for you, Gracie Miller. More than I thought I would. If you are in mind to, I would be ever so happy if you would let me court you."

Yes, her head was spinning all topsy-turvy now. Luckily, she found a nearby stool to quickly sit on.

"Are you all right, my dear? Shall I fetch my *mamm*?"

When he took up her hand, she faced him. Her *daed* would be grinning ear to ear that someone would offer to marry her, give her *boppli* a father to guide them in the right direction. Yet Grace felt faint and utterly numb.

"Freeman, I thought we were just *freinden*."

"We could be more," he sounded so desperate, so eager, and the way his eyes begged for her to give him the answer he sought, made her next words the hardest. Elli's, Betty's, and even her *Aenti* Tess's voice rang in her ears.

"I appreciate your honesty, but Freeman, I do not wish to court you. I'm glad to have you as a *freind*, it's a gift, but I will be leaving Walnut Ridge after my *boppli* is born." That was her best answer to stall him.

"We can court so in secret." He winked. All his eagerness was out there in full view. *Secrets.* That was another word that left a sour taste in her mouth.

"I will have no more secrets clouding over me." She cradled her belly and tried to ignore the way his eyes narrowed and his lips puckered into a perfect pout. Grace was only relieved when the voice of a woman hollered out that supper was ready.

...

"Why did you not tell me that your *daed* owned the shack?" Grace glared at Freeman in the buggy seat beside her. The whole evening had been a mix of prodding questions and uncomfortable moments. So much so that Grace had barely touched a bite of food. She was no longer under her *daed*'s roof, but Elmo Hilty had made it abundantly clear she was now under his.

"It matters not," Freeman replied. "He has let others stay in time of need. You are not the first. All that matters is that you have somewhere safe to stay while we talk about our futures."

Our futures? Had she not already settled that conversation? This whole evening was moving right along without her. Grace tried to remember patience, but it seemed she was dealing with someone who had none.

"Freeman, does your family think us to be courting?" Cullen's very words were revisited in her mind, making clear how wrong she had been. Freeman did have tendencies of jumping ahead, planning too far.

"They know I have an interest. You should rethink my offer and the future I have planned for us. You may never get a better one," he said, a bit more forcefully than before.

"I do not wish to have any offers," she said seething. "My *daed* expects me back in Havenlee. You should be honest with your family," she bit between clenched teeth.

They veered onto the narrow little road that led to the sinner's shack. The quicker she got out of Freeman's company, the better. Cullen had been right about him all along. Freeman's ready-made future and bold declaration was not part of their friendship and she settled right then and there to stretch some distance between her and Freeman Hilty.

It was plain to see the man was just desperate for a *fraa*.

As they passed Cullen's farm, Grace peered right. Cullen stepped out of the glowing forge, watching their return. Like a prick in her side, he was always there, always nearby. Did men like Cullen Graber plan futures? She figured not. Men like Cullen made them.

CHAPTER FIFTEEN

Two days later, the old cookstove burned hot with early morning baking. Grace raised the fog-stained window by the front door a few inches, hoping to lessen the stuffiness filling the room. A new snow had covered a world damp and brown and empty, and she marveled at the glorious change. From this height, she could see a scattering of Christmas lights in the valley below at all hours of night and early morn.

"Everything changes," she whispered. An assurance she hoped for herself.

The baby twisted, and she postured to give him more room to do so. She placed a firm hand on her belly, certain a foot was the cause of her current discomfort, and caressed the bulge.

"Now, my little one, be patient. I want to meet you, too." Grace glanced around the barren room. "I just hope I have a real home for you when you arrive." Looking at her only option for now, she worried she could not uphold those words. A tear fell, then another, and before she could cross the short distance from the front window to the sink, she was again a flood of emotions. She had made a mess of her life and in doing so, another would be forever infected by it. What she would give to hear Charity or Faith spring forth words to comfort her right now. Charity certainly would have seen right through the likes of Freeman Hilty, that's for sure and certain.

Her sisters' faces, one by one, came to her. Life had been strained in her *daed*'s *haus*, and she was not the only one who felt it, but they had all been close, as close as sisters could be, lessening the mundane. She missed them. Missed their voices. Grace missed late night chatter and girlish giggles that wafted into the late hours. All would be less lonely and far easier to manage if she had not been made to come here. Wiping her face with a dish rag, she remembered how *Aenti* Tess said the pregnancy would cause tears to come. Elli said so, too, when she found herself unable to contain them after church last Sunday when the Bishop Mast seemed to have spoken straight to Grace's heart. That's all this was. Her body changing, "hormones" Elli called them, and soon it would all be right again. *Soon*...the word brought forth a new run of tears.

Two hours, and a couple dozen not-so-perfectly-iced cupcakes later, Grace gathered her emotions, and stepped outside for another stick of firewood. The world of cloudy white took her a bit to adjust her eyes to, but once everything became clear, she couldn't help but feel in awe at the sight of trees bearing the weight of winter. It was a whole different view than yesterday at this hour. Cedars cascaded to the earth, frosted like the icing she spread just moments earlier on the cupcakes for the Country Kitchen. The sun peeked through, illuminating God's sprinkles of the season. Mercy always called them that. Charity said the glittering flecks looked like diamonds. Not having ever seen a diamond, Grace settled for God's sprinkles.

Christmas was just two weeks away, and there was still so much she wanted to do before her life would change again. Excitement welled up inside her, anticipating becoming a mother. Finally putting a face to where all her love was aimed. What wonderful *aentis* her sisters would make. No matter how *Daed* spoke to her on the day she left, once she returned, she would always have her sisters.

With memories of her sisters still frozen in her thoughts, Grace lifted a smile. She had made few wages but put them away in the old coffee can hidden where *Aenti* had instructed, and was recently able to purchase new gloves for each of her sisters, rare garden seed the local feed store still had lingering in a forgotten bin for Hope, and even new shoes for Mercy. That girl wore out any hand-me-downs given her in no time, and Grace thought it would be nice if she was given something new, and only belonging to her. Being a middle child, Grace knew what hand-me-downs felt like. But being the youngest, and certainly the most active, had to be worse.

She quickly added more wood to the fire, and resumed boxing the muffins *Aenti* Tessie agreed to deliver. The frosting set well this time, and she was glad to finally get better with the old cookstove. Burning so many delicious cakes and muffins already, she made it her top priority to master its aging decline.

"*Gut morgen*, Grace," Tess said, stepping inside the front door without the courtesy of a knock. Grace was just glad to have company. "You should get Cullen to tend to that," Tessie continued, willing the door to shut while shaking loose snow from her shoes. No wonder the door would never work well. It was meant to swing in, not out, and the confusion had obviously worn the thing down.

"*Danke* for delivering the muffins today. I hope the hill

did not give you much trouble," she said, not addressing the comment about Cullen. He had done so much for her already, including warning her about Freeman, and yet she'd practically called him a gossip and sent him away. She would be lucky if he ever spoke to her again.

Tess waved off the comment, too stubborn to let a snowy incline with ruts as deep as barrels sway her. The baby shifted again and a sudden urge to visit the outhouse sent Grace bounding out the same door, with less resistance.

When Grace returned, her *aenti* had loaded the three boxes for Sadie and was oddly waiting patiently at the table. "I'm sorry," Grace said, cradling her belly, "this little one has been a bit restless of late."

"That will only worsen. It is normal. You can wear those sanitation pads if need be." Grace grimaced at the thought. Being pregnant for nine whole months had freed her of that encumbrance and she wasn't in any hurry to return to it.

"Wait until your time does arrive. The pain you feel in your heart from that *Englischer* and my *bruder* will be nothing but a memory."

How was that supposed to make her feel better? Grace wasn't a child—she knew that birthing was a painful thing, but *Mutter* had told her often the memory of it faded the moment you held *Gott*'s gift in your arms. *Aenti* Tess seemed terribly confident for a woman who never had a husband or *kinner*.

"I will manage. Have no choice in that." Grace shrugged.

"*Nee*, you do not." Tessie reminded her. A long silence grew between them. Grace turned to the counter and wiped the already clean top.

"My *bruder* means well, you know. He is much like our *daed*. They mean well, but sometimes they forget about the forgiveness part." Tessie stared off as she spoke the words.

Grace blinked, taken aback by her *aenti*'s words. Maybe she understood more than Grace thought.

"Have you forgiven?"

The heat of the room shifted into a freeze, and a shiver ran up Grace's spine.

"I forgive my *daed* for sending me away. I brought shame to him and our family. It is just hard to accept what we deserve, I guess." Grace collected her baking dishes to ready for washing.

"And?" Tess's stern brow lifted again, drawing Grace out.

"I want to forgive Jared, for leaving me after promising me so much. I need to forgive him," she said, lowering her head, letting her own mumbling words take root. She did need to forgive Jared. She was just as responsible as he was for where she was right now.

"You should, though I expect forgiving a man like that will be hard. *Gott* instructs us to have forgiveness in our hearts, to offer it freely." Tess cleared her throat, and a dark cloud fell over her normally stern expression. "You must also forgive yourself. You made a mistake, you have done what you needed to for that mistake, but if you don't forgive yourself, you will never be able to move forward and live the life *Gott* has planned for you."

Grace hadn't thought of that. How could she consider forgiving herself when she wasn't worthy of others' forgiveness? She stiffened against her vulnerability and locked gazes with her *aenti*.

"*Daed* said anyone can confess a sin, but that *Gott* knows the heart and sees how sinful it is." She was glad they were able to share this time. Grace had no one to talk to, not about things so private. Tessie got to her feet and moved toward the door.

"Benjamin Miller doesn't know what it takes for a body to confess their sins publicly. He doesn't know how it feels to beg forgiveness of the church," she said with a lace of contempt. Tessie was capable of being more than she appeared. Kindling cracked against the forces of heat in the stove nearby, breaking their connection.

"I am leaving to deliver your things before it gets much colder." Tess pointed to a sack in the corner. "Your mail and some light reading. Do you have plenty of wood?"

Grace looked at the sack curiously. She had mail, words from home? She was eager to dive into the bag. "Yes and you already gave me a book."

"One can never learn too much," Tess almost grinned. "Rest when you can," Tess continued. "You will need your energy these next weeks."

Then as suddenly as she appeared, the slamming of the door followed her exit. Grace went to secure the door latch and couldn't help but find herself smiling. *Aenti* Tess was a confusing sort. One minute fussing, the next spouting wisdom. Could she forgive Jared? Really forgive him? Could she forgive *herself*?

Cradling her middle, she peered into the sack. She reached in and pulled out a book. *What to Expect When You're Expecting.* It was twice the thickness of the first book. Grace thumbed through the pages. Her eyes widened at the vivid pictures on display, and she quickly closed it again.

Light reading? She chuckled.

She set the book aside and sifted through the letters. The first envelope was from her *mutter*, most likely another list of Bible verses like the last, reminding her to beg forgiveness of her sins. She had—begged, that was. Lord knows she had. But not just in a room of the bishop and deacons that knew not of her heart, but in her own room with *Gott* as her only company. Was that what *Aenti* Tess meant? She set her *mutter*'s letter aside. She was in too good a mood to let words from home change it again.

A second letter was nothing more than someone wanting to lower her interest rates. She tossed it back to the counter for burning later. The last envelope was from her sister Charity. Faith and Hope had written her once since she arrived, but these were the first words she had received from her eldest sister. Being the eldest made Charity less fun and a bit harder, but her love was always present in her tender smile and caring arms.

At the sound of a second buggy climbing the hill outside, Grace let out a groan. Both letters from home would have to wait, and she went to the door. Stepping out onto the porch as the two work horses drew nearer, Grace couldn't help but smile.

CHAPTER SIXTEEN

Cullen tossed the last pieces of wood into the wagon. With a nod, he was satisfied it was now full. Tessie was not her usual self today when she stopped telling him that Grace was nearly out of kindling. Tessie Miller smiled at him. Something for sure and for certain was up. Grace made it clear she didn't want his friendship, but he couldn't let her freeze, now could he?

Muted sound and movement caught his attention. A blur rushing through the woods, and he squinted to see it more clearly. Whatever it was vanished out of sight, and he brushed it off as possibly a running deer most likely frightened by local hunters still plaguing the area. Just yesterday two men in orange vests and camouflage clothing marched out of the woods and down the road like they belonged there—one even so bold as to toss him a wave when he stepped from the forge and watched them leave.

The earth that formed the hillside drive had softened in the current weather, and he was glad he'd harnessed both horses to pull the load of wood instead of just one. He would need each set of muscles to get up there today. The wheels sank deep into icy mud, but both Jax and Rosey moved the load rather easily up the climb. Out of all his horses, the two worked perfectly together. Maybe that was the reason they made the best foals. He smiled considering it. Even in God's creatures, it was important to have the perfect helpmate.

Reaching the cabin, Cullen took a moment to admire the change. The porch had in fact made all the difference to the place. It was funny how one little thing could change something so much. "One little thing," he smiled, humoring himself. *Little Grace and her little bare feet in her little cabin.* That image of her was forever burned into his mind.

Grace was standing outside, her gray dress blowing in the cold breeze. From this distance he could see she wasn't wearing a coat. She should be wearing a coat, he silently grumbled. He took a long, deep breath, then swallowed hard against the apology he knew he owed her. He should have never said those things to her. Should not have let his feelings toward Freeman seep out in harsh words. It was none of his concern who Grace chose to befriend or not, but seeing her standing on the porch he made, watching him near as if coming home after a long day, did cause his heart to flutter.

He guided the horses forward and came to a stop beside the porch. For a moment they only stared at each other. She didn't appear to still be angry. In fact, Grace looked at him with a combination of awe and bewilderment.

"I brought you another load of wood. And by the looks of it, glad I did." The woodpile was gone, and her porch held so few sticks, he wondered how she would get through the next day as it was. "I didn't mean to intrude," he added quickly, noting her flour-coated apron. "Tess said you had only a little left."

"I'm sorry," she quickly blurted out. Cullen cocked his head to one side, studied the sincerity of her expression, and then nodded.

"It's me who should apologize. You did nothing wrong." Something flickered in her eyes he couldn't rightly read. "I should get this unloaded."

"I'll put on some *kaffi*. Please *kumm* in and warm up first. Then we will both unload the wagon." She offered him a second smile before stepping back inside. Cullen wasn't about to let her lift the first stick, but *kaffi* sounded wonderful.

Before stepping inside, Cullen kicked the loose wet snow from his boots. The house smelled loving with the aromas of her baking. Grace set a kettle on the stove and fetched two cups. Cullen wasn't a fan of instant *kaffi*, but he wouldn't be rude when she was being kind enough to offer.

"Do you want to talk about it?" She said with her back to him. He shed his coat and laid it on the chair. Did they need to talk about it? He removed his hat and ran his fingers through his hair.

"Not really. I was wrong." She turned sharply. "Talking about it will only make me feel worse."

"You were right. Freeman is who you said he was. I was so desperate for a *freind*, I didn't see it. I should have trusted you." She turned and quickly readied their cups, but Cullen didn't miss the sharp line of her lips before she did. Had Freeman said something to upset her as he had others? Suddenly Cullen didn't feel so sorry for what he said about him. Pouring *kaffi* into two cups, she splattered the hot liquid onto her thumb. Grace quickly retrieved a rag and pumped cold water on it.

"Did it burn you?" He stepped forward and then stopped short of her.

"*Nee*. I'm *gut*," she quickly answered and went right

back to stirring the granules. "It isn't very *gut kaffi*, but I have sugar if you prefer it." She handed him his cup and took a sip of her own.

"This is fine." Cullen sipped and they stared at each other over the brims of their cups, neither knowing what to say.

"*Aenti* Tess shouldn't have asked you to bring me kindling. You have work and your own wood to cut."

"I don't mind, Grace. It is what neighbors do."

"And *freinden*?" She grinned.

"*Jah, freinden*," he replied, offering her a warm smile. "And *freinden* can ask questions, *jah*?" Why was she grinning?

"You want to know what he said to me." It wasn't a question, nor his concern, yet Cullen nodded, hoping she wouldn't think him too forward, or worse, nosey. By the time he finished his second cup of *kaffi,* Grace told him about the dinner at the Hilty's. How Elmo Hilty informed her he owned her cabin, how Freeman suggested they begin courting in secret, and how cruelly he tried to use her circumstances to secure that. Cullen tried to bite back floods of anger, but was struggling. Freeman needed a good talking to. For years he preyed on every single *maedel* in the community in search of a *fraa*.

"I should speak to him. It is not right that he thinks to pressure you."

"He does not pressure me, Cullen. I told him how I feel and made him bring me home. I was surprised he said those things, but it isn't the first time my feelings were hurt."

He hadn't prepared himself for what he was about to

say, and *Gott* must have agreed that his timing was off because the sound of a buggy approaching interrupted his attempt.

He and Grace went to the door and watched it come up the hill. Cullen stepped from the porch and began unloading the wood so as not to draw attention to the fact that he'd been alone with her just moments ago. Elmo Hilty brought the buggy to a halt. Setting the brake, he let out a heavy grumble, sounding more bear than man. Tipping his hat, Cullen did the same.

"Cullen. May I ask why you are here with Grace alone today?"

Maybe it was a fair question, but he had been the one seeing to Grace's needs since the day she arrived in October. Not Tessie, not Elmo, and certainly not his spoiled son.

"*Aenti* Tess asked Cullen to bring a load of wood to me," Grace defended. Grace didn't like the way Elmo looked at her now any more than she had at his table. Freeman certainly favored his stern expressions and stiff posture.

"Figured it proper to see that a woman living alone did not freeze. And what brings you to Grace's home today?" Cullen kept his voice calm. Elmo's face crinkled; the man always wore a stern look, and Cullen never imagined it could grow stiffer, but it did.

"I suspect the two of you have a few things in common," he said, scratching his wiry bearded chin. "You should know Freeman has shared with me that he has an interest here." Cullen shoved the armload of wood onto the porch floor and marched to the side of Elmo's buggy.

"Grace, would you please go inside before you get a

chill," he asked, knowing full well she didn't like to be ordered about. To his surprise, Grace turned without questioning his need for her to do so and certainly without her regular defiant opposition to him.

Yes, something had certainly changed between them.

"Freemen will be here first thing in the morn with ya pay." Elmo's voice raised, his stubby neck craned to see her directly around Cullen. "He asked that I stop and tell you such, which I think I should do more often." Grace flinched. He could see she was trying to find the right words to say. She lifted her chin, clasping the sides of her apron.

"I had plans to speak with Cullen here about our next order, but he wasn't home working as he should be." His eyes set firmer on Cullen, now narrowing in a predatory glare. They were gray with no sign of blue lingering in his advanced years. "A man should mind his own *haus* and not that of others. I think now I might have to reconsider what I truly need, as should you."

Looking back to Grace, Cullen could see she knew what Elmo was implying. The man dared to threaten their business dealings if his son was challenged in his pursuit of a *fraa*. The Hilty buggy shop was his biggest customer. Her mouth fell open, and when she closed it, she continued to storm inside and slam the door behind her. It was for the best, considering she would be out of earshot.

"Mr. Hilty, we have done business since my *daed* made your first set of buggy springs." Crossing his arms, Cullen couldn't imagine the man capable of continuing business without him. "But if you have no further need of me, then I pray only the best for you and your family. As for tending to another's *haus*, I am doing as the Lord instructed. No one in our community would see that Grace is left to fend for herself, especially not me. If Freeman had such interest here, I would be chopping less wood. "

Elmo's teeth clenched, clearly stewing over his decision to force Cullen's hand in their business arrangement and defending his lazy son. With or without the Hilty family, Cullen had plenty of work.

"Bishop Mast preached just this Sunday about how we should each help our neighbor. I expected Freeman to do as such, but since he has not, I could not allow for one to do without. And since when did men make claim on others? She is not a horse, and no one should be taking it upon themselves to collect a woman's wages when she doesn't want them to."

Again, Cullen had stepped ahead of Elmo's control. Would God see this as disrespect? He hoped not, because his feet were planted firmly against the elder sitting above him.

"Freeman has many responsibilities. More than you even know," Elmo said matter-of-factly. "I do believe that shall be the last bit of help you shall be showing your neighbor."

"Ordering a man to go against *Gott*'s word? Against our own bishop?" Cullen gave him a quizzical look. Elmo was in no position to bark orders, and yet he wasn't bending.

"I own this land. I own this cabin. I decide who *kumms* and who goes." The warning was made.

With a slap of the lines against his horse, Elmo left before Cullen could argue such demands.

Was Elmo truly threatening him? And what about Grace? Was she to care for herself, or better yet, simply be tossed out into the cold until giving Freeman what he wanted? Cullen released the tight squeeze of his fist. How far would Elmo really go to keep Cullen off his land? Unlike Freeman's threats, Cullen had to think on this one. Or think around it.

Maybe it was time to pay the bishop a call. He was chosen by *Gott* to handle such complications, was he not?

Cullen watched the buggy clatter over the hill and drive down the narrow lane heading out of the holler before looking in on Grace safely tucked inside. Opening the front door and stepping inside, he found Grace crying. It was not good for a woman in her condition to be burdened so.

Taking a step forward, he froze. Elmo most likely would be visiting Tessie Miller and Bishop Mast before day's end to share his opinion with them as well. Cullen had always earned respect the honest way, but how would it affect Grace? She was all that mattered, and he couldn't leave her, nor could he be found alone with her again without causing her harm. There were rules, and he and Grace had bent them plenty already. What kind of foundation would they be setting for a tomorrow if they ignored the rules? There was a proper way of doing this. And Grace Miller deserved his best effort.

"I have caused you troubles, and you have been nothing but *gut* to me." Her voice quivered.

"So now you think me *gut*?" he teased, and she couldn't help but laugh through her hurt. It warmed his heart how she cared more for him than her own reputation.

"You are a smarty, Cullen Graber. Even after this, you

stay calm, crack jokes."

"Would you prefer a *dummkopp*?" He tilted his head.

"*Nee*. I most certainly would not." Good, so she absolutely had no interest in Freeman Hilty.

"Don't mind Elmo. He likes to bark orders to others when it is his own *blut* that he should be reprimanding instead."

"But he is your biggest customer, Freeman told me this." Her eyes lined with worry, and even that look of hers told him he could not trust himself to look deeper into them. "My troubles have spilled over onto you; I am afraid it has cost you."

"I have many customers, Grace. One less might be a *gut* thing. Gives me more time to chop wood." He winked.

"Cullen, be serious. Elmo says this is all his. He all but told me he was considering selling it before I came. He could change his mind." Her brows furrowed, worry etching her delicate flesh. "I should have never agreed with Sadie to let Freeman drive me home. I should act more like a sinner," she clipped.

"And how does one do that?" He asked sharply, crossing both arms.

"I don't know," she huffed, flinging a hand in the air. She was cute all frustrated like that. "It is what *Daed* said to do when he caught me smiling or laughing at something my sisters said."

"You are no longer a sinner, are you?" Their gazes locked. He liked when she did that.

"*Nee*," she said with a lifted chin. "But *Daed* says…"

He hushed her, holding up a hand. "Don't fret on acting like something you are not. Just be you, Grace. And you should smile more. That shouldn't be hidden." In her blank stare, Cullen felt his neck warm.

"Don't be worried about this. I will not let you go without the things you need." *Too bold, Cullen.* "No one will let you go without." *Better.*

"You really mean that, don't you?" The way she looked at him, with pure admiration, made him feel like a better man than the one he knew he was.

"I don't say anything I don't mean."

"No, I don't suppose you do." She tilted her head, staring at him intently. "Do you make promises?"

"I don't think one should. Sometimes you can't keep them, and I would never want to disappoint anyone. I don't want to disappoint you." *You have done it now, man.* Grace probably thought him too forward. Fingering the brim of his hat, he waited, his heart hammering in his chest for what she had to say to that.

"I can't imagine you disappointing anyone." Her deep blue eyes held a searching, like water flowing in a quest for a place to settle. Could he win her over, convince Grace to stay in Walnut Ridge, explore this thing growing between them, or would Elmo and his plans for his son's future stand in their way?

With chin up and shoulders straight, there again was that confident woman stealing too many of his thoughts. "I trust you, Cullen Graber."

Those words, from her, hinted at something strong and powerful and utterly vulnerable all the same. A tiny sprout of hope pushed up from the frozen soil of his heart at those words. Man wasn't meant to be alone, and he, for once, agreed.

Taking the door handle in his hand, he pulled. It was

just another broken thing that surrounded her. Cullen swung it back and forth, testing it. "I can fix this." He shot her a grin and stepped back out into the cold.

. . .

Watching Cullen drive his team and empty wagon over the hill, Grace marveled that his control over the large animals was as gentle as his touch. Hugging herself, she tilted her head and took in the scents of sawdust and smoke still lingering around her. She trusted him, and knowing that changed everything. He had defended her and, in doing so, changed everything. Cullen Graber had somehow taken part of her troubles and made them his own, leaving her less to carry.

That was how she had always envisioned a man to be, but she hadn't trusted *Gott*'s timing and had let the first boy who floated her a smile sweep her off her feet. Tessie was right. It was time to forgive the one person who needed forgiven most. Only then would she be able to face the past that came calling and a future that didn't look so scary. Closing her eyes, Grace bowed her head and began to pray.

CHAPTER SEVENTEEN

The following day Grace stood with fingers threaded tightly within one another as Freeman stood in her kitchen. It was clear Elmo meant what he said—that Freeman would be delivering her pay—which only caused her to worry whether Elmo meant everything he'd said.

"Sadie said the *Englisch* customers have taken a liking to your cinnamon bread," Freeman said. Grace doubted it was all customers but let Freeman continue talking as he deposited two large bags of flour and three smaller bags of sugar on her counter. "And they could use more pies for the holiday. Apple and pumpkin are selling faster than she can make them herself." He reached into his coat pocket and pulled out an envelope. "Your wages, my dear." Grace accepted the envelope with her weekly pay but didn't dare offer Freeman a seat or cup of *kaffi*.

Without invitation, Freeman removed his hat and sat down at her humble table. It was one thing to be alone with Cullen here, his presence helping mend the brokenness of the place, warming the coldness always threatening to enter, but Freeman could not be trusted.

"Everything looks smaller than I remember from when I was younger." Freeman eyed every corner.

"You spent time here with your family?" Grace straightened the pine boughs and cones she'd gathered before the snow. It made the sinner's shack less dreary and more hopeful for the season.

"Not time like you mean," he scoffed. "But *Mutter* would *kumm* to pick flowers while I played in the fields catching bugs."

"Francis likes the wildflowers, too?" Grace never before imagined the quiet woman had many interests. How could she with so many duties tending to her family? Francis Hilty showed no sway from being a dutiful *fraa* and *mutter*. A perfect Amish woman, Grace settled.

Finding joy and comfort in tending your own was just as important as an interest. An interest was something you picked outside the realm of duty, a distraction. Hers had been Jared Castle. From that first distracting smile to a path of roses over New Year's Eve snow leading her to the lake where she learned to skate. She let him take her into his world, lure her with gifts and compliments, until she let it all consume her. Enough to turn her back on all she knew and plunge into the darkness.

Yes, Francis Hilty was the epitome of a faithful, by the book Amish *fraa*.

"I do not know if she even liked the flowers. She picked them like a young girl but would just pile them up around some old tree on the hillside and we would go home. *Daed*'s allergic to them," he added to make some sense of his ramblings.

When Freeman had driven into the yard, Grace had peered out the window to see who had come. His buggy was empty, which meant he did in fact not bring wood for her to burn as his father had suggested. Cullen had brought plenty for a spell. Both sides of the porch were stacked neatly. Easy access for her to retrieve what she needed for a night. Cullen said she had no business trudging out to a woodpile in her condition, that she could slip on the snowy ground and no one would know. Cullen thought of every-thing.

Stop it. Grace needed to stop flirting with fanciful ideas of a man like Cullen Graber and she needed to concentrate on getting Freeman Hilty out of her house.

"*Mutter* is baking for the *kinners'* Christmas recital in a few days and wanted to invite you to *kumm* join my family. I think she likes you."

Freeman motioned to the empty chair awaiting her. Cullen had done more than just provide warmth and friendship since the morning meal they shared—he provided her an extra seat, too, for a guest. Did he hope to be a guest at her table again?

"Tell her that was kind of her to offer, but I will not be attending."

"A proper *maedel* should do her part, help in her community instead of waiting for others to help her, or else she may never become a *fraa.*"

"I have a job and I haven't taken advantage of others to be *faul*. It isn't proper to give your *mutter* the wrong impression that I have an interest in being married to or courted by you."

"You could be."

"I don't care for you, Freeman. You should look else-where." Freeman rose to his feet. The plump lines of his face pinched.

"Where did the firewood come from?" He knew where it came from, but she answered, nonetheless.

"Everyone knows that *Aenti* Tess asked Cullen to see that I have plenty. Not like I can go cutting down trees in this condition." She lifted her chin and planted both hands firmly on her hips. Freeman's obvious disdain for Cullen's help was apparent.

"I will be bringing your needs to you from now on. I will tell him so when I leave here today. Cullen Graber needs to find a *fraa* of his own."

She couldn't help but laugh aloud. Sure, Freeman made his hopes for a future with her known, but he clearly wasn't listening when she declined his interest.

"Cullen was only being nice. He is my closest neighbor," Grace defended. The way Cullen looked at her suggested that might be a lie, but surely in her situation that was only pity. "And I will accept his kindness."

"A neighbor? Is that all he is?"

"I told you I was not interested in your planned future. I should not have to repeat it again and again. I also hope you know how grateful I am for your kindness, driving me to work so often, but you don't need to bring my wages or drive me anymore. It isn't proper now that you insist we be more than *freinden*. My *aenti* will see that I have what I need and Sadie said herself she could have Matthew stop by and pick up my baking when I need him too." Her words were meant to be harsh, and she didn't care if he didn't like her tone.

"You will not see Cullen again," he barked in a warning tone reserved for children. His face was beet red as he bore anger toward her. Grace crossed the room, disbelieving that this man thought he could instruct her.

"You have no right to speak to me this way."

"We have been out three times, shared a meal with my *daed* and *mutter*…that is courting. You best not be letting that man *kumm* here anymore. I won't allow for it and it will give you a reputation." Like his father, Freeman's neck disappeared in his shoulders when his temper rose.

"Cullen fixed a roof and porch, brought firewood when you did not." Perching both fists firmly on her hips, she wondered when she had gotten so brave when a man raised his voice to her. She had only made one mistake in all her life and that did not mean everyone had the right to tell her what she could and could not do. It was Cullen, the man who delivered more than kindness and fire wood, but strength. The kind of strength Jared Castle never had. The kind Freeman pretended to possess.

"This is my home and I belong to no one. Leave, Freeman. Leave now!" Those words appeared to hit him differently than her last. His swollen chest, his beady eyes told her he would not accept her defiance so lightly.

"*Your* home?" A devilish smile crept over his wide face and she found that Freeman Hilty was the most spoiled, ill-tempered child she had ever encountered.

"You have no *mann* for your child and no home or finances to raise it. After the *boppli* is born, I will give it a name to be proud of, a future you cannot. You would be wise not to turn me down, Grace. You have so few options, you should not waste the best one being given."

" I will decide who will be part of his or her life." She was livid, felt the heat of it climb and settle in her cheeks. "I will pray for you, Freeman, but I will no longer speak to you. Now leave."

"Did you pray for this? Best be changing that stubborn mind of yours before it's too late. Nobody will want you. I am your only chance for that child's future." He eyed her body, and bit back whatever else he wanted to say before stomping away and slamming the door in his exit.

The breath she had held since coming to her feet exhaled.

. . .

Cullen added three more sticks of wood to the forge. Knowing Freeman was just up the hill made him sick to his stomach.

The sounds of Freeman's buggy rambled down the hill and Cullen stepped out from the shop. Watching Freeman slide over slick mud barely hidden under fresh snow was amusing to watch. The man had always lacked control. "Some things never change," he whispered.

Normally the short-tempered fellow drove past, nose in the air, stiff in the buggy seat. And after Elmo all but denied further orders from the buggy shop, why couldn't today have been the same? Cullen groaned deep from within as Freeman veered off the road and pulled up next to the blacksmith shop.

"Freeman," Cullen greeted, unimpressed, before crossing his arms. "What can I possibly help you with this day?"

"*Daed* had me stop by on my way from Gracie's to tell you he would like to renegotiate our next order of frames." The pains it took Freeman to will control was entertaining. One could just not imagine how a man could clench teeth and jaw while speaking like that, but it was possible. The words all but hissed out like a snake.

"Cannot find another blacksmith to help?" Cullen smirked and Freeman narrowed his gaze toward him. "I could give you some lessons." Freeman could use lessons in how to treat others more than blacksmithing, but maybe a little time with him would teach him both.

"I think wood chopping will be keeping me the next few days." Meaning, *stop adding to the pile on Grace's porch*, Cullen presumed, as Freeman eyed the sky to find something more interesting there.

"I know for certain she has plenty." Cullen reined back the inappropriate grin. No sense in making things worse than they were. He could handle the Hiltys, but it wasn't about him, really, now was it?

"I will be tending to any needs Grace requires from now on. She will *kumm* to her senses and see the wisdom of what I can offer her and her child." Apparently Grace had declined him once more. Cullen stifled a laugh.

What humor Freeman had brought to him on first arrival was now gone. "Grace isn't interested and won't be bullied. I won't allow her to be treated harshly," Cullen threatened.

With a crack of the leather in Freeman's control, the buggy slid away without slowing. Freeman just couldn't accept a refusal.

CHAPTER EIGHTEEN

Riding in the car with Elli, Grace was glad to leave the closed-in walls of the shack today, still tainted by Freeman's unexpected visit. Forty degrees with sunshine felt like a whole new world after being inside for days. Sitting alone, sewing newborn gowns and pondering Freeman's harsh words, what would be a better distraction than a day spent in the company of Elli and the women she had come to know and care for?

Quilting bees at home were full of focus and skill, but she had a feeling that the ladies of Walnut Ridge would be the fellowship she could use right now. "Best cure for the cabin fever is sunshine and friends." Elli bumped her shoulder and tossed her a smile.

The driver, an older woman Elli knew, fairly well by the way they teased each other, pulled into the drive and put the car in park. Elli tossed the woman a ten-dollar bill as Grace exited the car.

Three buggies sat outside Betty Glick's home. The door opened, and Grace was met with the scent of fresh bread and peppermint. In the kitchen, Grace found the source of the aromas. Betty's candy-making skills put anything created in her family home to shame. Christmas preparations had begun.

Grace popped a chocolate-coated patty into her mouth and let the minty flavors wash over her. After three days of an upset stomach, the peppermint was undoubtedly the best medicine, and hopefully the rest of the day would be the best cure for what ailed her.

"Look at you, my dear. You are glowing." Betty squeezed her shoulders.

Grace beamed. Betty was a ray of sunshine on any darkened day. The women doting over her recent growth made her feel almost happy. The house stirred with activity, and she watched busy bodies ready the quilting supplies. Hannah and Betty collected threads and needles, while she and her *aenti* spread the quilt over the kitchen table. Once everything was in its place, Grace found a seat and studied the pattern in front of her. Swirls had been quilted already and she had only to continue what another had started. That was easy enough. Even she couldn't mess that up.

"This will be *gut* for ya." *Aenti* Tess set a cup of tea down next to her and walked back to her seat at the large table. Since their last conversation her *aenti* seemed more pleasant to be around.

"I took out another dress for you," Betty interrupted her thinking.

"You are spoiling me, Betty. I can tend to such myself," Grace said. Though it was a job best suited for Charity, since she sewed the finest according to their *mutter*, but Grace had learned the skill as well.

"Don't discourage Betty, dear. I for one know all about her spoils. Want them or not she has a gift of knowing what we need and when we need it. Be thankful," Elli added and passed a smile across the table to her dearest friend.

"We hear Freeman Hilty has become rather enamored with you." Rachel was quickly replacing the thorn in her side.

"He has been very kind to me since I moved here," Grace said, not revealing that Freeman all but planned a full future without caring for her thoughts on it.

"Very kind indeed. He talks about you to everyone." Rachel sounded more informative than judgmental for once, and Grace could only stare at her from across the table in curiousness.

"He is very…what is the word? Determined. I have no mind to entertain his company other than being polite." *There*, she thought. *Point made.*

Rachel's regular tight expression softened. One could almost see the relief on her face. Grace appreciated the sentiment. Rachel must know firsthand all about Freeman's attentions, too.

"He has a history of being a bit pushy." Rachel added.

"I can see that." A smile floated between them. "He was even so bold as to tell me we were courting and had a future together despite my saying I had no interest in him. I take it he does not like being told no."

"That he doesn't. Even as a boy, he was not one for a no. He has flirted with every girl in the community and not a one accepted his efforts," Rachel said.

"If he is being a pest, you just tell us." Elli quickly lifted a firm brow.

"I made him leave this morning when he brought my wages. I don't know why Sadie gave them to him." Grace hoped she didn't sound too complaining, but Rachel was right; Freeman didn't take no for an answer.

"I will see to that," Tess barked. "That reminds me. Did Cullen deliver the sewing machine?"

Talk about timing. Tessie Miller was the queen of saying

the wrong thing at the wrong time. If they suspected she had feelings for Cullen, they would certainly be more stuck on it now. Rachel's raised brows were proof of that.

Grace gathered herself and slowed her breaths. Focusing on sliding the needle along the penciled line of the quilt, she answered. "He has not." Though she did have a new chair and the dish cabinet no longer leaned on the wall but held firmly to it. But Grace kept those thoughts to herself. Rachel scoffed in reply but otherwise kept silent.

"Very well. I think we will stop by and see that you get it. No point in putting others out when you can tend to your own needs. A busy man should not be bothered too often."

Grace nodded in agreement. Cullen had work, a living to make, and yet made time to tend to her so frequently. It spoke volumes about the kind of man he was.

"I do not need it. I have two hands," Grace said. Freeman said she should not sit and wait for handouts, and she hoped others didn't see her the same way.

"It was his *mamm*'s. He won't be needing it." Betty chimed in, then snipped a yard of thread and began working.

No, Grace didn't expect Cullen would need a sewing machine, nor have time for such womanly things, being the only blacksmith for miles, but one day it would be useful in his home again, would it not?

"What if Cullen were to take a *fraa*? He is still young. Why buy something that's already there?" With her needle threaded once more, Grace eyed the place she had stopped and continued quilting again.

"No one sees Cullen Graber ever doing such," *Aenti* Tess

snorted. "Do not worry, he thought it would be best for you to have it with the *boppli* coming and all." *Cullen's idea.* Why did that not surprise her? And why did it make her all tingling inside?

Grace did her best to concentrate on her quilting and not the handsome neighbor filling her every thought. "Why wouldn't anyone see him wed? He is strong, handsome, has his own smithy shop and home. He would be a *gut* catch for someone." As the words left her, she felt strangely affected by them. Cullen was a *gut* catch, and suddenly imagining him with another made her uneasy.

"I knew you thought him handsome. You should see your face light up at just the mention of his name," Hannah blurted out. Did her face light up at the mere mention of his name? Grace thought not. Hannah was being foolish and making Grace's face warm.

"You should know Sara Shrock and Beth Zook have tried catching his eye for years now." Was Hannah telling her she had competition?

"And Mary Beth Beiler and Bethany Zimmerman," Elli added with a knowing grin. Grace didn't know what to say and figured nothing was best. "They make certain to compliment the sign he made every time they stop in to purchase cheese for their *mamm*s." The women all laughed.

"You and Cullen Graber have much in common. It is not unlikely for you two to become *freinds.* Sara is my dearest *freind*," Rachel muttered. Loud enough all could hear, and Grace wondered why she even attempted keeping her voice down at all. Their eyes locked in defiance of the other, the friendly moment between them gone, broken only when Rachel pricked her finger. Elli slung a dishrag in her direction and Rachel quickly covered the wound before she bled on the white of the quilt top.

"Serves ya right," Elli barked. "Cullen is a good catch. All the available girls have tried for his attention, some still do. He has never taken an interest."

Did Elli know something of Cullen's well-kept thoughts that she didn't? "I do not understand." Grace paused, scanning the faces of everyone around the table for answers. Why would a man not want to marry? Was that not what they were instructed to do?

Setting her sights back to Elli, she watched the exchange. Elli looked to her *aenti* for consent before continuing further, and Tessie gave it to her. It was a bit unsettling to know the confident and forward Elli Schwartz required Tess's approval for anything. No, that wasn't it. The women worked as a team, a clutch of sisters. Was she part of that clutch? She thought not, but the idea she could be was pleasing.

"Cullen was a boy when he met Marty." Elli let loose of the quilt and laid her needle and thread next to a small silver pair of scissors. Everyone grew eerily quiet. Was Marty who Cullen meant when he said, "she's gone," leaving her with nothing more? Grace felt her heart ache just imagining Cullen giving his heart to another only to have her leave it broken.

"Marty was an *Englisch* girl. Poor little thing ran wild when she was young." Grace's eyes went wide. She tightened her jaw to make sure it didn't drop in astonishment. Cullen loved an *Englischer*, one he met as a child. The revelation was a jolt to her system.

Twice now she'd been told she and Cullen had

something in common. Grace suspected they shared broken hearts, but abandonment she would have never guessed. Who would dare leave such a man?

"Well of course with no *mamm* at home and no *daed* for that matter with all his drinking and gambling and such. *Kinner* need direction or they become wild," Tess added, rocking in her seat with every word she said. Grace noted that the tic of rocking like that only appeared when Tessie was upset. Not just her normal angry self but truly disturbed. Grace hung on their every word.

"Well, they grew up in this valley, and though Cullen's parents often warned him of such friendships, Cullen couldn't stay away from Marty, no matter the trouble it caused him." She never would have suspected Cullen was a wayward fence jumper. She certainly couldn't imagine him swaying from his faith. He was so solid in it. "The bishop even had to intervene when they became teenagers after Marty's father caught them fishing over at the lake. He beat Cullen bloody for being there." Grace gasped.

"Her daddy beat her that day, too. You all know it to be true and not idle gossip. The man was a monster to that girl." Heads bobbed in agreement with Betty's high-pitched comment. Betty wiped her face with a soft linen hanky and tucked it back into her sleeve. Betty had such a soft heart. So Marty was raised in an abusive home.

"That's what happens when you go mixing the separate worlds, *Mutter* says." Rachel passed her a judgmental gaze. She was right, yet her saying so didn't lessen the sting. Shame again coursed through Grace, leaving its bitter taste on her tongue. Grace raised the second cup of tea her *aenti* had offered and sipped the cold, awful stuff. It tasted of lemon and honey, which she had always liked, but something bitter, strong, and woodsy was in the brown concoction that made it hard to swallow.

"When she turned sixteen she began learning our ways. She talked to the bishop, and Cullen's *mamm* was teaching her cooking and sewing and all the things that make for a *gut fraa*."

"She was going to join our faith?" Grace asked. Jared had once made such a promise. With ears all in, Grace listened as a child waiting for the next chapter. Cullen's story was so like her own. No wonder she felt pulled to him.

"Grace, my dear," Elli said, touching her sleeve. "I myself was not born Amish. I became so after raising two daughters and burying my first husband. I was blessed with a second chance and fell in love with a good man."

That explained a lot. Grace realized her mouth was completely open and quickly closed it. "I had some suspicions." Grace quirked the corner of her mouth and patted Elli's hand back. "So did this Marty join the community? Was she baptized?" When no one answered, Grace lifted her gaze to the women again.

Elli got to her feet as Hannah and Rachel hurried back to quilting to avoid answering. Grace looked across the quilt. Betty was teary-eyed, and her *aenti* was simply staring at the colors before her as if the answers were all there. Something terrible had happened. Grace was sure of it, and just thinking it made her somber, too. Grace couldn't deny wanting to know more, yet she couldn't help but feel a pang of jealousy, too. She clutched her chest, waiting.

Elli cleared her throat again. "When Marty was ready to

leave her father's house, he stopped her, and she told him she was going to join our Amish community and marry the man she loved." Elli took a breath to regain her composure. "Her father was drunk with her in the car and they crashed into Twin Fork Lake. A couple of kids nearby said Marty tried to save him. He was stuck and the poor thing drowned trying to free him." Without a hand nearby to clutch, too, Grace squeezed her own together to lessen the emotions swelling up inside her. What agony, what pain Cullen must feel. "Then a few years back, Cullen lost both his parents in a buggy accident. He has lost much, but our Cullen is strong in his faith." It couldn't be ignored how much Elli cared for Cullen.

That was it, her mind proclaimed. Cullen waited for a woman he met as a child to make her his wife and she died saving a man who didn't care about her? It was the most horrible, tragic thing she had ever heard. Grace's insides screamed in protest. She no longer felt the urge to cry. If not for a few drops of moisture already, she wouldn't cry at all. What part of *Gott*'s plan was that? Cullen's loss had surpassed any she had endured. Jared was alive, but Marty was gone, never to return. Her parents were alive, despite not wanting her around. How could she even fathom one ounce of similarity to what Cullen Graber had endured? Life was so unfair.

She scanned the quilting table, damp eyes and solemn faces on them all. Grace felt her own vision blur. What was meant to be a beautiful story ended in heartache and utter tragedy. Where was the happy ending? Faith once read a story like that, but before the last pages were read, *Daed* had found the book, burned it in the cookstove, and punished them all for the disobedience before ever knowing the end.

What end would come to Cullen? He deserved the happiest of them all. Did she dare try to help him? Share her story in hopes he could talk about his own.

"Children always pay for their parent's sins." Tess muttered. Her chair fell to the floor as she marched out of the room. A pin dropped to the floor, and everyone at the quilting table heard it.

CHAPTER NINETEEN

Aenti Tess sat behind the driving lines holding firm to her usual brooding silence from Elli's house to Cullen's. Grace wasn't sure who tore at her heart more at the moment. Cullen Graber, who lost the woman he loved tragically, or her *aenti*. Something happened at Betty's house today. Something everyone understood but her. She wasn't part of the sisterly group, yet. *Aenti* Tess carried wounds, wounds that were not so well buried. But what those wounds were, Grace hadn't a clue.

The horse pulled into Cullen's yard, heavy dark smoke rising out of the blacksmith shop and traveling in a long train down the valley. The scents of heat and damp and iron landed in Grace's nose, but they didn't disturb her. She was no longer strangely affected by it and welcomed the smells her neighbor's trade carried.

Cullen stepped out into the open, gloves high on his thick arms and a heavy apron stretching to his knees. Her breath caught. He was more handsome than the last time she laid eyes on him. She exhaled, putting aside the thought only triggered by knowing more about him than she should have. How could a *Gott* who made such a man treat him so unkindly?

He eyed her peculiarly and she couldn't rein in a timid smile. Now who pitied whom? She had ignored him, thrown him out of her *haus*, snuck around his, and was smiling at him like he was her best friend. *Stupid.*

"You forgot to deliver the sewing machine we spoke of."
Aenti Tess never beat around the bush, and Grace was for
once glad of it. After knowing so much about him now,
private things, she couldn't disguise the pity that flowed
through her. She had never been one to hide well the
thoughts of her heart. Cullen saw it, too. The way his chin
lifted and his forehead crinkled, he was reading it all over
her face. After a long pause, he diverted his attention to
Tess.

"I have never ignored a request from you before." His
brow rose in correction and his gravelly voice did as well.
"I set it under the window so you could use the light." His
eyes shifted downward, giving a slight nod. How thought-
ful, Grace thought. Cullen always thought of everything.
Her heart beamed at knowing how carefully he'd considered the sewing machine's placement so she didn't have to
move it.

"I waited until you both left for your quilting to take it
to her sinner's, um, shack," he quickly corrected. Grace's
breath hitched. "I am glad someone will have use of it.
Mamm would have wanted that."

Grace didn't miss the nod Tess threw at him. It carried
the weight of complete respect.

"*Danke*, it is much appreciated," Grace muttered.

"Just being neighborly." He grinned, and Grace couldn't
help but grin back.

• • •

After her *aenti* left, Grace took out the bag of material
Betty gifted her and arranged it on the table. Betty had

given her more than enough to make what was needed for the *boppli* and Grace considered using the rest for a quilt. After today, she was in the mood for trying her hand at quilting again. Her sisters would be tickled to know such. Charity often fussed over her loose stitches.

Thinking of her sister, Grace remembered the letters from home she'd tucked away when Cullen arrived that day. So much had happened she almost forgot she had them. Grace went to the drawer to retrieve them.

Grace tore the letter open. Part nervous to see what Charity had written, part excited her sister hadn't forgotten her in this place, and part afraid.

Gracie,

All here is the same as yesterday and the day before. With the exception that Michael finally asked Daed's *permission to marry me. Yes, I am to be married come spring and hope you and my new niece or nephew will be here to celebrate it with us.*

Grace's heart leaped with joy. Charity deserved a man like Michael, a life beyond the home they grew up in. But how was Grace going to endure living under the family roof without her? Charity was the only daughter Ben Miller dared to reason with.

Michael says you are welcome to stay here, too. The house is small, but until you get your bearings, we will make do. It would be best for you to do this, I feel.

A subtle hint that *Daed* was still sore at her and may never offer the forgiveness *Aenti* Tess referred to. Grace felt her sinuses tingle.

Mother misses you in the kitchen, though she would never say so. Mercy has shown little interest in filling your shoes. Baking is not her talent at all. Faith is courting Alan Hamel and I feel she will be marrying shortly after I. I worry her heart is less in Alan's than in leaving home, but I cannot say a thing to her on my thoughts without a fuss on the topic. I guess she can quilt in peace if she marries Alan. At least they will never be cold.

Two of her sisters were to marry. A sting of good old fashioned jealousy washed over her. Grace would never have that joy, putting the cart before the horse as she had done.

Charity's offer was sweet, and living with her and Michael would be better than living under *Daed's* firm hand again, but that wouldn't be fair to Charity. What newly wedded couple wanted to be saddled with a mother and child? Charity hadn't made mistakes; she never faltered or swayed in her faith. She deserved a life all her own. Grace wiped her face with her sleeve and continued reading.

Hope still sings like always but has to do so in the barn milking now, not the gardens she loves. You know how she can get stuck indoors too long. We had snow finally and Michael took me sleighing with others. It was wonderful.

I have prayed daily for you and how you are doing alone in that place with Aenti Tess. She was so harsh when we were kinner. Is she still? We heard you lived in a charming little cabin in the woods near her and she wrote Daed and said you fit in well with the community there. I hope they love you as we sisters do. I know it is the last thing you want to think of right now, but keep an open mind. Sometimes a new place can be scary but it also can be a blessing. Meeting new people, making new friends.

That was true for the most part. Freeman might have turned out not to be what Grace expected, but the women, the community, had been kind. No one darted her disapproving looks. No one spoke of her sin freely and aloud. Yes, Walnut Ridge was a blessing in a time when she felt she didn't deserve one.

With all that being said, I have enclosed a second letter. I have lost much sleep deciding if I should burn it or see it delivered to you. I then realized my selfishness for your heart was wrong. Please don't be angry with me for sending this. It was only my intent to do the right thing, and under the circumstances, I did not know what that was.

Love, your always faithful sister,
Charity.

Grace reached into the envelope and fished out the second letter. What could be written inside that would cause Charity to wrestle with giving it to her? Grace took a deep breath and unfolded the paper. As she read each messy handwritten word, Grace realized nothing had prepared her for this. "No!" Grace cried out.

The crack of the fire matched that of her heart from the inside. How could a few simple sentences have such a damning effect? Her fingers loosened their hold and each letter floated to the floor.

Emotions scattering, she slowly crumbled to the floor. Had she not prayed for weeks to receive such word? Grace sobbed uncontrollably.

• • •

He shouldn't be here, Cullen told himself, but he had to make sure Grace didn't need the heavy sewing machine moved someplace else. Lifting his hand, he formed half a fist to knock on the door. Sounds of crying seeped from the inside and met his ears. His brow furrowed. She was crying again and just after Tess had left. He knocked softly the first time, but Grace didn't come to the door. A second, more firm knock had the same results.

"Grace," Cullen called out. The weeping stopped, faint movement stirred on the other side just before the latch he was just contemplating breaking lifted, and the door slowly creaked open.

Large blue eyes, rimmed in red looked up at him. Cullen felt his heart clobber him straight in the chest. The woman was going to be the death of him. Was it healthy for her child that she felt heartache, loneliness, despair? He hadn't a clue, but that troubled him, too.

"I'm so sorry," she cried out and took a step back. Cullen stepped inside not minding the snowy prints he was tracking through the cabin. If she would stop crying, he would take whatever raking she had to give him for the mess.

"Don't apologize for crying," Cullen quickly said. She didn't appear hurt—not on the outside anyway—and he studied the scene around her. On the floor were letters strewn about, he determined they had brought her to this low point. Grace's crying was spawned by words from home perhaps, and for the first time since she had arrived at Walnut Ridge, Cullen saw her for the completely broken thing she truly must be.

"Grace, talk to me," he said, slow and calm. He was

tempted to pull her into his arms, offer her a safe place until nothing made her sad, but that would be too bold. Wiping her sleeve across her face, he could see her hands were trembling. It was a hurt he wasn't sure how to fix. If she knew what a failure he was at helping damsels in distress, she wouldn't look at him this way.

Guilt, misery, fear…each took a turn dancing across her delicate features. Even so, she was beautiful. Last time, he helped her forget the things that tugged at her. Cullen hadn't even known he possessed such abilities. Practice made perfect, *Daed* always said. He could help eradicate all those crestfallen looks for good if he tried harder. He really did like that smile of hers.

His heart tugged and pulled, his chest burned with the workout. Grace had no idea she was awakening pains he didn't want to feel again. He had failed Marty, waited too long to make a difference in her life. His protective nature took hold, shoving a regretful past into a dusty corner, and Cullen hoped now that his timing had improved.

He lifted an arm, offering a safe place, and Grace lowered her head into the bend of it and continued the crying he had walked in on. "*Ach*, Grace," he said, his other arm following his first as he pulled her into a safe hold of security. How could he help her? "You are not alone, my Grace. Cry if you must. I will not leave until you want me to."

Her small frame melted into him and raised his awareness of just how much he had come to care for her. He held her gently, but she held him firmly, her fingers twisting into his coat so tightly, his flesh pinched into it. Was that what she needed? Cullen was made for just that.

He was something strong and safe and present.

Grace needed him, and suddenly Cullen realized he needed her, too. But she would be leaving. Suddenly, he realized that sorrow was the mood for the day.

Cullen's shelter was a warm quilt on a cold night, and she buried herself in him. Her breaths shattered as her options opened wider into view. Her child deserved a father, but would Jared fulfill his promise to join the Amish community? Could she count on him? It was the right thing, after so many wrong ones, but whatever she had once thought she felt for Jared had disappeared into the shadows of the man he truly was.

Cullen patted her back, small gentle taps like those meant for a child. There was no place safer, no place better for her to be than where she was right now.

Cradling her in his arms, Cullen found a refuge for himself and selfishly remained still, relishing how good it felt. It wasn't the mere connection with another; it was something more. He wanted to make things easier for her, help her through all this pain and guilt she was carrying. But Grace had become a healing balm to him, after years of drought and solitude. She made him want more. She made him feel.

Who was he kidding? Her presence brought forth a stirring he had long hidden deep inside. It was her, he knew. How could he let go now?

"*Danke*, Cullen. I am sorry you had to see that. But if you didn't make such a habit of showing up at the worst of times…" Clearly she wanted to thank him for being there but was embarrassed he had seen her struggling.

He understood. Was she also trying to make light of

what was shared between them, or had she felt nothing at all? He stepped back, offered her a hand. "I think you have fallen far enough. Now, it is time for us to get up, face the day."

Her lips curved into a smile that said she knew exactly what he was saying. Grace needed to look up, move forward, and let yesterday be nothing more than a memory. What she didn't know, when she took his hand, was that they were *both* climbing out of a low point and rising anew.

It was time to heed his own advice.

"Letters from home," she whispered. Cullen gathered the scattered mess. His eyes froze on the name at the bottom of the top one. Grace didn't snatch the paper from his hands, so he continued to read.

"This is from him, *jah*?" Could the man even be called such?

"*Jah*, he is going to be on leave from the military. It is the life he chose over us." Her voice cracked as she ran a trembling hand over her middle. "You must think I am childish to cry over such a person."

That was the last thing Cullen thought. Grace had been let down so many times, he feared this letter might be the light she deserved, that her child was deserving of. They both knew heartbreak, only the one he'd loved hadn't walked away. Marty died saving the only person who tried to keep them apart.

Handing over the letters, he thought she looked fragile, worn, and brittle. Not the fearless defender of her home he knew her to be. Stepping away before he took her into his arms again, he opened the front door, putting space between them.

"*Nee.* I would never think you childish, Gracie. I wish I could say something to make easy the hurt that letter has brought you." *Or help you forget it ever arrived*, he wished to say.

She raised her head and smiled at him, as if seeing him clearly for the first time — the real him, not the unpolished smithy neighbor over the hill.

"Was ya holding out he would return for ya?" he asked. He had to know her answer, and with bated breath waited for it. Imagining anyone else holding her, comforting her, sent a wave of anger through his core.

"In my heart he was no more. I do not know how to explain this hurt I feel now inside of me. Things are different. I am different. He wants to see me, talk with me after all this time ignoring me. Ignoring *us*."

Grace seemed to fight back the urge to cry again and straightened, brushing her hands over her apron. He wondered what her heart did feel for this man who had left her. He wondered what her heart felt about him. She shivered and he closed the door again — a fool for letting the outside in. Another thing he figured to remedy. The outside world had taken enough of her, and if she allowed him, Cullen would slam shut the doors, lock all the windows, and keep it at bay.

"I feared my *boppli* would never know the love of a *daed*. A *daed* to teach love and play games and wipe away young tears." She started crying again. "Now I fear…" Her words fell short, unfinished, and she cupped her face in her hands. Was it possible Grace feared welcoming this man back into her life?

"Don't fear anything. *Gott*'s will. We may not see His

plan, or understand it, but if we remain faithful, we will. Trust Him."

"*Gott* did not bring me here. I brought me here. He had no part in this," she said firmly, wiping away a few lingering tears. Cullen couldn't suppress a chuckle. "You find my shame amusing?"

"*Nee*. I find *you* amusing, my dear. I'm afraid, Grace Miller, you aren't that powerful. Sin or not, *Gott* is in control." As soon as the words left his lips, Cullen believed them himself. Bad things happen, mistakes happen, but *Gott* was always in control, and He alone had brought Grace to Walnut Ridge. He alone had seen to it that she be given the support she deserved.

"My wrong path forced my father's hand. It sent Jared running away. *Gott* did not do that."

"*Nee*, He did not. But you are not responsible for the actions of others. Just your own. *Gott*'s grace covers Kentucky just as it does Indiana. You should find forgiveness in your heart, then you will be ready to face whatever this is," he pointed toward the letters.

"I have forgiven," she said sharply.

"But have you forgiven yourself?" Something flickered in her sapphire blue gaze. An awakening so apparent he knew she had not. "And do you even need others' forgiveness?"

Grace stepped back. "I don't understand. Of course I need forgiveness. I'm a sinner," she said, a little too loudly.

"Are we not all sinners? Did Jesus not die for our sins? Isn't His forgiveness all you need?" She thought about that for a moment.

"Why have you not been like others? You do not point

fingers at this." She touched her middle.

"It is better to help with the whole hand than simply point the finger." A hint of humor colored his words.

"Elli says that, too." She grinned, looking up at him. She had an amazing smile, even when she wasn't trying.

"She is a wise woman and never points fingers." When Grace huffed a little laugh, his heart opened wide enough to welcome her in. How would he keep these feelings contained? How would he accept Grace leaving, or worse, leaving with the man who broke her heart? He needed to think. He needed to talk to *Gott*. Cullen needed a plan. There was no way he could simply let her leave, not without knowing how he felt.

"Do you wish to speak to him?" Cullen ducked his head. He didn't want to see her reaction to his question.

"A child needs a father. Families are meant to stay complete."

"That isn't an answer." He looked to her now and found her peering up at him, a curious searching in her gaze.

"You will think badly of me if I answer." *Impossible.*

"*Nee*, I won't," he encouraged. She let out a sigh.

"What I want doesn't matter any longer, but no. I don't ever want to see Jared Castle again." She would never leave her faith for a man—that's why Jared's promise meant so much to her. "I cannot bear to think of my *boppli* raised outside my Amish faith, or by a man who runs when things get hard."

When Cullen smiled at her answer, Grace's heart flipped inside itself. *Kinner* needed the kind of *daed* that would love them through mistakes, hold them when they cried, and never, ever abandon them. Cullen Graber was a man who still mourned his first love a decade after losing her. What a great and powerful love they must have had to endure even after the stings of death. He was the kind of man who didn't run or abandon.

CHAPTER TWENTY

Goose bumps climbed over every inch of her flesh as she finished her washrag bath. A bird bath *Mammi* used to call them. Tonight was the Christmas recital and Grace knew *Aenti* Tess was disappointed when she refused her offer to go along. Grace couldn't imagine riding in the buggy all the way to the Amish school across the valley, or sitting for hours on those benches tonight, despite knowing that watching the *kinner* recite their verses and poems and the sound of Christmas hymns would be a balm to her spirits. It had been a favorite part of her own childhood, next to baking, that was. With a mere couple of weeks away from having her baby, staying close to home was a good idea.

The scent of roasted chicken in the next room told her to hurry into a clean dress. She chose the brown chore dress, having no desire to try and squirm her way into one of her blue ones. It had been Charity's and two sizes too big three months ago, but now was a comfort to her tightening middle.

The scar on her upper arm had long healed, and she traced the reminder with one finger. So much had happened in such a short amount of time, the scar would always help her remember every part of it when she was gone. She hurried the brush through her hair, wishing she hadn't used the last of the lavender from Hope's garden, and hurried into the main room before she burned supper. Hopefully her family had received their gifts by now. Grace could imagine the smile on Hope's face when she saw the heirloom seed packets. Hope loved growing various breeds of plants.

One whole chicken, two biscuits, and a half pan of gravy—her eyes had certainly been bigger than her belly when she concocted such a feast. She would never get used to cooking for just one person. Her stomach growled as the scent filled her senses. Maybe she would be able to finish the whole thing herself, after all. The thought of it amused her enough to laugh out loud. Her hair, freshly washed, hung long and damp against her back and she squirmed against the moisture soaking into the brown fabric.

Mutter's letter still lay in the center of the table. After reading Charity's and Jared's, Grace hadn't the stomach for yet more news from home, but as she sat there with her plate overfilled with food she was blessed to have, she thought of her mother. The letter stared at her as she took her first bite, taunting her to read it. It disturbed her more today than the previous days it rested there. Grace eyed it again. It was time to read what was written inside. Maybe her *mutter* was going to tell her how much she missed her, like Charity insisted. Maybe there would be no mention at all of her disobedience.

Taking a healthy mouthful of chicken, Grace lifted the letter. The seal had already dried, since she had opened it so many times, but until now she'd never so much as pulled the sheets of paper from the inside. She lifted the flap once more, then dared to venture further.

My darling Grace,

I have missed you by my side. Mercy has never been as quiet and easy to work with as you. Your daed says you may come home before the weather turns, instead of waiting as he first demanded. He has a request that I feel is for the best for you. He wants you to marry Leon Strolzfus. As you know, Leon is without a mate after the birth of his son, and his three children need a mamm to raise them, as your boppli needs a father. His dairy is doing well, and your daed assures me he will be kind to your child and accept it as his own. They have spoken on this often of late, and Leon has expressed that he has a great respect for you. Your girlish hopes for anything more are no longer important and we hope you will set aside any false hopes you have entertained and return to the life required of you.

We are sending money for a driver to Tessie. We must know our funds are used only for the good of Gott and nothing more. The bishop and deacon have agreed to welcome you back into the church once you return and will bless your marriage with open hearts. I look forward to seeing you again. Please don't delay and don't disappoint your family any further.

Your mom

Suddenly chicken and gravy became a sour villain to her stomach.

Rising from the table, she took up a wooden spoon and lifted the round iron on the stove top. Dropping her mother's letter into the flames, she closed it up with a clang of iron against iron and tossed the spoon across the floor.

She was stuck. In order to stay, she would possibly be forced to find another place to live, and what Sadie gave her would not allow for such. If she returned, she would be expected to marry. And Leon Strolzfus? The man had always been cold and slower-moving than molasses. Charity offered to share her home, but Grace couldn't be so selfish as to take it.

It was expected that one was to marry, and Grace should be grateful she had options to provide her child with a father. But she couldn't bring herself to marry for the wrong reasons. Hadn't such thinking gotten her in enough trouble?

In another attempt to be heard, Grace bowed her head and prayed. "Lord, don't leave me, for I have never felt more alone than now. Guide me to the life you want for me, for my child. I will follow."

Who better to put her faith in than the one who knew all the right answers?

She needed someone to talk to. She peered out the window, rubbed her middle, and stared out at the evening. The sun had not fully retired, and yet the moon was trying to outshine it. One could see far in such light. Over the hill where blue moonlight bounced off pearly snow, Cullen's light burned. Not the lamp of his kitchen that was routine for him at this hour but the outdoor shop that filled his days. Did he not intend to go to the recital tonight?

The banging of his labors traveled through ash and oak and cedar. Grace wished she had an anvil and hammer, too. Then maybe she would have something on which to take out all her frustrations. She eyed the food left and moved quickly to secure enough to make a walk over the mountain worth doing.

Cullen deserved a meal, and she needed a *freind*.

• • •

"Betty left a pumpkin pie that we can add as dessert." The last thing Cullen had expected was Grace showing up at his door, and with an armload of food. She looked adorable in oversized boots.

"I can just set it inside. I know you have work to be done." Grace's dark blue shawl matched the color of her eyes. Her cheeks were red, her shoes thick with snow. There was no way she was walking back up the hill in this weather. If not for having the chance to see her again he would have tossed a fit that she walked this far at all.

"*Nee.* Work can wait."

She floated a grin—the kind he wasn't accustomed to. Something was different about her tonight. She looked... happy to be here. He could smell warm chicken, and his mouth watered as he took the plates and a bowl from her arms.

This was not her first time among his things, but it was the first time with him accompanying her. He stumbled past a messy foyer, cluttered with worn gloves, stained work aprons, three sets of boots, and into the kitchen his mother had spent most of her days.

"It isn't much; I just saw your forge fires glowing and knew you had not gone to the bishop's for the *kinner*'s recital. I hope this is okay." Grace was cute when she rambled nervously. He expected a few nerves himself, but none came.

"It's perfect. A man tends to get tired of eating alone. Why didn't you go to the school tonight? I thought Tess would have invited you," he said a little harshly.

"Women get tired of eating alone, too, and yes *Aenti* Tess offered. So did Betty, Elli, and even Hannah offered to

send Andy to drive me," she added, setting a small basket
of biscuits down at his table. "I really don't belong here and
it doesn't feel right joining in all the holiday gatherings.
Besides, *Aenti* Tess says it's best not to ride in the buggy
much now."

"You belong here, Grace," he said intently before
walking toward the refrigerator. She wished that were true.

Her eyes lingered over the pine boughs and cones.
Grace always found pine scents to be the scent of Christmas. She was glad to see he was the kind of man who didn't
mind the Christmas season scattered about. Her gaze softened. She no longer called him an intruder and accepted
the little touches he was slowly adding to her life. He could
only hope he was making her life easier, better, and by the
way she floated over the floor and gingerly pulled two
forks from a drawer to his right, he thought he had. He
wanted her to feel at home, both among his things and with
him.

"Water or sweet tea?" Cullen retrieved two glasses and
filled his with tea.

"Sweet tea would be *wunderbarr.*" He chuckled at the
way Grace stretched out her last word. "Don't laugh. I
haven't had sweet tea in months, and that was at a
McDonalds."

• • •

A buggy pulled up and Grace shot to her feet. She could
just imagine what some would say about her being here.

"You don't have to jump every time someone comes
around." Cullen got to his feet and shuffled toward the

door. "Finish your supper. It's too good to waste."

"I don't want to cause you any problems. I can just slip out the back and no one will know that I am here. Cullen stopped just as someone knocked at the door, and turned to face her. Did he have a better idea? She waited. Surely he didn't want whispers with his name carried in them.

"Please don't," he said before walking away to answer his door. She hadn't expected that. Grace fought between following his wants and doing what was best for him. Voices rattled in the foyer and she had only seconds to decide. Grace leaned on the back of her chair, feeling dizzy. Her heart couldn't take it, but just as she decided to flee, Cullen stepped into the room with Caleb and Mirim. When they both beamed smiles, she thought she just might faint.

"Grace is spoiling me. *Kumm*. Join us," Cullen urged the pair to sit. Mirim had introduced herself months ago at church, but since then Grace hadn't shared a single word with her. She didn't know Caleb well, but he had always been polite.

"We have a few slices of pumpkin pie left. Want a slice?" Cullen asked as he pulled two more plates from the cabinets.

"Never one to turn down pie. I thought you would be at the recital tonight." Caleb said.

"And yet you drove to my *haus* in the middle of nowhere?" Cullen gave him a sharp grin.

"Mirim had to work late and she mentioned she wanted to look in on Grace," Caleb answered and Grace stiffened. Why would someone she hadn't spoken two words to want to look in on her?

Sensing her confusion, Mirim reached out and touched

her sleeve. "I have been so busy with work and planning the wedding, I feel I have been a bad neighbor. I hope you will forgive me."

"Of course," Grace said. What was there to forgive? Mirim didn't know her and had no reason to feel guilty for not having the time to do so.

"I hear you make the best fried pies around, and from the look of this one, it must be truth," Caleb said as he helped Mirim to a seat. Grace'e eyes went from Caleb to Cullen. Did no one mind her being here?

"I heard you sent Freeman Hilty running home crying," Mirim added with a giggle. Her eyes were almost the same shade of green as her dress. Grace always thought green eyes were attractive.

"*Danke,* Grace. I always wanted to be brave enough to do that. If not for Caleb here I don't think I would have ever rid myself of him." She floated Caleb a sweet smile.

"I'm not brave, but I was glad to do it." Mirim and Caleb laughed. Grace turned her attention back to Cullen who was grinning ear to ear as he cut four healthy slices of pie and placed them on little brown saucers. He didn't seem to mind that it was a woman's duty, and she mentally struggled over whether she should take charge or leave things as they were. If she acted too familiar, Caleb and Mirim might get the wrong impression. Maybe they didn't see her sins as much as she thought. Grace took her seat and let out a breath.

"I say we play a game. How about Pictionary, or do you have a favorite, Grace?" Mirim was asking her like she mattered. Like she was one of them. Grace peered across the table while Cullen shoved a healthy portion of pie into his mouth. *He must really like pumpkin*. She mentally stashed the thought away. When he smiled with swelled cheeks, Grace almost burst into laughter. How did she ever get so lucky to be here with such good *freinden*?

"Pictionary is *gut*," Grace answered. Tonight she belonged.

CHAPTER TWENTY-ONE

"This will be my last trip into town, I feel," Grace told the driver Elli had sent to fetch her. The older man had no trouble climbing the hill to the shack and had insisted she would not be walking up it when they returned. Grace was surprised the small truck climbed the steep hill at all. His name was Hank, and he wore a shirt that looked like a checkerboard, and he smelled of musk and apples. The kind of sweet scent that usually came from spray cans and not the fruit. Hank liked to talk, too. He had no children but Grace knew exactly every gift he had bought for his lovely wife, Diane. Since the night of Pictionary and pumpkin pie, Grace was feeling invigorated. Something about the holidays always lifted her spirits. Hank interrupted her thoughts to show her a button.

"Right there. I push that thing and it gives my little truck all the extra horsepower it needs. Now you buy all the groceries you need and don't fret. I will get you right to your front door without this bloomin' weather interfering."

Grace smiled. It was cold and snowing, not blooming, but she understood the kindness meant.

She couldn't imagine how she would get her groceries and goods up the long drive when she could barely wobble without tumbling. Mere days before Christmas and in a little while longer she would be a *mutter*. She wouldn't be going anywhere, so she needed to prepare for what was coming. Excitement mingled with fear washed over her each time she thought about the big day arriving. Maybe she would give birth on New Year's. Wouldn't that just be the perfect way to begin again?

"Now, now, little one," she whispered, rubbing her stretched middle to calm the eagerness squirming inside, then turned back to the driver. "You can let me out here. Elli said she would meet me to help gather everything. I shouldn't be more than a couple of hours."

"Take your time, Miss. I'll be at the diner, just over there," he pointed across the street to a place called Shirley's Diner. Grace had not been in the restaurant, but everyone had told her she should give the place a try. "I'll watch for you."

Stepping out of the truck, careful not to slip in her descent, Grace walked into the I.G.A. and began her shopping. She was a few minutes early for meeting Elli, but if she knew the woman, she would find Grace fairly quickly. Grace tugged at one of the red buggies, loosening it from the line, and slowly began browsing the food aisles. Though the bananas were still green and hard, not the lightly brown spotted sugary look she preferred, Grace selected a bunch of them and set them in the front portion of her buggy. She had barely made thirty dollars this week, so shopping needed to be carefully planned, especially considering Christmas was just a few days away. She still needed thread to finish Betty's gift, and maybe another yard of material for a separate gift.

"Grace Miller."

She bristled at the familiar voice. Of all the people to run into in a grocery store, it would have to be *him*. Putting on her best smile, Grace willed herself to turn around.

"Hello, Elmo. Is Francis with you today?" She hoped so. Peering past the short bulky man, Grace saw no sign of Freeman's mother.

"Just me today. Had to get the salad dressing Francis had forgotten. Is Freeman with you?"

She wanted to say *most certainly not* but caught hold of her tongue. This man had made known his ability to snatch the roof over her head away in an instant. *Just be polite, your* boppli *is coming soon,* she reminded herself.

"I have not seen him for some time now. I am waiting on Elli, actually."

His frown deepened—the same look he wore the last time a word was passed between them. Crossing his arms, cradling a jar of salad dressing in a wide palm that looked too large for a man of his short stature, he clearly had something on his mind, and Grace wondered if she should wait for what it was to slip out or just push the red cart forward and leave him standing there.

She had decided on the latter when he finally spoke. "My Freeman feels you two make a match."

Of course he does, she wanted to blurt out. Grace had seen plenty of young women in the area during church meetings, so why would the Hiltys seem to go out of their way to target her? And pregnant as she was? It was all a bit disturbing.

"Freeman has been kind and has made his intentions known to me."

"And?" She could see where Freeman got his impatient tendencies. Grace had been taught to respect her elders, but this man was stepping over a line. Courting was private. But then again, they weren't even courting.

"These things are private, but if you must insist, I have no romantic interest in your son, Mr. Hilty, and told him just that. I have no plans to make such decisions while I am here." *Lesson learned.* Looking back, she searched for Elli. Taking in a slow breath, Grace started to maneuver the buggy forward.

"I think it best you consider making some *gut* decisions. A woman in your condition needs a husband," he said after her.

What was that supposed to mean?

Elmo lifted his bearded chin with authority. "Francis seems to like ya well enough and Freeman is of the age he can no longer run around idle. It is time he takes a *fraa* and makes a family of his own."

She had seen matchmakers work, usually with shy young people who could not find the words to take the next step, but this was something totally different. She felt like one of those heifers in a lot while menfolk talked over them and decided which best suited their need. She was livestock to this man, a selected heifer for his son. Her blood ran cold, sending a chill over every inch of her flesh.

The baby shifted, worst timing for sure, and she placed a slow, firm hand to one side of her belly and gripped the red shopping cart tightly with the other, all the while giving Elmo a grimace.

"Then that is what he should do," she said a bit too firmly. "Mr. Hilty, I am not certain what you are implying, but I am of no mind to court your son. I feel nothing for him but friendship." And even that was fading faster than the daylight hours these days. She would have pushed past him right then if not for the sting in her side, forcing her to continue facing the monster.

"I have a buyer for the cabin." A threat not even disguised in subtlety. "Nice gentleman, too." Elmo straightened. "Willing to pay enough to buy a worthy home for you and my son." Temptation was a sin, and one she would never fall to again. He was trying to tempt her.

"I hope you do not delay in making a choice. We both know Tessie will not allow you into her home. Few would take you in after what you have done. You should accept Freeman's offer; you will not get another." He chuckled and watched to see if she would squirm. *Like father like son*, Grace thought. She almost blurted out that her *daed* planned on marrying her off to Leon Strolzfus, but that wasn't going to happen, either. Nothing felt more pressuring than to be placed between two wrongs squeezing for dominance.

"There you are, Grace. Elli is over there." Abram Schwartz appeared out of thin air. Just as gallant and heroic as Elli whispered the man to be. Grace could imagine he had in fact swept her off her feet years ago as Elli said he did. His dark beard, sprinkled lightly with time, matched his dark eyes, now narrowed and looking down at Elmo. Abram had a good foot on Freeman's father.

Regardless of the pinch in her side, she pushed the buggy and hurried to the dairy section Elli was standing in front of, putting as much distance between her and Elmo as possible.

"How long have you and Abram been here?" she asked when she reached Elli.

"Long enough that Abram insisted he fetch you instead of me." Elli seemed upset. Maybe Elmo's threat was loud enough it had not been for her ears alone. "Come, let's get your shopping done, dear." Elli tugged on the buggy, urging Grace to the next aisle.

"What about Abram? I don't think..." She glanced back to see Abram, arms crossed, lips set, listening to Elmo rattle off about something, most certainly not confessing what he had said to Grace, and she realized she had little to worry for the man's sake. Like Cullen, the bishop, and most of the men Grace had encountered in her two months in Walnut Ridge, he could handle his own well enough.

"My Abram is exactly where he needs to be right now. I think you might want to start telling me what is really going on, though, Grace. One minute everyone thinks you've got eyes for Cullen—who is a great man, I might add—the next, I hear you have been courting Freeman and speaking of marriage. I know that this is private, so indulge an old woman who never had the luxury of courting."

Elli's face wore a hint of authority despite trying to be coy. She was no-nonsense and had a head for all complex matters. Grace could use all the help she could get before she was out in the cold.

"I will tell you everything, but first, tell me why you and Abram never courted." Grace couldn't help but tease. She felt comfortable around Elli, bringing out a part of her few got to know. Elli calmed at the comment, just as Grace hoped.

"We aren't young, my dear. Nobody has time for that when you've got so much living to do," she said, and Grace smiled. "Now, tell me why Elmo is threatening you."

CHAPTER TWENTY-TWO

Grace stood soldierly at the window. She had waited all day for Cullen to leave. It was Monday, and like all Mondays, he left to go to town. The buggy drove down the snow-covered country lane, Cullen high in the seat, signaling his departure. Grace placed the pot into a bag, a simple venison roast that she could in no way eat all by herself and fresh rolls into another so as not to smash them. She gathered her heavy coat and shawl. Looking out into the cold of December, she wished she had bought herself a warm pair of gloves when she had shopped for her sisters weeks ago, but she would make today's little venture out a quick one. She had so much to do yet, and her recent spurt of energy should not be wasted.

Pulling on her black shoes instead of her muck boots, for safety's sake, she peeked through the window once more to see Cullen was clear out of view. One set of buggy wheels had revealed he was.

Balancing a bag in each arm, she did well to make good time down the hill and onto Cullen's front porch. The crisp air tingling her cheeks felt better than the overly warm shack, and she welcomed it. Setting the bags of food down, she reached for the handle and paused. Things had changed; she had invaded his chosen solidarity, and Cullen had sneaked in and invaded her heart. Did she deserve to even fantasize about a better life, one with a man who deserved a better *fraa* than one who carried a child not of his own?

The scent of smoke drifted by, breaking her doubts and hopes further apart. Grace turned to the blacksmith shop; the long trail commonly seen from her mountain poured out of the top of the tin roof and aimed for the east as it generally did. So why was the scent so strong?

Turning back to the door, it became obvious to Grace that the smoke was coming from the inside of the house. She pushed through the door just as a flame rose out of a corner of the cookstove and swallowed up the top. The smell of burned grease told her that Cullen had probably not wiped away his morning cooking as he should have.

Daed had been persistent since she and her sisters were small to always clean the stove. It was a good thing she came when she did, she thought.

Coughing against the rising dark plume, Grace splattered the whole rounded plastic container, what appeared to be sugar, over the flames and smothered them out before they reached anything further. Pulling her apron front upward with one hand to cover her mouth, she waved a towel from the sink into the air with the other, urging the gray haze out the front door.

"Grace! Are you all right?" Cullen was at her side and guiding her out the door before she even knew he had returned home.

She coughed. "I smelled smoke." She coughed again and gagged against the thickness in her throat. Cullen rushed back inside to see if the flames were out. When he returned he was wearing that big goofy grin she had grown to appreciate and expect.

"I guess my cooking skills are not equal to yours." His

eyes moved to the bags still resting on the porch floor. She lowered her head and took a deep breath.

"I think it is your cleaning skills that are in question. I told you bacon is to be taken seriously," she tried on a laugh but ended up coughing instead. "I thought you would be in town, like all Mondays."

Coming to her side, he lowered his head to her. Taking the rag in his hand, Cullen wiped at her face. She must once again look a fright.

"Your *kapp* is dirty." He laughed until his hands could no longer remove the smudges.

"It is not that funny." She defended with a stubborn brow.

"Yes it is. Since the day I met you, Grace Miller, you have been a true mess."

He was right about that. She laughed, too. "I guess that's fair to say."

"You may *kumm* and go here as you please. No one will ever tell you otherwise. I want you to be comfortable here." He muttered the words and she willed her emotions under control.

Whatever had brought him home so quickly today, she didn't care. Cullen was here, once again, when she needed him. Or was it she that was here when she was needed?

He stood and offered her a hand. "Ready to teach me how to clean a stove properly?" Looking up she couldn't help the way his eyes sparkling at her caused her heart to pick up its pace. She took the rough callused hand more accustomed to holding a hammer than a another hand, and smiled.

"Well someone should," she replied and followed him

back inside.

By the time Cullen and Grace got the kitchen back to normal and all the smoke cleared from the house, evening was already upon them. "I will go ready the buggy and take ya home," Cullen offered.

Grace nodded and gathered all the washrags to add to his growing pile of laundry in the next room. Maybe she could come back and tend to that for him. The thought flustered her. She could see herself preparing his meals, mending his clothes, listening to the deep timbre of his voice late into the evening, reading.

With her thumb she rubbed the palm of her opposite hand, the one he touched earlier. Did he feel the little jolts, the warm sensations, the tremors she did every time they touched? And why was the thought of kissing him, of wanting him to kiss her, so strong? Surely her head was not clear after all that smoke. She was smart enough to know he cared for her, but as a *freind*. Or could it be more? Would he one day try to kiss her? She stared into her palm, letting the daydream steal her away, when the very subject of her daydreaming stepped back inside and gave his boots a fair stomp.

"You ready?"

"Ready?" Grace said, dumbfounded.

"To let me take you home?" He stared at her for a moment, then grinned as he went to fetch her coat and shawl from a hook nearby.

"*Jah*, I'm ready," she stuttered. Cullen tenderly helped her slip into the heavy coat before wrapping her shawl around her snuggly. A gesture that highlighted his protective nature as much as his affection. *Please* Gott *don't let me be reading this all wrong. He is a* gut *man.*

Lifting a heavy blanket from a corner shelf, he opened the door and they walked to the buggy outside.

"You should have shared the stew with me, especially after cleaning up my mess." Cullen said as he helped her into the buggy.

"I have plenty. It was a rather large stew for just one."

"For two," he corrected. He tossed her the blanket before disappearing around the back side of the buggy. Once settled in the seat beside her, he took up the reins. "Before I agree to take you home, Grace Miller, answer me this," he bumped her shoulder playfully. "Just where did you get the venison?"

"Matthew and Sadie came by with it yesterday. One of their younger sons is quite the skilled bow hunter, I hear," she said playfully. "Venison isn't my favorite, but I would never tell Sadie that." Cullen drew in one side of his face, playfully.

"Sadie has been trying her hand at matchmaking of late. Should I be jealous?"

"Maybe," she responded. "I hear Timothy can run faster than any of the other *buwe* his age," she teased.

Cullen chuckled. Grace wished her every day was filled with moments just like this. Cullen had a way of bringing out the happy inside her. She hoped in some small way, she did the same for him. He deserved to be happy after so many years apart from it.

"Life is certainly eventful around you, Grace. *Daed* would have enjoyed joshing with ya." Grace liked the way one corner of his mouth went a little higher than the other.

She knew about his parents' death in the buggy

accident. How a truck from the local feed store collided with their buggy, ending their lives. Cullen lost both his parents, and he rarely mentioned them without an emptiness clouding over him. It was an otherwise pleasant moment, and she wondered if she dared tread further, ask him about the kind of people they were, the kind of woman Marty was.

Everything he loved most in this world was taken, yet he was still strong in his faith. Woven in it so tightly, it was iron clad. She envied his ability. She had ignored her faith for far lesser things, and that alone told her she could never be worthy of a man like Cullen Graber. Settling into the seat, she felt her feet bump into the bricks on the floorboard. Cullen had placed four heated bricks there, probably from the forge, to keep her feet warm and dry on the little trip up the hill. Such an effort for such a short drive. Where had this man been when she was on the cusp of her own womanhood?

"What was your *mutter* like?"

The sun had lain to rest behind Sugar Mountain, just as it did most nights, and the ride across the evening snow was nothing short of enchanting. Grace listened to Cullen describe two people she would have enjoyed meeting, a *daed* with a strong faith and a sense of humor, and a *mutter* with a kind heart and a talent for baking. There were no words that could describe a night like tonight, nor how her heart raced riding in the buggy seat next to Cullen. This was how her life could have been if she'd had the patience to wait for it.

Peering over, she caught his gaze resting on the same quiet peace around them. *What holds his thoughts?* she wondered. *Is he thinking about his parents? Marty? Did they court on nights like this one?* The women all believed he could never settle down, not after the woman he loved was called home. She admired that part of him, oddly. And no matter how she was losing her own heart to him, for all the little things and precious moments he gifted her, at least he was the kind of man worth losing one's heart for.

Cullen Graber was worthy, like no other man she had ever known.

Beside him on the short buggy ride to her home, warmth radiated from him, and she wanted to slide closer and sink into it. "Tell me about Marty." If she surprised him with her forwardness, he didn't show it. His face held fast, and when they reached the top of the hill, he allowed the horse to decide the pace.

"What do you already know?" The timbre of his voice hinted no irritation.

"That you met when you were *kinner*. She had no *mutter*, and her *daed* was very unkind."

He studied the stars, glanced over the fields below. Moonlight had made everything so still and alluring. Other than the crunches of the horse's feet in the snow, it felt like they were the only two people in all the world. And if they were, even for just one small moment, she hoped he would share with her the things he held inside himself.

"She had a hard life, that is true. I fell for her the minute I saw her," he said plainly. Not hiding the truth of it.

"She was seeking, and"—he looked at her, but Grace knew what seeking was, now at least, after Elli explained the process of an *Englischer* deciding to become Amish, and nodded for him to continue—"she had her eighteenth birthday and was leaving her *daed*'s *haus* to live at the bishop's—"

"He was going to let her stay," Grace interrupted.

Cullen nodded, his shoulders appearing heavy with the weight of memories revisited. This community was so close and helpful to one another, Grace wished her own family would have been raised here all along.

"You for one should know how generous our community is." She did know. "After she planned to take her baptism and the allowed time had passed, we were to wed." He paused, glancing away, and she took his hand. It was warm and stiff and rough to the touch, but there was still gentleness in it.

The horse stopped far from the little cabin, but the view here was nothing short of spectacular. Grace took her own study of the valley below. Like a postcard, Christmas lights from *Englisch* houses lit up the valley. Huge farms and fields were blanketed in white—crisp and frozen in time— and she hoped she would have this moment they were sharing to carry with her for all her life.

"You do not have to say more. Elli told me about the accident. I am sorry you lost her. It must be hard for you after loving someone like that," she said.

His eyes locked on to hers, and something strange came from them she had not seen before.

"I'm sorry you lost someone, too. Marty is in *Gott's* hands, safe. Jared was a coward to do what he did to you." His words were suddenly harsh. Did she really like the angry side of him this much? His defensive nature and need to protect were foreign attributes she was coming to admire.

She stared out over the woods and one valley bleeding into another. It didn't matter what powers Jared had used to lure her into his comforts; she had accepted them, and it was time to forgive herself for being such a fool, or a fool forever she would be.

"Have you agreed to talk with him?" he asked.

Now who was being the bold one? His body shifted, eyes boring deep into her own. Every inch of Grace warmed at his stare. So much so, she thought she might explode. Looking into his brown eyes, Grace found there was nothing he could ask of her that she would not give. "I wrote him back. *Aenti* Tessie mailed it for me. I want him to forget we exist," she cradled her middle. "Like he did before."

She couldn't help but smile when the weight in his shoulders seemed to lift.

Cullen stared at her. Grace's face was puffy like a woman ready to have a baby, but even now he thought her the beautiful creature *Gott* created. The urge to kiss her was strong, a force like he'd never encountered. Maybe it was the way she glowed, all beaming and spectacular in the moonlight. Maybe it was the fact that she would rather raise a child alone than with a man of no faith, no values. Either way the urge to kiss her grew.

Heat surged up his neck.

"Did you ever think to leave," she quickly asked. She felt it. too. "I mean if she didn't plan on seeking, would you have left the Amish?"

"*Nee.* Were you planning to?"

"*Nee.* He broke his promise, but I haven't considered leaving. Some might think so, because of…well. But *nee.* I could never leave."

His strong hands were on her shoulders, then one cupped her face. Cullen leaned in, his lips carefully connecting with the cold flesh between two thin brows. Such tenderness from a man who held so much strength. Such affection without crossing lines. That kiss on her forehead meant more than a dozen on the lips.

Her pulse throbbed in her neck, and she was certain he could feel it. His kiss was soft, careful, but needed. Maybe for the both of them. "Cullen." Her voice was a mere whisper.

"I know," he said, still staring down at her with such intensity she thought her heart might burst.

His thumb traced the lines of her jaw, the tiny lobe of her left ear. The feeling was nothing short of bliss, and she leaned into his touch. Her breaths quickened, though his remained calm, so unnervingly calm, as he explored the curves of her face. She shivered, yet the night air did nothing to cause it. When his eyes landed on hers once more, his lips gathered and raised into that familiar grin that had so many times before only teased her.

"I wasn't prepared for this. For you. Now I can't think of anything else." His confession was like a balm to her soul. His warm breath steamed between them.

"I don't deserve a man like you. You deserve someone better. A woman who…" One hand gripping firm onto Cullen's arm, the other resting on her middle, she took a long breath.

The baby kicked, and her eyes widened from it, but she remained quiet. When his eyes locked on to hers, something new seemed to have awakened in him. She closed her coat more snuggly as the *boppli* stirred within her.

"You deserve a second chance." He cleared his throat. "Grace Miller, will you join me for Christmas and Second Christmas, and perhaps New Year's?"

She spewed a laugh through tears of joy.

"I would love to, Cullen Graber."

"*Gut*." He let go and gathered the reins once more. "Then it is a date."

CHAPTER TWENTY-THREE

Despite the sloppy mess of melted snow and softened earth, the day warmed well above freezing and everyone in the community gathered to fill the bishop's house in celebration as Caleb and Mirim became one. Cullen hung his long coat along with the other men on one of the walls Bishop Mast used for such occasions and scanned the happy faces of the people he had known all his life. Christmas always brought out more smiles than any other time of year. Even in the Plain world, glimmers of the season sparkled in young eyes. But today a wedding was the center of all the excitement.

Tess Miller brushed past, taking her place in the back of the women's seating area, without so much as a gruff hello. Still, Tessie Miller's face, etched with the lines of her years, rarely smiled, but today even she carried one with her. There was something about watching two people come together as one that lifted spirits.

Next, he met Elisha's gaze, and the two shared a small smile. He was not nearly the carpenter Elisha was, but under Elisha's watchful eye, the cradle for Grace had turned out moderately decent. Cullen had considered at length what his gift would mean to Grace. He wanted her to have it, she *needed* to have it, but he could not decide if he had the right to give it.

Grace declined coming and he didn't press, despite how he wished she was at his side. He hadn't talked about

Marty with anyone before, his parents either for that matter, yet, under moonlight and frigid temps, Cullen talked about both. Seeing tears when he spoke of his *mutter* only made him care for her more.

Timing was everything, but when she smiled at him, he fought the urge to claim her lips right then. He was becoming a weak man. Planting a kiss on her forehead hadn't been the *most* romantic gesture, but she had seemed pretty pleased.

Spotting Caleb, Cullen joined the men in the front of the room. "This is the day, my *freind*," Cullen greeted.

"That it is." Caleb and Mirim had courted only two years before they found themselves here in front of *Gott* and community. Cullen reached for Elisha's hand next, congratulating him as well. Elisha Schwartz and Emma Bontrager had courted six years, if no one counted that, they had been the best of friends since childhood. Double weddings weren't so rare in Pleasants, and Cullen mentally counted how many he had been a part of in his years.

"If you weren't so stubborn you would be finding yourself enjoying such a day," Elisha teased, poking Cullen in the rib.

"I am not stubborn, my friend. I am content in accepting *Gott*'s timing." But was he? He had thought he was. He had been for ten years in that regard. Then everything changed. In just ten short weeks, everything changed.

The bishop and deacon came together at the front of the room, and Cullen settled into a front-row seat, trying hard to put out of his mind what a day such as today would be like for him.

. . .

"Cullen, would you be a dear and do something for me?" Betty stepped beside him as Cullen dropped his empty paper plate into the trash.

"*Jah.* What do you need?"

"If I were to make up a plate, would you see that Grace gets it?" He nodded; he would relish any chance to see her. "She is such a little thing. Not half the size of what she should be."

"I am certain she will be glad for it. She eats more than you know, but I think she is tired of wild game and eggs."

"Then I am sure you can find something else that's pleasing." Betty grinned, challenging.

Cullen eyed the bishop and, along with him, Freeman Hilty and his father at a table behind where Betty stood. Both of the Hilty men were like hawks, eyeing him now like they had during the ceremony and the whole wedding meal. Betty turned to follow his gaze, only to turn back to him and let out a laugh.

"I think those two like to bend ears more than lend hands," she said.

He chuckled and knew she was not wrong in that observation. "Make sure to add a huge slice of cake, will ya?" He winked.

"I knew we women could count on you." Betty nodded and took up a plate as Cullen aimed for the main door. "I want to speak to the newly wedded and will be back to fetch that plate."

Outside, the sun felt like a warm blanket on a cold

morning. Spotting the group of men clustered together by the barn, he went to join them. Cullen slowed when he heard Freeman's voice in the center of the lot and would have returned back inside if not for Caleb catching his approach and waving him over. Freeman must have sprinted to get here so quickly. Like a gossip on a mission, Freeman stood front-and-center to hold all their attentions.

"First thing *kumm* spring, I will have my own *fraa* keeping me warm." His laugh was slimy, and Cullen stopped short of walking through him. "Full of vinegar, that one. But have you seen those eyes? Prettiest thing in the whole county, and she is mine."

The collar around Cullen's neck tightened. He took a calming breath.

"Cullen." Freeman's eyes narrowed, and Cullen looked down on the little man with a distaste everyone could feel. "I was just telling the boys here about my Grace."

"Your Grace?" Crossing his arms, he hoped to intimidate the boastful Freeman Hilty, but the man didn't budge. Intimidation was a game only the Hiltys played. Real men never had time for such foolishness.

"*Jah*. My Grace." Freeman reminded one of a puffed-up rooster, boasting and swelling until he grew into something besides a scrawny bird. "We are courting. Taking her as my *fraa* is only the next step."

Freeman's lips gathered into a grin at winning a game Cullen was not playing. The thoughts of this man taking Grace anywhere sent a flush of anger throughout his body and his fist clenched tightly.

"Putting the cart before the horse again, I see. She has already said she isn't interested. It would be best you look elsewhere and leave Grace be."

"Cullen, how has work been?" Caleb stepped between the two and Cullen wished he hadn't. Someone needed to put this puffed-up rooster into a stew pot and close the lid tightly.

"*Gut*," he answered, but his focus never shifted from Freeman.

"The sooner you get your head wrapped around it, the better. Grace cannot say no to me." Freeman blurted out.

"She has said no, more than once." Need Cullen remind him again?

"Wait, Grace said no to courting you?" Caleb stepped forward. "Freeman, you should leave Grace be, like Cullen says." It appeared no man, other than Freeman, would stand there listening to such nonsense. "Tess will not be having you trying to bully her niece into courting."

Freeman huffed loudly before turning on his heel and stalking away. Cullen wanted to reach out and pull the little man back into the group. A squeeze of his arm steadied his wrath.

"Do not let anger fill you, my friend. Freeman will be Freeman. Grace isn't the first *maedel* he tried that on, but Tessie Miller will tend to him once she gets word and put him in his place all and good." Elisha chuckled and Cullen had to agree with the logic. Tessie Miller would indeed see Freeman's behavior tended to if she had to drag him by one ear to the bishop's door herself. Freeman wore off on one quicker than new paint on a hitching post.

Then Freeman's words hit him again. *She cannot say no to me.* Cullen put the pieces together. The Hiltys were using Grace's circumstances, her living arrangement, to acquire Freeman a *fraa*.

"Elmo owns the land and cabin." Wasn't it a farfetched thought to think an Amish man to be capable of turning generosity into leverage? And if Elmo crossed such a moral line, he would pack her up himself and deliver her to her *aenti*, regardless.

"Well if I know you, and I do—" Elisha grinned. "You will have seen to it that Grace is taken care of. Don't think we all don't know how often you climb that hillside."

"She is lucky to have you." Caleb added. Cullen thought he was the lucky one but kept that to himself.

"I heard she was going back to Indiana, you know, after the *boppli kumms*."

"She might do that yet." But he was determined to change her mind; he had only a week to do it.

"Does it bother you that she is carrying another man's child?"

"I am one who would never judge another by their past. Made a few mistakes myself." He rubbed his chin. "A child needs a *daed*." If they asked him the question months ago, Cullen might have given a different answer.

"And a man gains strength from *kinner*. Best be changing her mind," Elisha added. Cullen nodded and turned to leave.

"Where are ya heading?" Caleb asked in a worried tone.

"I have got a neighbor to see to."

"Before you do, *kumm* to the barn, I got something for ya. Emma made me save the best for last." Elisha motioned him to follow.

CHAPTER TWENTY-FOUR

Cullen steadied the full plates Betty prepared in his hand and knocked on the cabin door. He wished Grace had been able to attend Caleb and Mirim's wedding, but he understood her need to stay close to home.

Inside his coat, the kitten had surrendered to being held captive and snuggled into his side for warmth. Elisha was right, the kitten would make a fine addition to the cabin, and he hoped Grace loved her. Maybe she would be less lonely, miss her family less, if she had something to help distract her for the next few days while she awaited her child's arrival.

When Grace opened the door, he found she looked nothing like the last time he saw her. She looked *happy*. After seeing her so distraught so often, he found this was just the way he hoped she would be—no longer broken. His heart skipped a beat as he returned her smile.

The house smelled of pine and bleach and warm chicken soup. A large book lay open on the table. She was finally comfortable and was making the cabin something that did not remind her of her failings. She had made it a home.

"What do ya think? It isn't much, but makes it feel more like Christmas." She motioned toward more pine limbs lining the window sills and on top of the cabinet that held a few dishes, adding to the one he had gifted her. In the center of the table was a red-leafed plant. "It is a poinsettia.

My *mammi* always had one when we were small. Elli got it for me."

Grace glowed so brightly, he quickly forgot his reason for coming in the first place. Stirred by her voice or the smell of warm chicken, he wasn't sure, the kitten moved and dug into shirt and flesh.

"You look to be feeling much better. Betty wanted to see you were included in the day and sent these over for ya." Taking a step forward, Cullen quickly handed her the plates before the next swipe of claws forced him to do so. Who would have thought something so small could be so lethal?

"I wish I could have *kumm*. I love weddings."

Watching her lift the tinfoil from one plate, he all but laughed as her eyes widened at the variety of sweets. "I have been craving sugar so much! I cannot believe how *gut* it all looks."

"I know, and Betty insisted on plenty." Fingering the brim of his hat, he squirmed slightly and when she took the food and turned, he adjusted the beast inside his coat. A good flick on the head is what the critter needed.

"That woman is a blessing. She knows how to spoil me. Did I tell you she made me two dresses after I came here?" Glancing down, Grace jolted. "Spider!" she yelled and with no effort or assistance, perched herself on the more sturdy chair of the two she had.

Cullen looked down at the tiny creature that had caused such a fuss and placed a boot there while trying to contain his laughter. Coming to her side to steady the expectant woman, he noticed that she, too, had found the humor in her reaction and began to wobble with laughter. With little effort, he lifted her down from the chair and back to the solid floor. His arms slid from under her arms but he didn't let go.

"Ya can single-handedly protect yourself against stray dogs with only a broom handle and yet need someone to kill spiders for ya? Grace Miller, you are a joy, my dear."

The kitten meowed just then, and Grace's head shot up in surprise. Cullen's heart picked up the pace of a racehorse at the look of her. Like a child on Christmas, innocent and full of joy. He reached inside his coat and pulled out the little yellow beast and presented it to her.

"Oh, Cullen, she's beautiful." Grace carefully took the kitten and brought her to her chest. After all that clawing and biting, *now* the little fur ball decided to purr. He rolled his eyes.

"I thought she could keep you company, and maybe kill any threats of spiders."

"She's mine?" Those larger-than-life blue eyes had the power to cut a man in two as quickly as they could make him reevaluate his whole life.

"*Jah*, she is yours, but I do think I should have the right to help name her."

"What did you have in mind?" The kitten nuzzled her cheek and Cullen felt a pang of jealousy.

"How about Stella?"

"Stella?" She made a face. Cullen made a nervous laugh. Was she trying to be adorable?

"My *mutter* had a kitten like that, and it was her name."

"Then Stella it is. What was your *mutter*'s name? I forgot to ask."

"Her name was Abigale."

"Oh," she cupped her belly and smiled as wide as the ocean.

"Are you okay?" How could he not worry for her and the safety of her child? She looked up at him in wonder and awe, in amazement of the miracle she had inside her. It shook his insides straight to his heart.

In socked feet, Grace moved closer to him and reached for Cullen's hand. In the warmth of her tiny fingers he found everything he had waited for but didn't even know he needed. He loved her—and he wanted to spend the rest of his life loving her.

When she placed his hand on her belly, he knew he had earned her trust, and that pleased him to the core. A trust he would not ever take for granted.

Movement grazed the palm of his hand, and he couldn't believe she shared such a precious and private thing with him. Forgetting himself, he placed his other hand there as well, and she laughed at his eagerness. Suddenly the movements sprang into jolts. "I can feel him," he marveled.

The life inside her jerked once more and Grace laughed until her whole middle shook. "I think *she* has the hiccups."

Cullen didn't care if it was a he or a she; it was Grace's child at his fingertips.

Joy passed between them, and his eyes moved from the smile on her plump lips to her wide, stormy blue eyes. Their breaths labored in rhythm from laughing, and when he got himself back to rights again, he found he could no longer control himself. He had spent so long holding on to the love he and Marty shared that he had been blaming loneliness for why Grace tugged at his thoughts so often. Looking at her now, he hoped his heart was capable of loving another, the way Grace deserved to be loved.

Grace Miller might not have been the first woman to steal his heart, but he knew as sure as he knew the sun would rise come morning, Grace would be the last.

Tracing the curve of her jaw with his thumb, she looked at him in a way she had never done before. Leaning in to her, he whispered, "Do not leave Walnut Ridge. Stay."

It was a bold, foolish statement, but the words were already spoken before he could consider them fully.

Grace remained at his fingertips, searching his eyes for something he only hoped she wanted. "Cullen." What she needed to say hung there between them, silent.

"I know about what the Hiltys are hanging over ya. I know you cannot stay with your *aenti* if Elmo sells this place." He knew so much more, but when her head lowered, so did the glow that surrounded her the moment he'd walked into the room.

"My family wants me to return. I do miss my sisters, but *Daed* insists I marry some widower with three *kinner*." Every hope and beat in his chest awaited her next words.

"You do not know what awaits me there," she said.

He didn't, and when she started telling him, he wished he'd never asked. Not only was her life under her father's roof strict, even by Old Order standards, she would be frowned upon forever unless she wed a man from her district.

"Leon Strolzfus has three *kinner*. The man is a stranger to me, and old. He is, like, thirty-five or something." She began crying, and he wrapped both arms around her. "I have ruined my own life so badly, *Gott* won't even show me a bit of mercy."

Stroking her arm, Cullen searched for the words she needed now.

"His mercy is for the weak and the brokenhearted. His grace is offered freely." She looked up at him, softening in his words.

"*Danke.*" She remained in the cradle of his hold.

"My sister Charity offered to let me and my *boppli* stay with her. It might be best…" Holding her safely in his arms, Cullen breathed in a hint of pine, broth, and fear. Where had the lavender gone, the scent that was her own?

"Do you want to leave Walnut Ridge? Do you want to return to the life you had there?" Had no one ever asked her what *she* wanted?

"*Nee.* I cannot marry to make *Daed* happy, nor can I be without a home for my *boppli.*"

"It does not need to be decided tonight." Cullen grinned and gave the kitten a friendly nudge with his boot.

"Christmas is almost here," he added. "What better time for new beginnings?"

"I like that." She smiled down at the kitten.

"Do you care for me, Grace?" he asked. She sucked in a breath before looking up at him again. He would marry her tonight if that meant she wouldn't leave. He would marry her tomorrow, if she would only say yes. Nothing would please him more than to offer her and her child refuge, love.

"I do care for you, Cullen Graber." She admitted. "You have been a *gut freind.*" She bit her bottom lip causing his pulse to race.

"Just a *freind*?" He stroked a finger over the kitten in her arms then lifted her chin to face him. "It is not a hard question. Do not be afraid to answer it."

"*Nee*, not just as a *freind*, but it means a great deal to me." He smiled, kissed her forehead, and stepped away.

Cullen retrieved his hat and made his way to the door, not masking the wide grin smeared over his face. "Well then, don't go running off and marry Freeman or any old widowers before I return." He winked and stepped out into the cold evening.

He really needed to cool down before he exploded. Hopefully the bishop was still wide awake, but if Cullen had learned one thing, it was never to put off what can be done right now.

• • •

Cullen disappeared behind the closed door, and the feeling of the cold floor on her feet mingled with the warmth of his fingertips, still fresh on her skin, meeting somewhere in the middle. It was a promise that, for the first time in her life, Grace believed might be fulfilled. When he looked into her eyes, she feared her heart beat loud enough that if he had half an ear, he would have heard it.

And maybe he did hear it, because she knew he not only cared for her but those eyes held a love that even a foolish woman like her would know without question. He was invested in her life and that of her child. Cullen was nothing like Jared. He was unpolished, rough around the edges, but it was Cullen's low timbre that stuck in her head from the moment she woke and carried through her dreams, guiding her, reminding her that she was enough and would always be enough. Did *Gott* truly offer second chances? And if he did, did she even deserve one?

She touched the soft spot on her face where just moments before, his hand had lain. The smell of heat and iron, of woodsmoke and leather, all combined into a scent that was all Cullen, and she craved it so much that she knew her life would remain empty until it was filled with those aromas every day.

In a moment of joy and insight into what she now trusted as her true self—the grown, wiser woman she was compared to a year ago—reality hit her. Her family would expect her to return to Havenlee. Could she disappoint them again? Shoulders slumped, heaviness weighed on her, and she felt like her knees could no longer handle the burden.

Thoughts of leaving Walnut Ridge made a tear in her heart no needle and thread could mend. She didn't want to leave the tenderness and love the women here had given her, the friendships she had made, or the man who awakened her to possibility.

Elli and all her interventions and smart advice.

Betty and her mothering hand, always seeing that Grace's needs were cared for in the absence of her own mother.

Hannah, who made her laugh, and like a sister shared her mothering experiences with Grace so the new title Grace would soon claim would be easier to carry.

Even *Aenti* Tess. Underneath that bitter facade and veneer was a mysterious past Grace was certain made her that way, yet Tess was still present and would come to her if the need arose. She might bark all the way, but Grace could rely on her for honesty.

If she dared leave those women, Cullen, this community that had welcomed her with open arms, she would crumble into that last crumb of pie on one's plate. Where was *Gott*'s mercy now? If God's will had brought her here, as Cullen and Elli insisted, then why open her heart to a new life only to make her choose between what her heart desired, a future she craved more than anything, and her own family? Hadn't she already resigned herself to a life with no selfish wants in it?

She stomped her foot on the floor, and the sting reminded her that she was still present, alive — and that she, and she alone, needed to make some hard decisions.

CHAPTER TWENTY-FIVE

"Twenty-three thousand! It is only a few acres of nothing but forest and one forgotten field. There isn't even good timber on it any longer." Cullen couldn't see why Elmo Hilty was asking such a price for the cabin and hillside, but he was. Bishop Mast patted his shoulder, but Cullen found he could only take a seat to steady the numbers bouncing around in his head, the price required to outbid the *Englischer* wanting the land for hunting.

"The bank said if you could settle for a higher number, they would help intercede the sale. Elmo should have known better than to use an *Englisch* realtor." Bishop Mast shook his head. "We all want to help you do this, Cullen. Within the realms of what is proper, that is." The bishop's half-hearted smile was encouraging. His mother had always said little got past the bishop and nothing got past *Gott*. She was right. Bishop Mast had always shown up the moment he heard Cullen needed him, and Cullen never once had to mention why he needed him right now.

"If Elmo knows it is me buying it, he will settle for the lesser amount from the *Englischer*." Of that Cullen was certain. Freeman would pout and stomp if Elmo even considered Cullen a buyer. Cullen had no chance even if he was willing to use his extra savings account for the land.

"*Jah*, he would. I still cannot see why he would sell it after everything." Bishop Mast scratched his beard and paced the hardened concrete floor of his barn.

"After everything?" Cullen questioned. The bishop's eyes widened like a swollen river at the shock of his own words.

"It is not for me to say; gossip is a sin, Cullen," he said.

Cullen still wasn't sure what the bishop was implying. "If you know something that will help Grace stay here in Kentucky, I should hope you would share that with me now." Cullen had never been so forward with the leader of the community before, but Bishop Mast was a sensible man, and if there was a way to keep Grace here, he needed to know it.

"I, for one, will not interfere with her staying or going. That is for Grace to decide. But talk with Tessie Miller. She will give you what you need." At that, the bishop clamped his lips tight.

"I will do that," Cullen replied. "I should go make my offer, before the bank closes for the holiday." Cullen stood and offered the bishop a hand.

"I will go with you," he said, and Cullen nodded appreciatively. Yes, Bishop Mast was a man who took his role in the community seriously. That, or he was trying to escape a houseful of chatting women baking Christmas cookies.

The bishop climbed into the buggy with a wide smile. "You're escaping, aren't you," Cullen teased.

"Going with you is better than hiding in the barn. It is winter ya know," Bishop Mast said, jabbing a pointy elbow into Cullen's side.

Cullen slapped the reins and aimed for Pleasants Community Bank. He had his savings, and hadn't meant to touch it until he was ready to expand the house for a family. He also had his parent's savings to lean on if the need ever came. He had almost forgotten about that, but he had always promised himself he would never touch it. Not unless there was a real need within his community for it. Buying a run-down cabin and land that served no use was not a real need; it was a want.

A want that might keep Grace at his side until she was ready to become his wife.

A horn honked, breaking his concentration, and Cullen veered off the side of the road to let the blue van pass. To his right, he saw the old forgotten house, yellow curtains blowing in a winter breeze. Cullen turned to it—it always called out to him—but instead of a mournful ache twisting his gut and blotting out his present day, he smiled. Marty would be glad he found someone worthy of spending his life with. She would say, "Now that is how life is done," as she had a habit of doing.

"You have grieved long enough. I am glad to see you are moving ahead." The bishop didn't keep to himself how pleased he was that Cullen was finally heeding his advice. Even if it was ten years waiting.

"I am." Cullen suppressed a wide smile. Just the thought of Grace becoming his *fraa* filled him with a fullness he had long been denied by his own hand.

"*Gott* does not want us to mourn so long, but there is no time frame on such a thing."

"I thought all I felt for Marty was gone when she was called home. I never thought I could care for another again." Cullen figured few men dared to confess raw emotions, let alone to their bishop, but that is what bishops and ministers were for, was it not?

"Took ya by surprise, did it?" The bishop nudged him and winked. "He sent her here. You helped her, and doing so you both got healing. *Gott* is *gut*."

He most certainly was. Cullen's love for Marty had been so strong, he did in fact bury it in the deepest recesses of his soul. He hid it in the aches of his chest, the center of his bones, and even in the places between teeth and cheek. Selfishly stored and haunting him all the same. But Grace changed that. She awakened that part of him that needed to be rebirthed.

"I don't know if she will even stay."

"I have seen the way the two of you sneak glances at each other. Everyone does. She will stay. Are you prepared to be a father to her child?"

"Yes. No child should be without the love of a *daed*." He couldn't imagine a childhood without his father in it. No one should.

"I agree." As they pulled into the bank parking lot, the bishop added, "You know, I have watched so many couples over the years fall in love, join in marriage, start families…"

"I know this."

"There is a common order to how these sorts of things are done, and you have yet to follow it," he said with a wink.

Cullen had loved an outsider and planned to help her enter his world before marrying her. Not the most traditional of Amish relationships. Now Grace, cast away by her family, with child, and not a widow. Yep, for a man who followed the *Ordnung* to his best abilities, in this department Cullen was lacking.

"I'm sorry to disappoint you." He really was.

"You have not disappointed me. You are a *gut* man, Cullen Graber, and you tend to be drawn to the destitute. No matter what path you take to reach that place inside you that brings you joy, *Gott* will smile on you all your days for that big heart inside you."

• • •

Tessie Miller lived in a small two-story gray house at the end of Walnut Ridge. The lot was barely an acre, but she had managed to fill every inch of it with gardens, flowers, and fruits. As a boy, Cullen had climbed the young apple and peach trees while his mother and Tessie sat in the shade, sewing and sharing tea. They had been good friends, and the woman had never once treated him like the other children around her. Oh, she scolded him a time or two, but she also gifted him smiles, soft kind eyes, and cookies, whereas she never did for others. Maybe because she and his mother were so close, he thought.

Stepping to the door, Cullen made a mental note to shovel her path to the barn before leaving, then knocked. He had no idea how to start the conversation he needed to have with her. The bishop had been so vague about everything, but felt Tessie held all the answers to solve his problems. He would be plenty grateful if she managed to simply solve one.

Inside, he heard Tessie walk across an old wooden floor. The woman was so small, he was surprised her steps sounded like the thud of a large man on a hollow floor. She opened the door, not looking surprised that it was him waiting on the other side. In fact, if Cullen were a betting man, he would say Tessie Miller had predicted his coming all along.

"I wondered how long it would take ya. *Kumm*," Tess greeted with a permanent frown. "The *kaffi* is about ready. You are a bit early." Had she been expecting him? Surely she hadn't a clue where he and the bishop had been. Cullen chuckled under a breath. Gossip traveled faster than a racehorse. By morning it wouldn't surprise him one bit if all of Walnut Ridge knew he just bought a worthless hillside.

He shook his head, freeing any concerns from taking precedence over the matter at hand, and stepped inside. Following her past the sitting room into the kitchen, Cullen shed his coat and hat before taking a seat at her table. He still had a few chores at home to tend to, and no way was he missing Abram's surprise birthday party this evening, but speaking to Tess, while the bishop's words were still fresh on his mind, was best.

"How did you know I would *kumm*?" He shifted in the chair as she poured him a cup of *kaffi*.

"I have eyes." Was it that obvious how he felt about Grace? "I see you busy about and tending to her."

"Then you need to bring her here to live with you." That would sure make everything easier, cheaper, too. "The Hiltys are threatening to sell the cabin if she doesn't agree to marry Freeman, and her *daed* wants her to return to marry her off to some widower with three *kinner*. A man named Leon Strolzfus." Tessie didn't seemed surprised.

"Those Strolzfus *menner* are slower than Christmas comin'," Tessie grumbled. "Talk at the same speed, too."

Cullen took up the cup of *kaffi*, blew the rising steam,

and sipped the strong brew. His adrenaline had already worked in his favor today and he made a mental note to not consume more than half the cup given to him.

Tessie never rattled easily, but he had expected a bit of surprise from her. Everything that was happening to Grace was not how things were—not fair or acceptable. And yet, Tessie Miller was not surprised to hear them.

"I know all of this. My *bruder* has forbidden me from interfering. He does a lot of that." Tessie slumped into a seat across the table with a defeat he had never seen in her before. She looked weary as an old quilt. The gray hairs slipping from her *kapp* had whitened more in the passing weeks, proof of how quickly life could wear one down. Cullen needed that fight she had always been known for, now more than any time in his life, and it was simply not there. Even with the bishop understanding his need to help Grace, and not forbidding him, it wasn't enough. He needed Tessie Miller and all that pluck that made her. Grace didn't want to disappoint her family again and Cullen feared she would return home as her father demanded. Who else could stop what was happening and convince Ben Miller to do right by his middle daughter?

"Why would one do such a thing to his own daughter, Tessie?"

"He is punishing her."

"I gathered. But she confessed and repented before her church. She endured weeks under the ban and is no longer shunned in her community. She has been forgiven, so why tell her she must marry?"

"It is what is expected. We are meant to marry, raise *kinner*, even if we go about it the wrong way. And *kinner* should be punished for doing wrong. Spare the rod, spoil the child." She darted wide and uncompromising eyes at him.

"Grace is not a child. She made a mistake, confessed it. We are to forgive one another's shortcomings. Is that not what we are taught?" Did they all not forgive Dave Shelter, the former deacon who ran off with all their money years back? "Shelter robbed us and we forgave him. Is her sin so much greater than his?"

Cullen couldn't slow the anger rising up inside him. This was not right.

"*Jah*, we are to forgive." Tess exhaled a shallow breath. "Ben knows no other way. It was the same way of our *daed*, and for me."

Cullen stiffened at her last words, but Tess simply sipped at her cup as if the revelation stirred no broad reaction. "Tess?"

Looking off toward the light shimmering through a kitchen window, rays bursting through panes of glass in a line of hope that reached the center of the kitchen table, she appeared to gather her thoughts. Cullen dug in deep for the patience he was known for and waited. Knowing Tess since he was born, Cullen had not once heard of Tessie Miller ever doing a thing that would deserve a punishment, other than a few harsh words on a bad day. She was profoundly faithful and stiffly obedient. She bent no rules, avoided all worldly things, and sat front and center with an open ear every other Sunday.

"He would see his *kind* thrown to the wolves for what she did?" The silence was killing him.

"*Jah*, he would." No explanation but a simple yes. Was

Ben Miller so unforgiving as to see Grace marry without love? Tess lowered her gaze to her cup as if something were there that would help her. "Benjamin thought our *daed* a great and *Gottly* man and does what he can to be much like him. They both share the same thoughts on such matters as this." No wonder Grace found Walnut Ridge so friendly and forgiving.

"You were sent here like Grace was," he muttered, trying to recall all he truly knew of this woman.

Staring into his own cup, memories long brushed away resurfaced. Tessie Miller had not been there since he was born; she moved here when he was young. "I remember little. *Mutter* would walk the hillside to the cabin to deliver cookies and fresh ham and visit." How could he have forgotten those long hours of digging in dirt and catching grasshoppers on that hillside? On Grace's hillside. The excitement he found remembering little forgotten moments with his *mutter* was quickly drowned by the current situation.

"Ya *mutter* was very kind to me, when no one back home was." Her dull gray eyes glistened. With guilt or pain, he didn't know. "It has been hard for me to know Grace was up there, alone. It can be such a lonely place." Her boney fingers rotated her cup. "Abigale knew that. She said she could see the lonely in my face. It took me two months before I dared open the door and let her in." The memory brought a smile. "Anyone else would have stopped coming, but not your *mutter*. No, she saw a young *maedel* who had made a mistake, a stained thing who needed cleansing. Your *daed* helped, too. You remember that old *hund*, Buddy?"

"I do. He growled at the wind but let me climb on his back till I was too big to do so."

Tess leaned forward, pinning him with a grin. "He was my company like that awful fur ball you gave Grace." She leaned back in her chair, her eyes still on him. "Grace is lucky to have you and Elli and Betty. I was blessed to have your *mutter*."

"But you do not have *kinner*. Why were you sent to live away from your family?" It still amazed Cullen how one could do that to another. Next to God, family meant everything to the Amish. Even in matters of fallen souls and sin, they did not simply toss a member out without leaving a door from them to re-enter.

Being shunned wasn't the end unless the shunned wanted it to be. Its purpose was to isolate without harm, and in love, to bring the fallen back to the fold. And when they returned, all was forgiven and placed in a past that could not be revisited.

A tear fell down Tess's cheek. Then another and he wished he had not made the statement. "I can leave. I am sorry if I have hurt you by speaking of things that are not for me to know." Cullen stood.

"My *boppli* did not take its first breath." Hand trembling, she lowered her head. *Like Grace*, he thought. The past had repeated itself. Thirty years from now, would this be Grace sitting here? He thought not. If his mother could help Tessie Miller, he could certainly help Grace.

"We do not have to talk of this if ya cannot." Her story was hers, and she needed to know she did not have to share any of it with him.

"I was alone when my time came. In the very cabin our

Grace is in. I was young and knew nothing of having a child. I thought I had time." She looked off again, and he handed her a hanky he had taken from his mother's drawer just recently. One never knew when Grace would have a day when it would be needed. With all the tears that were being shed in his presence lately, he fussed at himself for not doing that sooner. "Your *daed* found me and hurried me to the hospital, but it was too late."

She was crying, her hardness broken by a memory, and Cullen shortened the distance between them and took her hand. He did not need the details surrounding her hurt in order to feel for her. One look at her face did that good and well.

"I am sorry that happened to you, Tessie. If I had known—"

"Few do. And I expect it to stay that way." She sniffed and wiped at her damp cheeks, returning to her straightforward posture and the frown that made her. In a short moment, she had surrendered her past and the hurt that dwelled there, but she would not allow it to consume her.

"You think me hard on her, but I pace the floor each night praying for Grace. Praying the Lord sees fit that things are different for her."

Cullen could see that in her. "Was it an *Englisch* man, just like Grace?"

"*Nee*. It was no *Englischer*." Tessie's snarl told him she was not so inclined to sin past the walls of her community. "We both made a horrible mistake." Cullen wondered how any of this would help Grace. Tessie seemed to read his mind and answered that for him. "My sisters and I had *kumm* to Pleasants for my cousin Matthew's wedding." He assumed she meant Matthew and Sadie Miller, the owners of the Country Kitchen, but did not ask. "We were permitted to stay for a *gut* long time, a month to help with the harvest and the wedding," she added defensively.

"I met a man who said all the right things to someone raised so plain and private. I was very unruly and disobedient back then," she said.

He couldn't imagine a young Tess being unruly or disobedient. Snarky and opinionated, but not disobedient.

As Tess came to her feet, Cullen thought she would end the story there, not revealing any more of her shortcomings to him. He didn't blame her. It was a hard thing to admit failure. It had taken him years to admit his failure to steal Marty away from her father and run away with her as soon as he discovered she was being abused.

"I did not know he was to be wed soon after Sadie and Matthew. We wrote back and forth every day for three months, before he told me he had taken a *fraa*." Cullen couldn't imagine the heartbreak she would have felt at the news. Amish or *Englisch*, man was simply a creature he could not understand.

"I never saw him again until I was sent here to watch his life continue around me and not be part of it. It was my punishment, you see." She pinned him with a grave expression. "Grace was sent to see how lonely I lived, what her disobedience would gift her. That was hers."

Cullen felt a rage creep into him that he had never known before. This was another father who found no worth or room for error in his child. If God ever was to bless him with *kinner,* he would never make such mistakes, he promised himself right then and there.

"The man hid me away in hopes that few would notice me. I never left the cabin unless visiting your *mutter*. I did not even attend church then." The revelation was like a bolt of lightning, raising the hairs on his arms and neck.

"Did this man know you were expecting before he married?" She nodded, and Cullen stood to give the floor a good walking over, too. "Tessie, are you saying…?"

Turning away from Cullen, she continued. "I buried our son in the back field. Bishop Mast and your parents were the only others there that day. I was told to return home, but after all of that, I could not allow for it. My punishment was to forever be reminded of that mistake, so I stayed. I have never allowed myself to look past *Gott* and have followed his word the best I could since. Your *mamm* was my dearest friend—I could not leave her side, either. My heart broke just as yours did when we lost them. I still weep for her to this day."

She was trying to convince him of her loyalty since her womanhood began, but Cullen needed no such convincing. Tessie Miller had been as strong in her faith as any he had ever known. He would not judge her for the sins of her youth any more than Grace's or his own. This was not who they were now.

"And you would let that, or even worse, happen to Grace?" It was bold, stupid, and a little pushy, but Cullen had to try.

"I know what you and the bishop have been planning. I saw him at the bank talking with that Sherman Wilson fellow. But Elmo will not sell it to you, and I cannot go against my *bruder*'s wishes. Benjamin says we women cannot change after giving in to sin. He says you can yank all ya want on a duck's neck, but it will never be a swan."

They were at a standstill. Trying to wrap his head around the mystery this woman had kept all his life and the fate of Grace and her child, Cullen dropped back into his chair and lowered his head to the table with a thump. How could he court Grace and eventually marry her if she was forced out of Walnut Ridge?

"Do not be knocking that thing around." She smacked the back of his head with her palm. "We need it to *kumm* up with something smart."

So she wouldn't go against her brother's wishes, but she was still invested in helping Grace any way she could. Cullen looked to the heavens, then back to the coffee cup again. There had to be some way around all of this. A way Grace did not have to leave Walnut Ridge.

"Can I ask you two questions?" She nodded, and a slow grin began forming on her lips. "Do you love her?

"*Jah*, I do love her. I want to help. I just do not know how I can be of any assistance without going against my family." Her hands were tied, he knew that, just as Grace thought *her* hands were tied. His were not, but he couldn't do much on his own. This would require something out of the ordinary, but not pushing the boundaries of the morals that he had been raised with. If his idea had some worth, and Tessie was willing, they would still need more help.

"If I gave you a Christmas present, would ya accept it?"

"What are you talking about?" She raised her voice. "Christmas is in two days. Can we not focus on this matter first?"

"Would you like to own the property where your child was buried?"

CHAPTER TWENTY-SIX

Elli and Betty carried the long birthday cake to the table as everyone crowded around to admire the monstrosity covered in icing. Cullen had to admit that he had never seen such a cake in all his twenty-eight years. Three in one, that's what it was. His stomach had been growling all day — he couldn't eat with so much yet to get in order for Grace's sake, but for now he needed to settle the beast in his belly. Could he even wait until Second Christmas to give her both gifts?

Elli's husband, Abram, a man who looked years younger than fifty-five, stepped into the kitchen with a look of panic on his face, noticing the cluster of family and friends about. That was, until his eyes caught sight of the cake. Surprise birthday parties weren't common, but when you married a woman who wasn't born into the Plain life, it wasn't uncommon, either.

Cullen tugged at his shirt to loosen the tightening around his neck in the heated room. He spied Abram shooting an enduring look at Elli and smiled. He admired the love shared between them. Knowing Elli for at least six years now himself, he had come to find her just the breath of fresh air Abram Schwartz had needed. Caleb thought so, too, and loved her as if she was his second mother from *Gott*.

Abram had been a widower for longer than Cullen could remember. Like most of the Schwartz and Glick families in the area, and at least two Miller women, they had all come from Indiana, the town of Havenlee. Abram's first wife had died when Caleb was only a boy. Cullen remembered his *daed* speaking of it the night Abram lost his *fraa* in a house fire. Looking at the wiser and older man, reddened from embarrassment among friends and family, Cullen found him the perfect example of a heart willing to find a second home. Elli was his second chance at love, and it wore well on him. Elli crossed the kitchen with a knife to cut the cake and Cullen studied her. Confident in stride, content in soul. First and foremost, she loved Abram. He was the center of her everything, and this evening was just another example of it.

Yes, second chances had happy endings, too.

"Cullen, help me set up more tables. Matthew and Enoch are getting chairs from the storage room," Caleb said. Cullen nodded and followed him to the hall where long white folding tables leaned against one another. "I take it Grace is not getting up for such things with her being so close to her time and all."

"She wanted to finish some sewing," Cullen replied. Truth was, Martha, the local midwife had looked in on her and thought it to be best that Grace stayed close to home from here on out. Caleb put a table under each arm, hooked his fingers into the closed-up legs, and aimed for the large kitchen.

"You tell her yet?" Caleb winked and set the first table down. Cullen hadn't.

"She knows how I feel, but not what I've done, if that is what you mean." Once the tables and chairs were all set up, Cullen stepped in line to receive his own slice of cake. It was part chocolate, part vanilla, and as the cake began disappearing, he could even see pink at one end. Elli had in fact made one cake out of three. The thought amused him.

Bishop Mast motioned him over to a table, and Cullen weaved through the kitchen and took the seat next to him. A couple of boys bumped the back of his chair as they scurried out to gather with the children in the neighboring room. "I think today I can eat that fast, too," Cullen joked and took up a large plastic forkful of chocolate and filled his mouth with it.

"You were never one to rush as they do." The bishop smiled, and Cullen came to realize how important the man had become to him. Bishop Mast was not only the head of the church, but after sitting and talking with him so much in the last few days, he found he was a *gut freind*. He answered all Cullen's concerns without judgment. He even helped Cullen find scripture to support the thoughts in his head, and his heart. Everything would work out just as *Gott* had planned it, the bishop told him. And Cullen believed that to be so.

• • •

Evening came, and people began saying their goodbyes. Abram and Elli held the door to the cold snow falling outside and thanked everyone for attending. The sitting room had been tidied up from the children's playing, and Cullen found a table in the back of the kitchen to sit and just take in the day. Looking a bit weary himself, the bishop came and joined him.

"I think from all the work ya been doin' lately, you

might need this." Betty winked, handing him a fresh cup of *kaffi*. "I am glad you have worked hard to do right by others as you have." For a people who had no cell phones or landlines close, it amazed him how fast word traveled among the community.

"Well, we both know some of it was selfish," Cullen winked.

"Not selfish to fall in love with someone you lent a hand to. Not selfish at all, right, Bishop?" Betty asked. Cullen didn't need to look to know the bishop was nodding.

The front door closed. Abram, still wearing a wide grin from ear to ear, marched over and joined them. Betty flashed a giddy smile and scrambled away. The Schwartz house had three stories and it surprised Cullen how they warmed it so evenly from attic to basement. He watched the busy room about them as Abram began talking about the weather. Elli was handing little Noah back to Hannah, but not before planting a few sloppy kisses on both his chubby cheeks. Tess was following Hazel Shrock into the sitting room, where a few men sat talking, a tray apiece in each woman's hand filled with hot chocolate and *kaffi*. Betty stopped mid-duty to straighten her daughter Ruth's *kapp*, and Elli urged Hannah to take the children into the next room to play as she began straightening the kitchen. Caleb and Mirim were whispering something back and forth to each other in the far corner where a large cabinet, glass displaying old pottery, sat. They were in perfect bliss and enjoying the early stages of the newly wedded.

Eyeing the room, Cullen thought of his parents, how they would have wanted to be here. How his *daed* would have said, "This is what community is all about." Love bloomed around him as snow fell outside, and for the first time since Marty, Cullen felt a part of it. He wished Grace were here, helping Elli wash dishes, laughing at Noah trying on his legs to toddle about, and possibly throwing him a smile across the room the way Elli did Abram.

Soon, his heart whispered. Grace's well-being and that of the baby's came first and bouncing around in a buggy was out of the question, according to Martha.

The front door slammed with a bang, raising heads in a jolt. An elevated voice, one everyone knew well, along with Elisha Schwartz, quarreled. Elisha's spoken plea to leave well enough alone came from the foyer. Cullen shifted in his seat and his eyes met the bishop's. He, too, had a look of concern. And though both men expected this moment, neither expected it on such a night of celebration. But since when did proper ever get addressed by Elmo or Freeman Hilty?

"What is the meaning of this?" Elmo Hilty stomped into the room like a deranged man about to unload all his fury on every soul remaining in the Schwartz home. Bishop Mast remained as calm as Cullen had always known the older, much wiser, man to be, and slowly came to his feet, his actions as good an example to follow as his wisdom.

Betty stood and leaned on the back wall, and her husband John came to stand next to her. Elli and Abram gathered at the sink, pretending to wash the few utensils used for the evening. Both turned, giving the intrusion their half-hearted attention. Elli gave an eye roll that would make Rachel Yoder jealous. As if the room wasn't warm enough, the anger Elmo had brought into this house, Cullen thought hot enough to melt all of Elli's pretty cake frosting.

"Elmo. I see you have something that has upset you. *Gott* can hear our whispers and the thoughts of our hearts, so raising your voice will not get you answers any quicker than if you would just simply say what it is on ya mind," the bishop said.

The birthday gathering was no private gathering—everyone in the community had been welcomed to attend Abram's celebration—so Cullen knew most couldn't understand Elmo's abrupt anger. And what was meant to be an evening of celebration and good food, Cullen felt had slowly become a reckoning.

Elmo's eyes found his and narrowed into a hate that seeped like lava from his crimson face. It oozed from his every pore. Freeman entered close behind, following his father's lead. Dressed in damp black from hat to boot, Elmo raised a finger, pointing Cullen out as the sole cause for his temper.

"You have no right to go behind my back and ruin the sale of my property. Bishop, this man interfered with a sale I had made with another. How, I do not know, but we are about to." Elmo crossed his arms, not taking his focus away from Cullen. The stubby man marched confidently across the room and positioned himself to stand near the bishop. His face was that of a man having the upper hand, but he was so sadly mistaken.

Pity should have been his first emotion, but instead Cullen shook his head, shamed in the behavior that had forced his hand. Giving Elli and Abram a nod, a silent apology for what he had invited into their home, he quickly returned his eyes to the men. He was glad Grace hadn't come now, sparing her from this hardened of hearts display. And Tess was in the sitting room with the others, also free from dealing with the scene.

The Hiltys were bullies. Always making demands and wheeling things to their favor. It was time for them to be reminded how real men behaved. They were like two matching bantam roosters, full of—what was it Freeman called it? Full of vinegar.

"No one has cheated you, Elmo. You hired that realtor to sell your land for top dollar, ain't so?" the bishop said. Elmo's head slowly tilted toward him, and Cullen suppressed a grin as Elmo slowly realized the bishop knew why he was here tonight. "From what I hear, the woman did just that. You should be glad to be twenty-four thousand, one hundred and sixteen dollars wealthier for it."

Cullen stood and took a few steps forward, closing the distance just as Freeman stepped in front of his father and closed the distance with Cullen. "Gentlemen, Abram's home is not the place for such." Freeman looked up at Cullen, a threat begging to lash out.

"This means nothing. You will not have what you want." Like his father, Freeman smelled of tobacco, and Cullen scrunched his face from the horrid stench of it.

"Men, this is a day of celebration. Have some cake, I will pour you some coffee, but I will not have any arguing in my house." Elli stepped between the two men, and Cullen could see the amusement on Abram's face behind her. Grace was like that, too. She did not think herself as strong as Elli Schwartz, but the same fire that burned in Elli burned in Grace, too.

Cullen took a step back to indicate he had no intention of bringing any further embarrassment onto Abram's *haus*.

"Since you, Elmo Hilty, decided to use an *Englisch* realtor to sell your land to an *Englischer*, then you should have known all would not go as it should. If Cullen bought land to join his own and you profited from it, then I see no quarrel to be made. It is still Amish land and will be handed down as such. No man in this community would see wrong in this." A glint of mischief flickered in the bishop's eyes. "Unless there is something else that has upset the two of you." The bishop lingered on his last words, ensuring each man knew what he was saying in full. "I think the matter is settled."

Cullen was certain that neither Elmo nor Freeman would willingly share how they planned to use the land and cabin to retain Freeman a *fraa*. They were bullies, not stupid. Yet, from the look on both men's faces, he wasn't so sure.

"What's all the rattling and fussing about?" Tessie Miller pushed past the door Elli had first closed and entered the room. Elli rolled her eyes, chiding herself. Cullen figured she wished she never left her post of guarding the door to step between men at odds now—he certainly wished she hadn't. Tessie didn't stop to take in the room but went straight to the center of the calamity. Maybe Grace was right. Walnut Ridge had a lot of strong women in it.

"This is not of your concern, Tess," Elmo ordered, his face red with fury. Elmo and Freeman were the only two in the room who weren't smart on how the next minute would play out. A door opened, silencing the room, and Betty pushed little Aiden and Sue Graber back through it before closing it again.

Even she would not miss Tessie Miller finally saying her piece. It had taken a lot of years for this moment to come full circle, and no one was willing to take it from her, nor would they miss it. It was not vengeance Tessie Miller sought—that was the Lord's. It was closure. It was burying a past and a mistake she had long been forgiven for.

The room held on to the quiet as Tess remained where she stood. Elli took a seat, as did Abram and the bishop, but Cullen remained where he was. Tess did not need his support, but he wanted to stand by her nonetheless, just as he would for Grace. Tess had once been alone to deal with Elmo and the judgments of others. It had made her bitter and lonely and maybe even a little afraid to feel any joy she believed she wasn't deserving of.

"All this fussing about land and run-down old shacks and *Englischers*. I do not know why you must always be stirring up trouble, and on our sweet Abram's birthday, at that." Tess shook her head, the stiff white *kapp* swishing left to right. "And to think you thought my sweet Gracie would ever choose to wed that boy." Her hands rested firmly on her hips as she scowled over Freeman with her commonly known frown of distaste.

"That girl has tempted my poor Freeman. And this man has tricked me out of my own land." Elmo shook a fist into the air toward Cullen. "I demand these sinners be shunned from our community before they corrupt us all."

"You should not speak of Grace or Cullen that way. *Gott* does not bless a man who bears false witness, and Cullen only gifted what he could to help out an old woman." Elmo froze stiff at her words. Never had anyone in Pleasants found a way to bring Elmo Hilty to silence, and Tessie Miller, in just a few simple words, did just that. The room fell into a strained silence, and no one moved even a hair to stir it.

"What are you talking about?" He clenched his teeth, almost to the point of crushing, and anger once again turned his ashen skin to crimson.

Leisurely, as if the world ran at her own timing, Tessie pulled the envelope from her dress pocket. She straightened her *kapp*, as if it was important to look her best right now of all moments. Someone snickered behind him, but no one dared take their eyes off the two in the center of the kitchen to make out the guilty party. Cullen shifted his feet; he would explode if Tess didn't get on with it.

Gathering her lips as if to hold back a long-awaited cry, she opened the envelope, fingers trembling. Cullen stepped close enough that she could sense his support. Betty sobbed by the door, quietly wiping the cascade pouring down her cheeks. He glanced to his right. Abram took Elli's hand in his, giving her his support as she watched her friend. It was too bad Grace wasn't here. She loved these women, and to see them now would only deepen the admiration she had for them. Cullen knew then that Tessie's secret wasn't such a secret after all. These women had held her secret, comforted her hurt, and tolerated the woman it made her. Walnut Ridge was blessed by these mothers and daughters and the people they had created.

Tessie Miller deserved this moment more than anyone ever deserved anything, and even Bishop Mast watched on, as a bystander, unwilling to interrupt.

Taking a deep breath, she finally said, "Cullen Graber did not buy the hillside and cabin to defy you or your *sohn*. He is not that kind of man. Did you know that money in his parents' savings came to total exactly twenty-four thousand, one hundred and fourteen dollars? I gave him two dollars to buy out his interest in the place. It was a bad investment for a man hoping to start a family, but for a spinster like me, it was a *gut* deal."

"How is this possible?" Elmo rung his hands together, attempting to remain steady on his feet, but this sturdy oak was rattled.

"*Gott's* will. Down to the last penny," the bishop said.

"*Mutter* and Tess were close friends for all their lives. *Mutter* helped Tess when she needed her most, and *Daed* said I was to always do the same. So, I did just that. I have more than I need, but there are some who have so little." Cullen knew he should not have spoken, but when Tessie began to lower her head, he feared she would not finish, would not use what she had finally been given after all these years: a voice. He wanted to say more but if life had taught him one thing, it was to never argue with people and simply let them be wrong. And Elmo Hilty and his son had been wrong about how they handled themselves.

"Ya bought my land to give to her?" His voice pitched an octave. Then Elmo shifted into a laugh that protruded from his mouth, mocking both him and Tessie. Freeman joined him in laughing at the idea of it.

"It was an early Christmas gift." Cullen smirked.

"He bought it, so I could tend to our *boppli*'s grave.

So, I could put flowers on his stone without fear. And I will tear done that cabin you left me in. I have paid dearly, while you—" She paused. "You are forgiven. I forgive you without your apology. But I will not allow the past to repeat itself."

CHAPTER TWENTY-SEVEN

The next morning, Cullen hammered away, more to think than to see his that horseshoe stock remained full. Grace would be joining him for Christmas breakfast at Abram and Elli's and if she felt up to it, they could go to church together. Tonight he needed to finish her gift. The sanding was complete, but the cradle still needed at least two coats of varnish.

The sound of an engine broke through the quiet valley morning. Moving the slightly bent length of steel aside where it would not cool too quickly, he stepped out into the open as the red truck pulled up to the house. *Englisch* came often to see his work or to order steel and welded signs for their homes or business, but the day before Christmas told him this *Englischer* wanted him to perform a miracle. Some men just didn't prepare as well as others.

He walked toward the truck, a nice cherry red with all the bold elaborations money could buy. At least maybe this person could afford last-minute gifts, but if it would make him late for dinner at Grace's, he would decline. The door swung open and just as Cullen sided the vehicle, out stepped a man, a few years younger than himself, wearing a uniform. Cullen slowed to a stop, his welcoming smile swallowed up by good ol' gravity, right before the earth stopped moving. Even the cardinals that had chirped playfully all morning were as silent as a snowflake.

The man turned, just now catching Cullen's presence.

"Good morning." The soldier went to meet him and offered an outstretched hand. When his dark eyes took in the full look of Cullen, his pace slowed, his hand suspended in air. Cullen followed the target of his unease to the hammer still clenched in his hand. To a man like that, Cullen must look like the perfect enemy. Maybe he was.

"Sorry to disrupt whatever you were doing. Are you a carpenter?"

"A blacksmith. Carpenters usually don't use this kind of hammer." Cullen replied, his tone absent of its normal friendliness to strangers.

"I should have guessed by the size of ya." A laugh spilled from his young face. He moved forward again, offering that hand. "My name is Jared Castle. And you are?"

"Cullen Graber." Cullen shook Jared's hand a little more firmly than usual. Jared tilted his head curiously, studying him in full. The apron, the straw hat, all foreign by the look of him. "You're a soldier?"

"Yes. Well, sort of." Jared scoured the landscape, the structures, Cullen's house, then settle back on him. "You live here alone?" That was none of his concern, and Cullen lifted a brow to say so without the words. "Sorry. I'm sure you don't get many normal people visiting out this far; I was just needing directions. If you can point me the right way, I will be out of your hair and you can get back to hammering away."

"*Normal* people?" No wonder this man had left Grace as he had. She was not even considered *normal* in his eyes. The thought burned inside Cullen, and surely his face reflected the insult.

"Oh, what is it you call us again? English?" The hint of sarcasm was recognized. "Listen, I'm just looking for a friend. She's supposed to be living with you people. I stopped at a few houses back there—" He pointed back out of the valley. "And after two door slams, one old lady growling at me and telling me I didn't belong here, and a kid who refused to speak to me but pointed this way, I kind of hoped you might give me a straight answer."

"Does this friend know of you coming?" Cullen crossed his arms. Did he dare lie, send this person along to keep Grace to himself without the temptations of the man she once loved to influence her? No, that would not be right. No matter how easily Cullen could make this problem go away, it was not his decision to make.

"No. It's a surprise. Couldn't very well call Grace up, ya know." He chuckled again. Jared's disrespect was astounding. How Grace had ever fallen for such a man was beyond him.

"Grace has done well here," Cullen said. Jared laughed again, dark eyes dancing. Cullen snapped silently.

"Grace is a resourceful gal. I imagine she can do well, anywhere. Is she here? You have her locked up inside that house or something?"

Was that humor? Cullen worked out a challenging grin but refused to speak until he could decide between what was good and what was right. He didn't like either scenario. Where was his faith now?

"Listen. I take it you know her." Jared paused, appearing as if he was trying to read Cullen's thoughts. *Good luck with that.* "And that you know who I am, by the looks of you. But Grace and I have some things to discuss, and they

have nothing to do with you, or anyone else here in Amish-
ville. I have traveled a long way, and I will find her one way
or another."

That was what Cullen was afraid of.

• • •

"Betty, you and John didn't have to *kumm* up here and
check on me. Martha said I am doing fine, and I can even
kumm to Christmas breakfast at Elli's," Grace said, as John
helped Betty out of her coat and black bonnet covering.
Betty held a plate in one hand and a white bag looped
around her arm in the other. She offered the plate to
Grace. "You do too much for me. Makes me *faul*."

"You should know by now that she worries about you
up here alone day and night," John added. "She worries
half the community will starve and figures to feed them all.
Just accept the fudge, Grace; you can't tell her *nee*." John's
dark hair and brows appeared to belong to one man while
his deep auburn beard looked like another. Much thinner
than Grace thought someone living under Betty's abun-
dant cooking skills would be, but he did work construction
full time and ran a calving operation from home.

"She spoils me," he said. Grace accepted the plate of
fudge—peanut butter, chocolate, and maple, all arranged in
checkerboard fashion.

"John and Matthew butchered a few of the older hens
yesterday." Betty held out the bag. "I thought you might
want one. Nothing like fresh chicken soup before a winter
snap to keep a body warm and healthy."

Grace's mouth watered at the thought, and she accepted

the bag with gratitude. She had already planned on cooking rabbit this evening, thanks to Cullen's good hunting skills, so she tucked the freshly butchered chicken in the fridge she finally had afforded a propane tank for.

"You ladies visit; I'm going to sneak over the hill and talk to a man about some horseshoes," John said before tipping his hat and stepping back out into the cold.

"I see you have been preparing for the wee one," Betty said, sifting through the small baby gowns and cloth diapers and burping cloths.

"I wish there was more, but…" Grace paused, hoping she didn't sound ungrateful for what material Betty gifted her.

"*Kinner* don't care about abundance, except in hugs and love," Betty said.

Grace hoped that was true, because her child would have little but love and hugs. Yet she would supply them amply.

"So have you decided?" Betty laid a small light-green gown down and settled into a chair. Grace brushed away one of her *kapp* strings tickling her neck and pulled two teacups from the cabinet.

"Decided?" Grace poured two cups of peppermint tea and set one in front of Betty before sitting at the other end of the table. Betty's dark hair framed her oval face. In the lamplight of the room, a few shimmers glinted to life.

"If you will make Walnut Ridge a home for you and your *boppli* or if you will both be leaving us." Put that way, Grace felt the stab of guilt she was certain her friend had not meant to deliver but had nonetheless. Betty was far from cruel, but it was apparent from the moment she and

John had stepped into the room that Betty was downtrodden. Did she really care that much if Grace stayed or went?

"*Daed* expects it. He wants me home after I am able to travel."

"So you will be leaving us?" Her head lowered.

"I don't want to, Betty," Grace admitted, reaching across the table and taking her hand. "You all have been so kind to me. You have made me feel like…"

"Family? That is because you are, Gracie. Tess has never been happier all her life until you came to live with all of us. I think having you near and the *boppli,* would be good for her." *Great, more guilt.*

"I don't think I had anything to do with *Aenti* Tess being happy."

"But you did and she is. Tessie has just been a certain way for so long, it is hard for her to show it. You should know she sees that we all know what you need, how you are feeling each week, and how many times our sweet and handsome Cullen delivers wood to your door. He has fine skills in carpentry, too, does he not?" Betty eyed the cabinet, the chair, even the table that now supported considerable weight. Betty would have made a right good salesman. Grace blushed.

"I didn't think Tess noticed *that* much." Grace replied.

"She can see the hillside from her kitchen window." Betty laughed, her teacup clattering on the tabletop but surprisingly, none spilled. "We women thought maybe you would stay now that you have so much reason to."

"You mean Cullen." Little got past these women, indeed. Did they truly see something between them worth pursuing?

"*Jah*. We all have prayed for his healing and all these years nothing came. *Gott*'s timing, not ours," Betty said woefully. She sipped at her cup and lifted her gaze to Grace again. "We see it is time now, and not only for him but for you as well. He cares for you—that is plain to see— but we don't know how you feel about him."

Instead of feeling bothered by this, Grace was pleased these women cared about Cullen so much that they would dare inquire about such personal information. Betty made a good spokesperson for the group, despite being the softest heart of the lot.

"I care for him also, but he deserves a *gut* woman. One who has not jumped the fence and brought shame to her father's *haus*."

"But you are a *gut* woman. You have confessed before your church and endured the weeks of shunning placed on your shoulders. You are forgiven. Why do you still feel as if you are not?"

A tear slipped down Grace's cheek. Forgiveness was not the issue, not any longer, but Cullen did deserve better, not a ready-made family.

"May I speak freely with you, in confidence?" Betty took her hand this time, squeezing it gently, and Grace nodded. "I would like to help you through this. I know a lot troubles your mind and your heart. Share thy troubles and the weight of them will be measured in halves." Betty added the old saying all Amish knew by heart.

Grace floated her a smile and shared her troubles. "The father, the man who left me and wanted nothing to do with our child, wants to speak to me now after all this time ignoring me. I wrote him that I did not want to talk to him.

Do you think that was wrong, sinful? He is the father."

"Do you care for him?"

"*Nee*. He gave me attention I never had. It's stupid, but I felt important with him. I thought it was love, but I know better now. And I could never leave my Amish faith. I could have left when I found out I was pregnant—we have family in Michigan who no longer belong to the community, and I could have written them for help, but I am Amish and endured the punishment I deserved in order to stay Amish. It was a bit harsher than I expected."

"That it was." Betty added. Grace reached behind her and rubbed the soreness from her back. Perhaps she had sat behind the sewing machine too long today.

"But Jared would never join our community as he once promised he would. It is not something he will do. I want my child to be raised Amish. I know so little of what tomorrow will bring, but I have faith that no matter, my *boppli* will be raised Plain." A tear slipped down Grace's cheek. "What I thought I felt for him was childish compared to..."

"Compared to what you feel for Cullen?" Betty asked.

Grace bit her lip at Betty's continued questions. She did care for Cullen—loved him, she knew—but how could she admit to such after the way she had behaved already?

"Love is easy to recognize when it is real, is it not?" Betty asked.

"*Jah*, it is. No one has ever treated me like he has."

"I have known that boy all his days. He was heart-hurt over Marty. He was just a boy then. And when his parents died, well..." Betty wiped her cheek with her sleeve. "It is hard to understand *Gott*'s will, and sometimes it's harder, even for big strong men, to accept loss like that. But Cullen did. He took his time, but he dealt with all those losses the best way he could. And Grace, dear, he is ready to love you now."

"I don't know if I can even make a man like that happy. I mean, look at me."

"I agree. You are hideous, little Grace." Betty laughed again, and this time Grace did, too. "You are much of the same, Cullen and you. Stay with us here, Grace. I know you miss your sisters and you are being called home by your parents. But *Gott* has a plan, and it might be right here. You are old enough to decide for yourself. So I just ask that you pray about it and decide after talking to *Gott*."

The sound of John returning with the buggy broke their sisterly time. Grace got to her feet and hurriedly added, "The Hiltys own this place and will not allow for me to remain now that I have refused Freeman."

"Don't you worry about that." Betty waved her off and got to her feet. But that was a big part of it. With nowhere to live, how could she stay?

"*Kumm* to Christmas dinner. Cullen can bring you." Betty stood to retrieve her coat and black bonnet. "And pray for guidance. Pray for direction. I think you will find all the answers there."

"*Danke*, Betty. *Danke* for being such a *wunderbarr freind* to us." Grace helped Betty into her coat and black bonnet and wrapped the woman in a hug. Yes, Grace really loved these women of Walnut Ridge. After Cullen, she might miss them most of all.

CHAPTER TWENTY-EIGHT

Grace folded the few gowns and the small quilt she had sewn together for her baby and placed them in the cardboard box. The treadle sewing machine had been a great help, considering she had never sewed as well as Charity. The stitches were tighter and stronger than if she had attempted them by hand. She eyed the greens and blues of the fabric and anticipated her baby wearing something she had produced with her own hands. That made her smile.

It was a shame there would be no dresser to store them in. She slid the box under the foot of her bed, careful not to crush Stella in the process—a yellow puff, the same color as the fudge Betty brought her wrapped with a red ribbon when she invited Grace to join her family for Christmas dinner. Elli had already secured Second Christmas. If Grace was going to be away from her own family this Christmas, she couldn't imagine more suitable substitutes than those two.

Betty made her think, more than she had, about leaving versus staying. Was it selfish to want to stay, to want Cullen and a life with him? Was it selfish to have written Jared that letter? She knew what she wanted, what her heart longed for, and all of it was right here in Walnut Ridge.

While still on her knees, she rubbed her middle and spoke softly. "Hiya, wee one."

Stella tilted her head as if the words were meant for her.

But since the hiccup episode, the vibrant life growing within Grace was moving less often, and she tried to stir it. An assuring pressure from her bladder to her backbone, evidence all was well, just growing cramped, eased her concerns. Did all women worry like this?

She had barely a week left, if all went as it should, and soon after that she was expected home. It would be a new year in an old life. She would write her mother and explain her decision to not marry Leon Strolzfus. She knew this news would be taken as disobedience, but Betty was correct—Grace was a grown woman, and she couldn't be forced to marry.

Grace bit her lip until the warm salty taste of blood forced her to let go. Did she dare write her *mamm* and also tell her that she would not return at all? That everything she could ever want, even the sinner's shack, was right here in Walnut Ridge? Her father had sent her here as punishment. He would surely be angry if she claimed to have fallen in love with Cullen.

Infatuation was a trickster on a young heart, and in these few months away from her family, among people who nurtured her into adulthood, loved her without consequences, Grace now spotted the difference. Her feelings for Cullen ran deeper than she ever thought possible. So deep, his needs blotted out any of her own. To see his loneliness fade, to make his heart flutter at a smile as hers did, to feel his strong presence beside her every day and be his in turn, to laugh with him over silly mishaps, was somehow more important than anything she could hope for. Cullen never criticized, only complimented, and they could truly enjoy a life together. Her baking, him blacksmithing, and the long walks she could easily imagine would be nothing short of bliss. She shook her head free from overworrying. What she felt for him was not selfish.

The small room that always held more heat than required to keep the cold away had fallen to an uncomfortable temperature. Betty said a snow was moving in. Cullen would fetch her for morning breakfast and service tomorrow so as not to risk her safety or that of her *boppli's* by walking over the hill in such frigid weather, but she wondered if the weather would taper off before then. She glanced out the window, heavy clusters of snow raining down like a waterfall.

She stepped out to gather as much wood as she could before the cold took over. Looking across the hill in search of the lantern that reminded her daily she was safe and watched out for, she could see nothing but a hint of yellow through blowing white. The weather had come in faster than she'd expected it would. In only a couple of hours since Betty's leaving, two inches of snow had fallen. And that was on top of the three still crisp from this morning. By midnight it would not surprise her if the valley would be blanketed in a foot of the stuff. Carrying only four sticks at a time, she was glad Cullen had cut the slices to half of what she had been accustomed to.

"Calm, little one," she whispered again, dropping the wood into the box that had just appeared out of nowhere the day she went shopping with Elli. Cullen was good for that, dependable, seeing to her every need as she made certain little needs of his were tended to as well. "You must not be impatient, wee one. We have another week before meeting." The words were not only to convince the soreness of her back to ease, but also her mind.

She massaged her lower back and after a few minutes, the stiffness had eased. Shaking her head, she put aside the concern and went to pick up her sewing, the material scraps for a quilt she had set aside upon Betty's arrival.

Pumping the treadle, she felt the pain return once more. It was the sewing machine that had made her muscles sore. That made sense, she told herself. Retrieving a pillow from her bed, she carefully positioned it on her lower back and relaxed farther into the soft feel. The quilt had to be finished in time. She needed to press forward.

Once the rhythm of the sewing machine needle flowed into cadence again, Grace focused on the birth of Christ and how tomorrow it would be celebrated with friends. Christmas made her homesick for *Mutter*. "Christmas," she whispered. She had never known a Christmas without her family. The cookies and pies, the ham she and *Mutter* prepared. Everyone was always smiling, and people gathered and visited one another on Second Christmas more often than any other time of the year. This year she would not be with her family, but she was thankful she wouldn't be alone, either.

The smell of baking bread reaching a point of ready, spread through her room, and she slowly got to her feet. She opened the oven door, and a wave of heat rushed her face. "Perfect," she said, smiling at the single loaf tucked in the center of the oven's warmth, its perfectly toned top browned to perfection.

Cooking on this beast of an old stove wasn't so bad any longer. Cullen loved fresh bread, and she loved the look he gave her when she made it. He also liked her gravy, and she

glanced at the cast iron skillet on the back of the stove
where fried rabbit lay smothered in thick pepper gravy.
Thinking of him, she glanced toward the door, as if just
thinking of him could make him appear. The pounding of
hammer, steel, and anvil had quieted long ago, muffled out
by the growing wind. Why he was working on Christmas
Eve was beyond her. The man never slowed, another
admirable trait of his.

He insisted she not travel any longer, but Grace insisted
he join her for at least one meal a day for all his kindness.
She hoped he would come but understood if he had other
obligations with the holiday. With both feet slightly apart,
she bent forward and pulled the pan from the oven.

The front door blew open, smacking into the wall
behind it. Grace jolted upright, sending the hot pan to the
wooden floor.

"Grace!" Cullen dropped an armload of kindling in the
box and was at her side in a matter of seconds. "Let me get
it. You might burn yourself."

Clutching her chest from the sudden startle, Grace
smiled at him. His black hat was now clumped with white,
his burly shoulders, much the same.

"Or *you* might burn *yourself*." Here he was, just as she
hoped he would be. Strangely, instead of his sunny smile or
flirtatious grin, Cullen's lips were pursed tightly, his teeth
clenched. "Are you mad at me for dropping the bread?" He
didn't seem to be the kind of man who ruffled at such an
accidental thing. He had been the one who startled her,
after all. "You know, you did come bursting in here and
gave me a fright." He closed his eyes, sighing heavily.
Opening them again, he scooped up the loaf and pan and

deposited them on the stove.

"I could never be angry with you, Grace. Never." On bended knee, he reached for her hand, the dry callused flesh of a man who worked hard for what he had, and he gave it a squeeze before letting go. A tingle ran from her hand, up her arm, and straight to her hairline. "It was my fault. I should have knocked, but my arms were full and the wind is picking up out there. And maybe I was a little eager to see you." There was that boyish grin, smoldering out whatever first consumed him. Cullen retreated back to the door and secured it.

"Then you are forgiven," she said playfully. "Now don't be running off. I made your favorite. Unless Beth Zook or Sara Shrock have already seen to your supper." She lifted her chin, a grin spreading like warm butter across her face. Under the brim of his hat, his eyes smiled before his lips did. Stella crossed the floor and went to him, licking snow from his boot.

"Neither cook as well as you do," he said matter-of-factly. There went the tingles again. She turned from him, from eyes that had a way of sucking her in, to set the table.

• • •

Grace did make the best gravy he had ever eaten, so why did his stomach still sour? He knew why. He needed to tell her what he did, how he interfered. Not telling was as good as a lie, and no relationship needed to start with lies.

"*Daed* always read from Luke this night," she muttered, picking up their plates and depositing them in the sink. She was homesick. Missing the family she had been away from.

"Do you still miss your parents the way you did that first Christmas without them?" She turned to face him, a look of regret on her face.

Cullen lifted the empty cast-iron pan smeared with bread crumbs and went to her. "Let me take care of this. You cooked. I'll clean while you rest."

"I'm sorry, Cullen. I should not have asked such a thing."

"I will always miss them. But no, time makes that easier. I will never forget them, but they are with the Lord this Christmas. What a thing to be so privileged."

A few black strands escaped her *kapp*, dancing and tickling her delicate neckline. The urge to reach out, brush them away, warmed him just as it did the first time he lifted her in his arms.

"Fetch your Bible," he suggested. She looked up, wide-eyed and hopeful. What man couldn't find joy in that?

"Really?" The way she spoke it, lifted his heart, his soul. She was so easy to love. Would she still look at him with such admiration, such wanting, if she knew he had sent Jared away? He had to tell her. No future could be found where secrets stood between, and he wanted the chance for that future, the one he was dreaming of more and more as days passed.

Grace disappeared into her bedroom and reemerged with her Bible. Plain and perfect, just like her. She flipped to Luke and set the Bible down on the table in front of the sturdy chair he built, then rounded the table and eased into the other chair.

Cullen took his seat and cleared his throat. His *daed* also read about the birth of Jesus when he was young.

Cullen had set aside the thoughts that one day he might do the same for his own *kinner,* but now hope replaced that acceptance. Would this be the first of many, or after this moment would he never have the chance again?

He needed to tell her and face the consequences.

• • •

Fifteen minutes later, lamplight flickered over the cabin walls, and Grace wiped a tear from her eye. The miraculous birth was better than any romance novel her sister had shared with her. What a strong faith Mary had; what a stronger faith Joseph had. If everyone trusted the Lord that flawlessly, there would be a lot less sin in this world.

Cullen's voice had a way of soothing the soul. The story of Mary and Joseph had given her something she had not expected when she first mentioned the family tradition. Regardless of how she knew the story by heart, tonight it, as well as the man sitting across from her, had given her a glimpse of hope.

She could never leave him. She could never leave Walnut Ridge. She could see no other life before her without this man by her side. "*Danke*, Cullen," she said quietly.

He nodded. "Grace, I have something I need to tell you."

"Okay." She stood and went to retrieve her Bible.

"I have done something I shouldn't have. Something that might upset you." What could a man like Cullen Graber possibly do that would upset her? It couldn't be too serious.

She chuckled. "Then maybe you shouldn't tell me. Likely it would be best I never know."

He stood and took a step back, lowering his head as if burdened with shame. All humor died in her, seeing him so defeated.

"I care for you, Grace. I don't think this surprises you," he said.

She smiled bashfully. Was he afraid she would think less of him for caring for her after what she had done? Quite the opposite, she admired his ability to see over her past mistakes and find himself willing to be present in her life.

"I care for you, too," she admitted.

"Then you have to know this. I was selfish…and did something I shouldn't have."

"If this is about you and Freeman, you don't have to tell me. I figured you said something to him, since he has stopped pestering me," she said with a grin.

Cullen stepped closer and took both her hands. Worry and regret marred his handsome features. Grace felt her heart go out to him. He was serious and troubled. Now she was starting to feel a bit worried about what he was about to tell her.

Cullen opened his mouth, looking as if he was carefully deciding the words he needed. Grace found it adorable. Cullen was always so calm and never flinched at what needed saying. It was nice to see this side of him. He had seen so much of her messy weaknesses, and now she was seeing his.

Three knocks shattered Cullen's next words, and the door behind them opened.

"Hello, Gracie." That was the sound of the last person

Grace had ever expected to be standing in her doorway. Taking a deep breath, sending up a prayer for strength, Grace turned from her future to face her past.

Jared looked even more handsome than she remembered in his military uniform, compared to the boy in jeans and T-shirts she was once accustomed to. He looked older, and larger than before. He was grinning, as if happy to see her. She blinked away the shock of his presence, and the true him reappeared. That disappointed look she had carried here with her when he said he didn't love her and that he had no plans to love the child inside her, either.

Six months had changed a lot, for both of them. Had he not received her letter?

Grace swallowed hard. Jared was a reminder of a place and a family she had missed in the loneliness, and he was also a past that had caused her many tears. She turned to Cullen and slowly lifted her gaze to meet his.

"Is this the bad thing you did. Did you tell him where to find me?" Her voice was shaking, but there was nothing she could do about that as betrayal ran like fire through her veins. What had started out as a day of sewing and baking and fellowship with the people dearest to her had turned faster than a twister on laundry day.

"He certainly didn't tell me a thing," Jared snarled. "In fact, he refused to, as did the rest of your neighbors, but now I can see why." Jared narrowed his gaze at the nearness of Cullen next to her. "I stopped at some Amish buggy shop down the road and they told me where to find you." Of course Grace could count on the Hiltys for this visit. "Now *those* Amish have no problem telling a man what he needs to know."

Grace closed her eyes and swallowed the acidy bile climbing up her throat. With wrecked nerves and an aching back, she wanted to go to her room, slam the door shut. She knew this day might come, hoped it wouldn't, but wasn't truly prepared.

"I wanted to see you," Jared said, stepping farther into the room. "I got your letter."

"Then you should have not *kumm*," she said sharply. "I wrote you not to. We have nothing to say to each other." She didn't dare turn around to read Cullen's thoughts on the matter. She still hadn't decided whether she was angry with him or not.

"You look beautiful," Jared said.

She was as round as a volleyball and swollen from cheeks to toes. It was just one more lie to add to his list of attributes.

He cautiously came closer. Grace took two steps back until she felt the strength and warmth of Cullen against her. He placed a gentle hand on one shoulder and she straightened taller in it. This time, facing the hardships of her life, she knew Cullen was letting her know in his own way that she didn't have to face them alone. He had just admitted to caring for her. Despite already knowing this, she felt the words had been a balm to her scattered concerns.

Like Betty said, *some things in life we have to face head on*, and she was stronger now thanks to Cullen and the friends she had come to know.

Jared shot Cullen an angry glare. "Mind if I talk to the mother of my child alone?" Jared moved closer to her, and

Cullen moved in front of her, directly in Jared's line of sight.

"I have dealt with bigger than you," Jared said to him. "Grace knows I wouldn't put a hand on her, and this is none of your concern. We have things to talk about, so you best scuttle back down to your little cave and play with your hammers."

Cullen stepped forward, and Grace tugged his coat sleeve. "*Nee*. This is not our way."

"I can fix this," Cullen turned back to her and said.

But it was not their way to entertain violence, and knowing Cullen would never let anything or anyone bring her harm brought a lone tear to her eye. The love she felt for this man was overflowing. Those four little words meant more to her than reliable doors and sturdy chairs.

They meant everything.

He *could* fix this, she had no doubt. Proof of his ability to fix the broken stood beside him, looking up at him, and admiring him.

"I know you can. But this is not for you to fix," she said honestly, conviction in her voice. "You didn't break it. Some things a person has to fix by themselves."

His eyes acknowledged her reasoning, and Grace knew he agreed with it, but she also knew he didn't like it.

"Cullen, it is *all recht*." She forced a grin. "Trust me," she said.

Jared cleared his throat. "Grace."

Neither she nor Cullen broke their connection at the sound of Jared's voice. The man who ran away from her, from his responsibilities, wasn't even in the room at all. The same tingle that went from her hand to her hairline returned. She watched Cullen's lips move, avoiding eyes that were lacking faith, and wished she could kiss them and let him know just how much she loved him.

"I don't want to make the same mistakes I once did. There are things I wanted to tell you, things I have…"

"And there are things I want to say to you. But first I must do this. Can't leave the henhouse door open, now can we?" she joked.

One corner of his mouth lifted slightly, but she could see he wasn't convinced of her ability to handle Jared alone. "Go back home. I will see you at Christmas, *jah*?"

He perked up at that, a secret confirmation that she still intended to join him. If he asked her to promise, she wouldn't. The sky might fall or something, and she was no liar. But unless that sky fell, she would be sitting across the table from him at Christmas breakfast. Stella purred against her ankles and Cullen lifted the kitten from the floor and stroked her buttercream coat with a gentleness she knew even a giant his size possessed.

"I will go." He handed her the kitten, his gift on days he was busy making a living. The thought warmed her heart each time she entertained it. "But I won't be happy about it." He grinned and lightly brushed her cheek with the warm crack of his knuckles, his eyes finding her lips.

If they were alone, she imagined he would have kissed her right then. The very thought sent shivers all through her. If the last four minutes were any indication of what a life with Cullen Graber would be like, she was the most blessed woman on earth.

Cullen slowly walked to the door. Jared didn't dare watch him leave but stood like the soldier he was, waiting for Cullen's exit. When the door shut, Grace whispered a silent prayer. "*Gott*, you led me here. You had a plan all along, and I am thankful I can now see it, but please give me your words, for mine are not worthy for what I am about to face."

CHAPTER TWENTY-NINE

"Is that your Amish boyfriend?" Jared jeered, tugging uncomfortably at his dark jacket.

"Why have you *kumm*?" Grace caressed Stella against her to keep her hands busy. Jared stepped farther into the room, stopping short of the chair Cullen had been sitting in all evening.

"I came to see you. So you've lived like this for months, alone?" His dark coffee eyes, now duller than Grace remembered, scanned the room in the time it took her to slow her racing breaths. *Calm*, she reminded herself. She wished she had Cullen's talent, but hard as she tried, Grace knew she didn't.

"I am not alone. I have *Gott* and I have *freinden*." She nuzzled the kitten. "And Stella, of course."

"Friends? Like that blacksmith? Does he come here often?" He lifted a brow, his short-cut hair made an eerie V in the front.

"That is none of your concern. But there is also Elli, Betty, Hannah—she has a little one and we are the same age—and *Aenti* Tess. I have many *freinden* despite being left here," she said in a clipped tone.

"You say that like you're happy." Regret filled the lines of his gathered brows. Was he doubting his reason for coming here?

"I *am*. I will not let you take that this time." She lifted her chin to portray strength.

"Grace, I…I've missed you." His voice had softened. Did he? She once felt that longing. While writing three letters he didn't bother to respond to, she pined for him to come stand by her, commit to her and the future he had promised. Did he know how she assured her family he would, only to have his lie become her own? Now, as he stood there, the epitome of a man capable of doing good, she wanted nothing from him. Felt nothing for him.

"Where have you been, then? A man who misses his family would not be gone so long, would not say he did not care for you or the child he helped create."

"I was in Texas. I still am in Texas, actually, just on leave for a few more days." He wiped his hands down his dark blue britches. He hadn't aged a bit. He looked younger, stronger, and capable of breaking many more hearts.

"What is in Texas?"

"Goodfellow Air Force Base. After basic training in Missouri, I did a four month basic course there. I attend the D.O.D. Fire Academy now."

Grace had no idea what any of that meant. She didn't care.

Sensing her confusion, he added, "I'm training to put out fires and save lives." Was this what Cullen referred to as ironic? She believed so and reined back a grin threatening to surface.

"I am certainly glad you have changed, grown up," she said, hoping to end the conversation.

He crossed the room and took her hand. The dark eyes that once enticed her revealed a hurt. "Grace, I *have* grown up. I can't apologize enough. Please forgive me."

"You are forgiven." She pulled her hand away with a

yank. He had no right to touch her.

"Really? Just like that? I can see you're still angry. You never were one to hide your feelings."

She hated that he knew her that well, but she *wasn't* angry. Not anymore. *Gott* had forgiven her, she had forgiven herself, and anger had no place in any future she wanted for her child.

"I forgive you. No need to yell or stomp. It is *our* way; we are to offer forgiveness to all. If that is what you have *kumm* for, you have it now and may leave. I have much to do." She turned to walk away, at least as far as the sink. Being this close to Jared was now uncomfortable.

"Come back with me," he pleaded.

His request brought her beating heart to a halt. The thought of leaving Walnut Ridge to live with a man she didn't love sent a ripple of pain through her middle. *Not now*, she silently encouraged her anxious *boppli*, stretching inside her. It was enough that her back ached all day, and now the tension of this unwelcomed visitor was spurring what she expected to be a tremendous headache.

Arching her back ever so slightly as to not draw attention, Grace lifted her chin and took a deep breath. She was no longer the girl who trusted sweet words and promises, but a woman, and soon to be a mother who would choose to do what was right and best for her and her child. She had wrestled long enough with deciding whether letting Jared back into her life was right or not.

Jared lived for adventure, for chasing dreams, and she had seen it in him the moment they met. Funny what we chose to ignore when blinded by what we wanted. Grace suppressed a smile just thinking what an adventure she had been sent on. A journey, really, finding herself, meeting wonderful people, gaining wisdom, all the while *not* becoming part of Jared's tempting world, as her father had predicted.

"I want to do the right thing now. We will live near base—it's a bit bigger than this—but you won't have to live the way you always had to. I mean, if I knew your father would send you to live like this, I would have come sooner," he added in a rushed breath. If he truly read all three letters she had written him, he would have known. Another lie on the serpent's tongue.

"You want me to leave the Amish. Leave with a man who ran at the first sign of hardship?" This was who she was. Plain. And Plain was who she would continue to be.

"I said I'm sorry about all that," he said. There was the boy she knew, temper quick to unleash when one couldn't see his way.

She wouldn't indulge him this time. "I am Amish. There is nothing out there worthy of losing that."

"But what about my child? Will you force him to live like this, too? I should have some say in that." Grace had accepted being her child's only parent for so long now, she hadn't considered that. Would he challenge her? She had heard how many *Englisch* divorced and shared their children. Would Jared dare put her through more than he already had? A bead of fear slid down her right temple.

"She will be happy and raised to trust *Gott*."

"You can't possibly want to stay here! Look at this, Grace." Jared waved an arm over the room. "It's not even the size of your *daed*'s smokehouse."

"I won't live here forever." Oh course she wouldn't. The

moment Elmo Hilty saw her in a buggy with Cullen tomorrow, it would all come to an end. Grace could only hope Tess would go against her *daed's* command and take her in. *The Lord will provide*, she whispered to herself.

"Where will you go? You can't do this alone."

Now she allowed herself to smile.

"I am never alone. And where *we*," she patted her middle, "go is up to *Gott*. He will provide just as He has been all this time." And she believed that with all her heart. "When I thought I would go hungry, food was provided to me. When I thought I might freeze, I was warmed by an endless fire." Jared's mouth was open, his eyes wide and looking at her like she was some exotic creature. "When the literal wolves came to my door, I was protected. When I felt lonely and afraid, He sent me *freinden* and safety. I can do all things through Him."

"God won't put a roof over your head, feed you. Come with me," he pleaded now.

How had she ever fooled herself that Jared knew what was best for her? And had he not listened to a single word she had just spoken?

"Why now? Why should I come with you?"

"Because I love you. I still love you. And I don't want to be known as the man who left his pregnant girlfriend to rot on some Amish hillside." That was it—the real reason for his return. Guilt was a hard swallow and she for one knew its resistance.

"Because that would make you look like less of a man?" she asked.

He threw his hands up in the air. "I should have known this was stupid." Jared paced the floor, leaving watery puddles everywhere. "Doesn't our child deserve a father? To be raised with both parents? Thought you believed in that sorta thing."

He was playing on her weaknesses just as he had a winter ago, but he was right, and the weight of it sent tears falling. Jared rushed to her, enveloped her in his arms. "I'm sorry."

Stepping out of arms she had once ached to be held in, Grace wiped the tears from her face and cleared her throat. "I know you are, and I am sorry, too. I see this is hard for you, but I will not leave with you, nor do I want a life with you. We both made a horrible mistake, but we don't have to let it follow us for the rest of our lives. You have this life, a life you talked about endlessly, and I have a hope. If *Gott* had wanted us to be together, then He would not have made us live in different directions. You wanted my forgiveness, but now I think it is time to forgive yourself and make peace with this." Tess's wisdom slipped off her tongue.

"How do I do that?" He hung his head. "How do I walk away? How do I face the men I work with knowing I can never measure up?"

"We can start by praying." She motioned to a chair. "I can show you how to do that before you go."

• • •

Cullen brooded all the way down the hill. Surely Grace would want what was best for her child. And what was best was for them to be raised by their father. Even if she had feelings for Cullen, hopes in a future beside him, Grace would choose the father of her child. Wouldn't she? It was the right thing to do.

Here Cullen thought his heart could never ache more than it already had. He was wrong about that. Grace said she could never leave her faith, but that was when Jared Castle was a distant thought. Now he was a close competitor.

Cullen had to trust Grace, and leave it all in *Gott*'s hands. Grace was right that some things in this world he could not simply fix. "I give it to you, Lord," he said as the flying snow pounded his face.

At the base of the hill sat a cherry red truck. The impulse to kick the tires as he stormed past entered his thoughts. Childish, yes, and the way his day was going, Cullen would most likely break a toe. Not only had he interfered, telling Jared nothing of Grace's whereabouts, but Grace was angry with him for it. He passed the truck and trekked through the growing inches of snow underfoot, looking out across his fields. In the flurry of white the lamplight reflecting from his kitchen window beckoned him in the right direction to the warmth of his home. The home he had hoped just yesterday Grace would one day share with him. Shrugging his coat up higher on his neck, Cullen grumbled all the way through the storm to his empty house.

A woman was the center of the home, the nurturer, the life giver. She would be lost out there in a world that could never love her as he did. The thoughts of her child raised in a world that treated its women so disrespectfully heated his already fueled anger. And what about her child, in that world, instead of here where he would be loved by many?

He brushed away any evidence of fear and worry along with quick-melting flakes still coming down heavily over him and all of Walnut Ridge.

• • •

Grace stepped out into the windy snowfall and wrapped her deep blue shawl around her shoulders. Taking a breath, she listened to the sound of Jared's boots crunching through the snow as he walked over the hill to retrieve his truck parked at the bottom. He should have known by now tires weren't as trusty as a good hoof in matters of snow and mountains.

In hindsight, Grace was glad Jared had *kumm.* Years from now she would never have to look back and regret not getting closure for the both of them. And to know she might have made some difference in his life instead of being the burden he once called her felt surprisingly good.

In the blink of an eye, life changed, and Grace finally felt ready to face it.

The events of the day had worn her ragged, and despite the longing to talk to Cullen filling her, Grace needed some rest. Tomorrow was Christmas, and if there was one thing Grace knew, she could depend on Cullen to show up. She shouldn't have overreacted as she did. Of course he wouldn't have been the most informative when Jared asked for her whereabouts. She hoped he didn't lose any sleep over it. And what better way to share the Lord's big day than with the man she loved by her side? And she did love him, more now than ever, and she would no longer make him wonder if she did. Tomorrow she would tell him how she felt and pray he still felt the same, too.

Pouring herself a warm cup of tea to soothe her nerves, Grace sipped gingerly and readied herself for bed. The ache in her back had not fully disappeared and she hoped for a scratch of sleep regardless of it. She untied her apron and hung it on a nail nearby. Tugging to lift her dress over her head took more effort every day. The wind outside began blowing against the small frame of old wood and time-worn windows. She slipped into her nightgown, leaving on the thick wool socks that would fend off any chill and crawled under the heavy quilt Betty had gifted her.

Hopefully the old shack would not fall so easily as the porch had under Cullen's strong hand. She touched the place on her cheek where his callused knuckles had grazed. Grace closed her eyes, faithful that tomorrow would bring the best Christmas ever.

CHAPTER THIRTY

Grimacing against the ache in her lower back, Grace cautiously rolled to her left side to keep from squashing Stella, who was snuggled against her. The kitten purred and found a warm spot at the lower end of the bed. Moonlight filtered through the foggy window above the mattress, filling the room with a dull blue hue. Comfort was nowhere to be found.

Rising up and sitting on the edge of the bed, Grace rubbed her lower back, massaging firmly the tightness that came and went all day. Perhaps it wasn't the treadle sewing machine that had caused all this discomfort. She took a long breath, trying to remember everything she had read about labor pains in the book *Aenti* Tess had given her.

"It cannot be that," she mumbled to herself. Her stomach may have felt a bit tight, but the pain was in the wrong place for birthing. And did she not have a week still to go? Martha had promised another week. Grace didn't know Martha Shrock all that well, but she couldn't imagine the local midwife who had delivered so many babies being wrong.

The warmth of the cookstove did well to keep what was going on outside from coming in, and she thought maybe she should take another look through the pregnancy book. Surely it held answers that might explain away such pain.

Coming to her feet, she felt every muscle, every organ, and every breath constricted into a knot unwilling to be loosened. When her body slowly regained some sense of normalcy, Grace knew.

"I am in labor!" she shouted. But no one would hear her.

She was alone, and the reality of that forced her to sit back on the bed. Stella appeared at her side, her big smoky eyes and tilted head offering comfort. "You might be making a new *freind* soon, Stella."

Her stomach tightened and her back radiated another wave of pain, as if she had just grabbed hold of her *daed's* solar fencing for the hogs, but didn't let go. She tried to rationalize her next move. If she was in labor, it could be hours; that was what all the women had told her. First time was always the hardest and longest. There was plenty of time to get to Cullen's and wake him to get her to Martha's. The midwife would know what to do.

"It's too soon," she cried in panicky breaths. She needed to get to Cullen. She could depend on him despite the weather, but first she needed to rely on her ability to get herself to him.

The pain only dulled but never left completely. Grace clumsily managed to get into her heavy coat and the oversized chore boots Hannah had given her. Willed by anticipation or by worry, she wasn't certain, she took three calming breaths to slow her racing heart.

Hand palmed against the shack wall, she gritted her teeth through another round of pains. The moment the pressure eased, she quickly wrapped her scarf around her head and neck, gathered up her lamp, and tucked Stella into the folds of her gown under her coat. "Don't be scratching me now. It's behave or be left behind," Grace ordered between gritted teeth.

If Grace and her child were to get through this, she was going to have to walk down this hill and get help for them both.

Another pain and she held the door handle, squeezing it through all she was enduring. What felt like an eternity passed, but when the pain eased this time, a warm liquid poured to the wooden floor. Like a bucket tipped over, it spread all around her, dampening her socks and now the inside of her boots. There were no doubts now.

Grace sprang into action. There wasn't time to change into fresh clothes. Her child was coming into the world—tonight.

· · ·

Cullen flipped over again. He couldn't slow his mind enough to get any sleep tonight. There was so much muddling it. He had been eager to tell Grace how he felt, what he and Tess had done for her, but Jared had interrupted that. If his smooth tongue had enticed her before, Cullen feared it would again. He eyed the cradle in the corner, and for a moment he wished it could remain there. Running his fingers through his dark hair, he pondered what a life with Grace would be like. If he kept his wits about him, he could convince her to stay. Even if he had to make a fool of himself and beg.

Surely she had to know his love for her would never fade or retreat in hard times; it would always be present. He flipped again, pulling an extra pillow to his chest.

The wind outside was picking up. A faint cry carried

into the night, and he listened intently to what poor animal had found itself outside in distress. He couldn't imagine even coyotes willing to scavenge on a night like tonight.

The sound came again. He alerted. Not a cry from a wounded animal but a person.

This time, Cullen was on his feet without a second thought. Jumping into his pants and heavy coat, he scooped up his hat and flashlight. Outside, snow pelted his face, and he pulled his hat down tighter, more to keep it from flying away than serving as a shield against blowing snow.

It was Grace he heard, he was certain of it.

"Grace!" He bellowed through the wind, but no reply came.

Squinting against the elements, he shouted again. The moon dodged in and out, playing tricks with the shadows, but he kept searching ahead, hoping he had not lingered too far from the road leading up the hill. Snow slid inside his pull-on boots. "Grace!"

He slid against something firm and righted himself back to his feet. His flashlight served little use against the beast of winter. His body froze when her scream came again. Lifting his gaze to the center of the hill, Cullen made out a small, darkened shape. He dragged through the three feet of drifting snow with determined urgency. It was like pushing through water.

Thankfully, God had made him strong. Her cries were painful to hear carried on the howl of this horrid stormy night. Jared had left hours ago, so what could have forced Grace from her warm little cabin to go tramping out into the storm?

There could be only one thing that would send Grace

out here. A new kind of panic washed over him when it all became clear.

Cullen reached Grace, but she was nothing but arms and damp hair under a bed of white, buried beneath the snow. A trail of patchy crimson stained the snow all the way down the hill, and he feared the worst. Tess Miller's account of her own terrible ordeal flashed in his mind's eye.

"I am here," he said in deep breaths. Not taking time to ask her condition, for all evidence proved that Grace was in serious need of help, Cullen scooped her into his arms and made his way back to the house. Her head fell to his shoulder, and she muttered something he couldn't make out. He peered down at her briefly, seeing Stella poke her head out of Grace's neckline. He should have known she would not have left Stella behind, even in her condition. It was just one more reason he loved her.

With the house in sight, Cullen pushed himself harder through the wind and snow to get Grace indoors. "I need to get you inside where it is warm, then I will go fetch help."

Her body tensed, and with a strength he now knew even a woman her size could possess, she squeezed his neck and shoulder until her muscles loosened again. A week early or not, this child was coming. Caught somewhere between fear and anticipation, Cullen plowed forward with more determination. Babies were born every day, under all kinds of circumstances, and this was the strongest woman he knew. Still, the need to do everything he could to ensure her safety and that of her child pressed down on him.

Once inside, Cullen carried Grace straight to the room

that once belonged to his parents. Laying her carefully on the bed, he felt her arms refuse to let go of the death grip she had on him.

"Cullen!" Another pain appeared to come, and the tiny soft-spoken voice he had come to know for months now rose, filling the whole house with an agonizing cry. Stella freed herself and darted at lightning speed from her cloak of cover, hitting the floor with inherent agility before disappearing into the next room.

He knew the feeling. Fleeing had its advantages. Seeing Grace in pain was his undoing. No wonder many men chose not to participate in such a horrid thing. Grace released him and fell back against his healthy stack of pillows.

"Grace, my *lieb*, try to relax," he encouraged while removing her shoes and damp coat.

She was barely clothed, in nothing more than a gown and thick, damp socks. He shrugged away any need to avoid seeing her in this hair-down, barely-dressed state. Grace needed his help.

Cullen shed his own coat and hat and quickly removed the wet wool stockings from her tiny feet. Fetching a pair of his own thick socks from the nearby dresser, Cullen worked them over her frozen toes. The storm outside picked up momentum again, crashing its heaving breath against his home. It was nothing short of a miracle that he had heard her at all. Another few minutes and she would have had frostbite for sure.

Once her feet were dry and warm, Cullen covered her in a heavy quilt. The wild look in her eyes, the bewilderment of what was happening, tore at him.

"I'm here." Leaning down, he kissed her forehead, hoping something in him transferred, helped her. Her eyes said it did and she even offered a weary smile.

"I need to hitch the buggy and go for help." But who? His mind scrambled for what was best right now. "Should I go for Martha? She is on the other side of the valley. Or your *aenti*? What about Elli? I can make the hill if I hitch Jax, and she is the nearest behind Tess." At this point he wasn't sure, but he had to get someone. What did he know about babies and what needs women had while birthing them?

"I thought my back was hurting all day because of the sewing machine, or Jared showing up out of the nowhere, and you and rabbit gravy and reading Luke."

Cullen didn't understand her rambling, interrupted by another wave of pain. She gritted her teeth through a held breath.

"Grace, tell me who you need."

"I have been in labor all day. It is too soon, Cullen. It is not the right time." Her eyes widened in fear and worry, and when her small frame lunged forward again, he held her there. Sitting on the edge of the bed, Cullen supported her as best he could. He would fetch Tess, bring her back, then go for Elli—that's what he would do. If it took the rest of the night, he was committed to have every woman in Walnut Ridge helping her. It was a good plan. Grace needed them and needed him to decide for her. No sooner had her body relaxed, Grace lunged forward again.

"I need to…" Another cry for mercy. Cullen's heart couldn't take it much more. The woman he loved was dying, or at least he thought she was. Surely it wasn't supposed to be this way.

"I need to get you to a hospital, Grace. I will go ready the buggy," he said, rising to his feet, but she grabbed his hand. Was she having another pain so soon? No, nothing felt normal about any of this.

"*Nee*," she said as her face dampened from the workout her body was putting her through. Did she not see if she was not at the hospital, she could lose her child and maybe even her life?

"Grace, this is no time to be stubborn. Your and the *boppli*'s life depend on it. I have to get you to the hospital regardless of this storm."

She shook her head, then quickly used his hand to pull herself forward again. "This is not happening," she screamed. He waited, though he thought best against it, until the pain slowed again.

"I love you, Cullen," she cried out. Was she delirious with pain? When she reached out for him, Cullen kneeled by her side. Her small fingers gripped his shoulder and despite what agony her body was enduring, she smiled. "I love you." It was probably not the best time for it, but Cullen couldn't help but lean over and give her a quick hard kiss.

"I love you, too, Grace Miller, but dear, I need to get you to the hospital so I can love you longer."

Those big blue eyes depended on him. "I will go hitch the buggy." He leaned forward and quickly kissed her lips again. It wasn't the first kiss he had hoped for, but it did wonders to calm his racing heart.

"Cullen." Her eyes widened once more. Her hand left his shoulder and slowly gripped the quilt into a tight ball.

"I do not know how to say this to you, but there is no time for a hospital. I need to push!" That, Cullen knew the meaning of.

He sucked in a deep breath and took a step back, wrapping his head around the situation. "*Gott* help me, help her," he prayed. Cullen gathered his wits and surveyed the situation at hand. She needed calm Cullen, strong Cullen. He could do strong and calm. He would just have to pretend.

Clutching the sleeve of his arm, she lunged forward again, and this time Cullen knew she was pushing to bring the child forth. The moment she relaxed, he stacked pillows behind her and rushed to the kitchen. Setting a pan of fresh water on the stove, he dipped two washcloths in it and went to fetch fresh linens from the hall closet, leaving wet boot prints all over the house. Watching farm animals birth over the years, he knew he would have to cut the cord and clamp it shut. *Daed* sprayed the cords, but he wasn't going to do that to his child.

My child.

The sudden thought hit him like a wave, fast and sure. If Grace accepted him, this would be his child, as he promised the bishop he was ready to claim. "My *boppli*," he whispered. The hope of knowing he was about to meet him or her, sent his heart pounding in a whole new way. He and Grace would both be welcoming this new life into the world. Hope filled him so full, Cullen couldn't help but smile.

He quickly scrambled through his father's desk drawers and found the scissors. Was this really happening? "You got this," he muttered to himself—a self-assurance greatly needed right now. There was really no time to do more than handle the matter at hand.

With arms full, he began to pray like he had never done before. Not like this, and certainly not since becoming a man. Nothing else mattered but the two people in the next room, and he prayed *Gott* gave him the wisdom and courage to help them both get safely through this night.

Inside his bedroom, Cullen placed a cool rag on Grace's head. She looked up to him and smiled. "You are about to meet the love of your life, my dear." Despite what she was enduring, the thoughts of finally holding her child in her arms clearly outweighed them. She was excited, ready, and now so was he.

"I am sorry you had to be —"

He stopped her. "I am not. I want it no other way. To be here with you, waiting for this little miracle to *kumm,* is more than I could have ever hoped for." He melted in her gaze and she took hold of his hand again.

"Me neither," Grace confessed and squeezed his hand. Every inch of his being warmed in the love that had grown between them, and soon that love would grow a little more. "There are so many things I want to say to you," she started, and rose forward again.

"Remove your *mutter*'s quilt," she said. He quickly did as she asked.

"Are you ready to meet your *sohn*, Grace?" He certainly was.

"*Dochder*," she corrected sharply. When her chin tucked towards her chest again, Cullen knew to help her lean forward. Grace brought her gown to her knees and locked her hands tight. In one long held breath, she let go to reach forward and retrieve what she worked so hard for.

Cullen was in awe. It happened in a blink, not the lengthy time he always thought such things to be. And Grace had never needed him at all. The woman was remarkable.

He hurried to cover the baby's dark pink flesh as Grace swept the infant's mouth. Crying filled the room in a parade of joyous pulsating wails. Nothing sounded more pleasant in all his life than the cries spilling out of the tiny body in her hands. Cullen chuckled.

Grace peered up and met his gaze. Tears of pure joy filled the bright pools of her eyes. Wiping his cheek, Cullen tended to Grace's dampness as well. Every detail, from the flush of her labors warming her delicate skin, to the soft elated laughter spilling from her, reinforced that Grace was the strongest and bravest woman he had ever known.

She had fallen and sinned, repented and confessed. She had faced harshness, abandonment, and loneliness. Grace had fought off wolves at her door and those inside her soul. Most importantly, Grace had healed a man who thought all his love had died years ago, awakening him to a second chance and a new start. Grace had walked through a snow storm to get help and delivered her child practically alone.

"She has your lungs," he said playfully.

CHAPTER THIRTY-ONE

Morning brought with it a calm after a night of blizzarding calamity. Cullen wrung his hands over and over for so long, they became raw. "You're gonna need those, might wanna treat them kinder," Abram teased. When he and Grace hadn't shown up at Elli's for Christmas breakfast, half of Walnut Ridge arrived at his door. "Where did the kitten come from?"

"She belongs to Grace." Having Grace in the other room with Tessie and Martha for over an hour was more stressful than the moment he realized Grace was going to give birth.

"Cullen, where is the coffee?" Elli asked with a bit of impatience in her tone. He shook his head, glad she was in the kitchen and out of view of him doing so. Poor woman had paced the floor more than he had, and he was glad she finally made use of her energy. He stepped into the kitchen doorway.

"Second shelf, of that cabinet there," he pointed to the old cherry cabinet his father had built before he was born.

His bedroom door opened, and Cullen, Abram, Bishop Mast, and Elli all came to attention. Propelled forward to inquire about Grace and their daughter, Cullen didn't concern himself with how desperate he appeared to everyone. "How are they?" This had to be what a new *daed* felt like, all anxious and afraid, overjoyed and blessed.

"Well, I believe she was a fortunate one for sure and certain, but Grace and Abigale seem to be doing just fine."

Abigale? Cullen lifted a brow in surprise. His mother's name.

Martha patted his arm and smiled. "I will return to look in on them again. Abram agreed to bring me, so you just keep her warm and fed and keep her to that bed. She is quite the stubborn one," Martha said with a grin on her face. He knew that, and it made him smile, too.

Martha reached for her heavy coat and shawl, her plump cheeks reddened from the cold burn of the wind, and motioned to Abram that she was ready to leave.

"But Grace said it was too early. Isn't there a chance of complications?" The baby was so small, how could one be certain. Was he questioning a woman who had delivered dozens of babies, a woman who had delivered *him*?

"Rest assured, that is one healthy set of girls you got in there. You can go see them now." *My girls*. What a lovely sentiment. "I don't suggest that she move around much today. As with all women after birthing, she needs to limit her outings. Stay close to home, I mean. She will need a few things, but I will speak to Elli and Tess about that."

Cullen looked back to the bishop. Grace wasn't his wife, and this wasn't her home. This would not be a proper arrangement, but if the bishop insisted, he already decided he would leave before she would have to return to the cabin up the hill. Everything she needed was here, and here she could be looked over much easier than at the cabin. Maybe he could convince Tess to stay here until Grace was up on her feet.

Bishop Mast stepped forward, "I am sure Cullen will see to it that Grace follows your orders. And the womenfolk will stop in and see she and the *boppli* are doing well and have the things they need." A smile passed between them. Bishop Mast leaned closer. "Shall I return after Second Christmas to speak with the two of you?" The bishop was referring to the counseling he offered to all courting couples who planned to marry.

Cullen blushed at the comment and nodded. Of course he hoped the bishop would be announcing an upcoming wedding soon, too. That was, if Grace meant what she said. He shook off any lingering doubts. She loved him. Not just her lips confessed it but her eyes spoke it, too. He cleared the disturbing thoughts and anxiously swept by Martha, pushing his way inside his bedroom. A parade of laughter followed him.

"Hey," he whispered, not wanting to wake the bundle sleeping in her arms.

"I can't believe we did it. She is perfect. Just look at her, Cullen." Grace's eyes were the brightest he had ever seen. No longer were they stormy and wild but the color of sapphires and deep blue lakes, glimmering with hope and excitement for the future she would have with her daughter. How she was not exhausted after everything amazed him.

"Can I see her?" he asked.

Grace grinned and nodded. Cullen went to the side of the bed and sat gently on the edge. Round cheeks, dark hair, lips kissed by roses. The child was beautiful in every way, a perfect image of her mother. She stirred and began crying. Like her mother, she could go from sweet to angry rather swiftly.

Cullen chuckled under his breath and lifted her into his arms, surprising himself by how comfortable something so weightless and fragile felt in his large hands. Abigale quickly quieted and nestled into comfort, sucking her bottom lip, and he marveled at the overwhelming cuteness of her. After a few moments, his attention went to Grace, surprised to find her staring at him, a look of contentment on her face. They locked gazes, lingered there.

"I like the cradle," she said, not taking her eyes off him. With everything happening so fast he forgot to put it away before she noticed it. Then again, it was Christmas now, was it not?

"I hoped you would." He couldn't decide who he wanted to look at more and settled on Grace.

"I am sorry I intruded on your house. Martha says I can go back to the shack in a couple days."

"You can stay here. I want you to stay here. I can go fetch your things shortly. I just want to hold her a little longer." He rocked slightly and took in the fresh, innocent scent of Abigale. "I got you another gift as well."

She smiled shyly and sat up, closing the space between them. "You have done plenty for the both of us."

"Don't ya wanna know what it is?" He wanted to kiss her right now, insides bursting, and instead focused on the little girl still resting in his arms, an easy distraction.

"*Aenti* Tess told me about Elmo's land and the sinner's shack," she said. "I had to beg her not to burn it down after all the work we put into it." He wished she would stop calling it that. "Tess told me a lot of things. I cannot believe all you have done for us. You changed my life, Cullen. I don't think you will ever know how much that means to me." She pulled a small chunky arm from the blanket and caressed it.

"You changed mine as well," he brushed her cheek and warmed at the ease with which she leaned into his palm. Suddenly her head jerked upright.

"It's Christmas and I never finished your gift."

"*Jah*, you did," he smiled stroking a small finger with his. "And she is perfect. But I have another gift."

"Cullen, you have given so much." Her voice shook with tenderness.

"I want to give you my heart." He shook his head. "You have had it since the day I found you with a hammer in your hand trying to dismantle the porch," he confessed. "I want you to stay, here, with me." Her eyes glistened, her breaths quickened.

"I come with a *boppli*. With a past and…" Cullen hushed her with a finger to her lips.

"We all have a past. I want all of this. I want you and her. You gave me a reason to want to be more than I was. You wouldn't just let me be. You kept bugging me to worry about you," he said. She laughed, a sound he found as pleasing as songbirds in spring. "You made me hope, forgive, and remember."

"Remember?"

"That I still have so much love to give. We cannot take it with us, so I might as well use it." He was nervous, rambling. Why couldn't he just get out the words he practiced?

"You sure are a romantic, Cullen Graber." Grace said

playfully. God he loved this woman.

Both looking down at Abigale, he felt some of that love already attached. "*Gott* has blessed us. We thought we didn't deserve second chances, and here he gave us both mercy and a little Christmas grace."

"He did," she said as if just now feeling His mercy and grace upon her. With tears slipping freely down her cheeks, her radiant blue eyes stared at him as if he were the only man on earth. He leaned forth and gently thumbed away the moisture on her left cheek. "I can fix that." His hand cradled her neck, his heart thumping as wildly as her own pulse.

"I have no doubt," she leaned forward and met his lips halfway. Voices rose in the next room, more visitors having arrived, but neither of them cared. When they parted, Cullen leaned back and admired every detail of her swollen lips and bursting blue eyes.

"Marry me. Marry me, Grace Miller," he said in a labored breath. "I need you in my life. I want you beside me in all things." He had rehearsed sweet words, practiced what he would say when the time came, but if there was one thing Cullen learned in his years it was that life didn't always go as planned. And he was so grateful for it.

"I cannot imagine a life without you beside me. I love you, Cullen Graber and nothing would make us happier than to be yours."

In the open doorway, Elli stood holding two cups of something warm in her hands. Cullen watched her and Grace exchanged grins, like some secret he wasn't privy to.

Grace turned to him again. "You want to tell them, or

should I?" He would never tire of that smile.

"I think they already know." With Abigale in one arm and Grace in the other, Cullen thanked the Lord out loud for his abundance in blessing.

"Merry Christmas, little Grace."

Elli stepped into the room, followed by all the souls that had helped them along the way.

EPILOGUE

One year later

"Look at them," Charity whispered. "We have been blessed." Grace leaned down and reached into the cradle, tucking the soft blanket around Finley's small body. Her nephew was the image of Charity, but those pouting lips were Mercy's for sure and certain.

"*Jah*, we have sister," Grace said with a full heart.

"Abigale has more hair than you did. Do you think she even knew it was her birthday?"

"She knows any day with ice cream is special." Grace suppressed a chuckle.

"Have you told him yet?" Charity passed her a knowing grin. Grace blushed. She still couldn't believe that after a year of marriage she could still blush.

"It was Abigale's special day," Grace said.

"A Christmas present perhaps." Charity nudged her shoulder. Grace laughed off her silliness and stepped toward the door.

"*Kumm*, let's let them sleep while we finish the dishes." The sisters slipped from the bedroom, leaving the cousins to slumber until Christmas morn.

In the kitchen, Cullen and Mike were finishing off the last of the cake, while Mercy and Hope were seeing that the ice cream had no chance of melting. Grace couldn't help but smile. She long thought staying in Walnut Ridge, marrying Cullen, would have put further distance between her and her sisters. She had been wrong about that.

The decision to allow Grace and Cullen to marry in February had been met with delight by her sisters and the community. Faith and Charity both stood as attendants while *Mutter* cried and *Daed* sat stiff. Betty was right saying Grace couldn't change his heart; that was for *Gott* to do. But his presence felt like a beginning.

Since the wedding, he hadn't visited again, but *Mutter* had come when Faith and Hope visited in the spring to help with spring gardening. Abigale would never know how her very being put a light in *Mutter*'s eyes Grace had only caught flickers of over the years. A *boppli* was a miracle, in so many ways, and *Mutter* took her *mammi* role seriously. Her first grandchild, and now with a third on the way, Grace expected many more visits with her *mutter*.

"We have three more cabinetmakers in our area. Makes it hard to provide for your family and I was worried I would have to find another trade, but Abram says he could use the help," Mike said, stopping Grace in her tracks.

"What are you two talking about?" Grace asked. Mercy and Hope snickered. Cullen leaned back in his chair and smiled that way he did when he was about to deliver good news.

"Well, my dear, I was hoping to have Mike here help with adding to the *haus kumm* spring in exchange for me helping them build their own. I just hope Abram doesn't keep him too busy working at the furniture shop to do it," Cullen said.

Grace pivoted around to face Charity, beaming. "You're moving here?" Her voice hitched.

Charity burst with equal emotion. "*Jah. Aenti* Tess is

letting us stay in the cabin now that the Weiss family who lost their home in that fire has left to go live with family. Abram and Elli Schwartz are as kind as you wrote about. Abram has been talking with Mike each time we visit, and well…" Charity lifted her shoulders. "He wants Mike to work in his shop and we found land nearby that is perfect."

Grace flung her arms around her sister's neck, tears pouring happily down both their cheeks.

"Finley and Abigale will grow up together," Charity said with a happy sob as they pulled apart. "We will be returning as soon as the weather breaks. That will give us time to get things in order."

"This is the best Christmas present I could ever receive. My sister will be living here with me." Grace turned to face Cullen, who was wearing his most trusting grin.

"You two cry at the drop of a hat," Hope teased, coming to her feet to join in the hug. "And don't think I will be moving. I love my job at the market too much to live in a shack on a hillside. Not enough land to plow a flower patch." Hope quirked a grin.

Mercy rolled her eyes and joined them. "Sister hugs." The lot of them stood there, heads connected for a time. "Grace, don't be disappointed, but I like that you live far away. Lets me travel with an excuse." Mercy never could sit still long.

"And now you will have twice the reason to travel often." Grace kissed her cheek.

Cullen scooted his chair back, making a loud scraping noise as he did, and got to his feet. "Well, my dear, I think now is a *gut* time to take my beautiful *fraa* for a ride."

"I need to finish up in here and we still have sweet rolls

to make for Christmas breakfast before church," Grace said.

"Abigale is asleep and you know nothing wakes her once she is down," Cullen grinned shyly. "Charity and Mercy are tending to all the baking."

Grace turned to find both her sisters smiling. Did they know something she didn't?

"Now *kumm* and don't give it a second thought. I have something to show you." He lifted her coat from the hook and held it out to her. Grace choked up as she recounted her blessings. She was surrounded by love on all sides.

"Just go, Grace. We got this. It's Christmas; spend some quiet time with your *ehemann*." Charity smirked as if she knew what was coming.

The ride through the snow-covered valley reminded Grace of the night Cullen almost kissed her. Moonlight illuminated the fields and forest in a bluish hue. When Cullen turned right, instead of left out of the valley, Grace shifted in her seat.

"Where are we going?"

"To where it all began." He leaned over, kissed her cheek. Grace felt her stomach flutter just as she had that night, too. He would always stir butterflies within her.

Once they reached the cabin, Cullen helped Grace down from the buggy. He clasped her hand in his as they both stared at the little house. The window boxes no longer held the vibrant flowers they had all summer, thanks to Claire Weiss, but new wood, the added laundry and bathroom, gave it a charming appeal that she figured Charity would enjoy. Just the thought of her sister, brother-in-law, and nephew living nearby sent another wave of joy jolting through her.

"This feels all too familiar." The corners of Cullen's mouth tugged up in a suggestion of a smile. His hands were warm, his clasp firm. Was he thinking, too, how far they'd come since that first meeting?

"More than you know." Grace smiled back. "Now, *ehemann*, tell me why we are here?"

He urged her up the long porch and turned the brass knob without saying a word. She didn't protest his secrecy; in fact she felt giddy about it.

When they stepped inside, Grace was surprised to find the cabin warm and welcoming and smelling of pine. On the table sat pine cones and candles and a poinsettia like the one Elli gifted her one year ago. Two lamps lit up the small space that now sported a couch, four chairs, and a new sink. The Weiss family had made little improvements here and there, blessed to have a roof over their heads when all was taken from them as their home burned months ago. Grace remembered the feeling of such a blessing, and the quilt over the couch, like the dishes in the pantry, were her little touches added, too.

"I was hoping to spend a little private time with my amazing *fraa*. Maybe discuss Abigale becoming a sister." Cullen's gaze grew dark, in that way that always made her insides tremble. Her cheeks flamed, but she welcomed the warmth. He leaned down, brushed his lips over hers softly, and then deepened the kiss. Grace melted under his hand, felt dizzy on his love. When he had snuck away to do this for her, she didn't know. Cullen was more the romantic than he let on. When they parted, she led him to the next door and paused.

"I should tell you that isn't necessary. We don't need to discuss it." She touched her middle, looked up, and smiled. Cullen's brown eyes went wide, then he lifted her off the floor and spun her while his lips rested on hers. Holding her suspended, he leaned his forehead into hers and laughed.

"We could pretend I haven't told you yet," she said playfully.

Cullen reached behind him and turned the handle. "I like the way you think," he said, and carried her inside.

ACKNOWLEDGMENTS

I would like to offer my heartfelt thanks to the following:

The Amish communities of Fleming, Kentucky, for answering questions and teaching me just how imperfect we all are.

My mother for pushing me forward.

My husband, Mike, for being my proofreader and cheering me on.

My children for inspiring me. I cherish our every adventure together.

My agent, Julie, for seeing potential, offering guidance, and believing in me. I am forever indebted and look forward to our future ventures together.

The amazing Entangled team: Stacy, Heather, Curtis, Elizabeth, and Liz for taking a chance on a debut author. We learned a lot from each other on this endeavor.

What happens when a female horse whisperer butts heads with a traditional male wrangler within the quiet Amish community of Honey Brook?

Turn the page to start reading The Amish Cowboy's Homecoming *by* USA Today *bestselling author Ophelia London*

the
AMISH
COWBOY'S
HOMECOMING

CHAPTER ONE

Isaac King slowly ran his finger down the center of her nose, ever so gently.

"Morning, sweetheart."

He felt her take in a breath, responding to his simple touch.

When she made a sound, he stepped closer, placing a hand on the side of her face. "I know, I know," he whispered, looking into her eyes. "I hate to leave, but it's something I have to do." With both hands now, he gently caressed all the way down her neck. Then, when there was nothing more to say, he touched his forehead to hers, taking in a deep breath. She smelled of earth and energy but mostly like…oats and molasses.

"Easy there, girl." Isaac laughed as the surefooted, petite Haflinger horse shook her head. "You know I could never leave you for long. It's just a day or two, and then we'll see what happens—probably nothing." He exhaled, trying to stay optimistic. He looked up into the blue-sky morning, feeling a slight flutter in his stomach.

This could be it, he thought, though not wanting to get his hopes up too high. *This could be my way out.* Our *way out.* With a lump in his throat, he glanced toward the house. No one was awake yet. That was good. He'd said his goodbyes to Sadie last night before he tucked her in bed. That had been hard enough—he didn't want to go through it again.

After giving his *gaul*—the one he'd had since he was just a boy—one more stroke down her nose, he knew it was time to stop procrastinating. Sunny wouldn't be coming with him on this trip, though she'd accompanied him everywhere else he'd ever gone. She was getting on in age, and this time, he wouldn't be needing a horse to just pull a buggy. Scout would be his travel mate.

From just thinking the fella's name, he heard the deep *neigh* coming from two stalls over.

Isaac grabbed his saddle, reins, and the rest of the tack off the back of the gate. "*Jah, jah,*" he said while approaching his white mount. "You excited, boy?" He laughed, patting his strongest, hardest-working horse—the one he could always count on. The one who would see him through what might be the most important moments of his life.

After leading Scout out of the barn, Isaac gave him a few extra minutes of brushing. Yes, he was stalling again. "Okay, time to go." He threw another glance toward the house. If he didn't hurry, his in-laws would be waking up soon and maybe try to talk him out of this. The buggy was already packed for an overnight stay if needed, and he had a fresh change of clothes on a sturdy wooden hanger in the way back of the carriage. He smoothed the front of his hair down and slid on his favorite straw hat. The one shaped more like an Englisher "cowboy" hat than a traditional Amish one, with the round brim.

He easily recalled when that hat had been given to him as a gift. As he clicked his tongue, prompting Scout to walk, he pulled down the front brim, ready for business. He could've had one of his Mennonite friends drive him the thirty miles in a car, but the four-hour buggy ride would give him time to think, more time to mentally prepare.

He'd been over every angle dozens of times. He'd sought counsel from his brother and good friends, but mostly he'd prayed his heart out. This route, this very road he was on right now, was the path that felt right. This brought a certain amount of peace to his heart, though potentially taking his little family away from home might be the hardest thing he'd ever have to do.

The early-morning spring sunshine shone down an hour or so later—time to give Scout a break, and Isaac needed to stretch his legs. Maybe do some jumping jacks, try to pop that tight area on his lower back. He might've worked the new draft horse too hard yesterday. If Isaac himself was sore, Nelly would be, too. His stomach dropped slightly, always regretting when he overworked a horse—he cared so much about the animals, especially the ones that had come to him from rescue situations. Those were always extra special to Isaac.

He gave Scout a few additional rubs and scratches down his neck. When the retired racer had first been brought to him, the poor horse had been worked nearly to death. Even though violence had never been a part of his personality, Isaac would've loved five minutes alone with the person who'd done that to a helpless *gaul*.

All these thoughts were still going through his mind when he arrived in Honey Brook. Following the careful directions given to him, he took the last stretch down a long, winding road past several well-kept dairy farms. While at the top of the hill, Isaac easily saw the horse ranch—the large telltale pasture ring in the front of the property giving it away. As he drew near, he noticed someone was in that ring with a horse. Probably John Zook, the owner of the property and the man who just might be his future boss.

Wanting to quietly observe the man's technique — wondering how well it would match up with his own — Isaac slowed the buggy, then tied Scout to a nearby hitch. The closer he got, the more he noticed how tall the horse was. The caramel-colored gelding looked to be about twenty hands high. A giant.

Isaac neared the white fence, his curiosity getting the better of him. But now, the closer he got, he noticed it wasn't that the horse was tall; it was that John Zook was short. Very short and quite slim, more like a teenage boy than a grown man. Isaac tilted his head. Was John Zook wearing a…dress? That was definitely a blue top with a long black apron. The skirt of the dress, however, was hiked up, tied in the back. And were those pants underneath?

Isaac felt a smile slowly spread across his face when he realized it wasn't a grown man or a boy working with the horse but a young woman, though she was petite and probably no more than nineteen years old at most.

"Good day," he said, using the Englisher greeting instead of "*Guder daag*," the traditional Amish phrase, though he was pretty sure she was Amish. She dropped the long stick she was holding and spun around. He hadn't meant to startle her. Even her horse let out a little whinny.

"Oh," she said, sounding out of breath while pushing back loose strands of hair that had fallen out of her *kapp*. "Morning." She looked at him for another moment then began dusting off the layer of dirt from the front of her dress. After probably realizing it was no use, she lowered her chin and smiled—but it seemed that smile hadn't been meant for Isaac. By the way she was looking off to the side, she was smiling at something personal. A private memory?

For some reason, this intrigued Isaac.

Without speaking again, she returned to her task, working the pretty gelding to trot in a circle.

Isaac leaned an elbow on the top rung of the fence and watched, a bit captivated now, for she seemed to know what she was doing. Though the stick never touched the horse, she kept it right at his peripheral vision, so he would know it was there but receiving no harm.

"This the Zook's Horse Training Farm?" Isaac asked.

"Aye," the woman said without looking at him. The ties of her black prayer *kapp* were caught in a breeze as more of her hair came spilling out. It was brown, reminding Isaac of someone else in his life—someone who used to be in his life. "If you're looking for John Zook," she added, "he's in the house."

She switched the stick to her left hand so she was holding the lead rope in her right. Without missing a beat, the obedient horse did an elegant turn, his hoofs keeping perfect time, trotting in the other direction, steps high.

Isaac was taken aback. He hadn't known many Amish who preferred the English style of riding over the more common Western, especially if all you needed was a strong horse to pull a plow or an obedient one to lead a buggy.

"Impressive," he couldn't help saying. "How did this *gaul* come to you?"

"Pardon?" she said, tossing back her skirt in a manner that seemed unexpectedly feminine.

Isaac stepped onto the bottom rung of the fence so he could observe her more closely. "Where did you get this horse?"

Before replying, the woman began slowing the gelding's speed, gently pulling in the lead one inch at a time. When he was close to her, she leaned in and whispered something Isaac couldn't hear.

"Honey Pot came as a new foal," she finally answered, leading the horse toward the fence.

Isaac couldn't help lifting his brows. "Honey Pot?"

The woman was close enough now that when she smiled again, he noted a dimple in her right cheek, making her look…maybe not younger but much more innocent… and rather pretty, despite her tomboy exterior.

Even simply noticing that another woman was attractive caused an illogical knot of guilt to form in Isaac's stomach.

"I think it fits him quite well," she replied, turning to the horse, running a hand down his neck. "Though I didn't name him."

"So he didn't come like that?"

"Like what?"

He was about to say "so well trained" but didn't. "Nothing," he said instead, not wanting to insult her if she'd helped train him in the English style. But how likely was that? Isaac knew very few—if any!—Amish women who took more than a passing interest in horse training.

Martha didn't, he couldn't help thinking, that misplaced guilt returning. But then he forced a smile, thinking of Sadie. There wasn't a bigger horse lover than her, and she was always very interested in what he did.

"What's the joke?"

He looked over at the woman. She was shading her eyes from the bright afternoon sun. "Joke?" he asked.

"*Jah.*" She patted Honey Pot. "The way you're smiling, like you're thinking of something funny."

"Not funny exactly," he replied, noticing that the loose strands of her hair had flashes of red. And her eyes were blue. What was the sudden impulse he felt to wipe the streak of dirt off her cheek?

Not wanting to reveal what he was thinking, he blurted, "Yes, I was remembering a joke."

She turned to face him squarely, one corner of her mouth lifting. "*Jah?*"

"Uh." Isaac dusted off his hands, stalling. "Ever heard the one about the Mennonite and his favorite cow?"

After a short pause, the woman lifted her chin and started laughing. It was loud but also purely female, maybe because her voice was a lovely soprano, high like a bell. "Oh gracious!" she said between laughs. "You sound like my brother." She waved a hand in the air. "And all his friends." She cleared her throat and dusted off one shoulder. "Aye, I know all about the Mennonite and his cow."

While watching her, Isaac grew even more intrigued. Who was this woman? And how could she be both feminine *and* act like one of the guys?

"Anyway," she said when the silence stretched on for too long. "Best be getting back to work."

Isaac nodded. He needed to pull his thoughts together so he would be prepared for his meeting with John Zook. Last thing he needed was to be preoccupied by a dimple and a pair of captivating blue eyes.

The woman clicked her tongue, causing Honey Pot to stand at attention. She then clicked another three times, and the horse began to trot in the same circle as before, front knees high, chin tucked. Despite how he needed to focus elsewhere, Isaac couldn't stop watching.

She lifted the stick, reached it out, and tapped at the horse's chest. Suddenly, the *gaul* reared up. The woman stepped toward it boldly, tapping at its chest again. "*Hör mir zu,*" she said in a strong, commanding voice, though the horse continued to rear.

Just as she lifted the stick again, Isaac leaped over the fence and grabbed the stick from her. "What are you doing?"

She whirled around to him, those blue eyes flashing. "What do you think *you're* doing? Give me that."

Isaac held the stick away from her. "Not if you're going to be cruel."

"Cruel?" She pointed her chin toward the horse. "You consider that cruel?"

"I do."

"Then you don't know the first thing about training horses."

Isaac almost laughed, but seeing how angry she was, he quickly handed back the stick. "They respond better to positive reinforcement, you know. Just like people."

"No one asked you."

Surprised at her brashness, Isaac took a full step back. Was she always so loud and bold? Well, never mind—his business was with John Zook, and not some ornery woman using the man's ring to beat down a horse. Though knowing any animal was being mistreated caused his hands to clench into fists. Maybe after his meeting, he'd talk to her.

Looking her in the eyes, he tipped down the front of his straw hat. "You said John Zook is in the house?"

"*Jah,*" she replied, petting the horse's nose. "That way."

"*Danke,*" he said simply, then walked back to his buggy, giving Scout a few tender pats. "She's a lunatic," he couldn't help saying under his breath, though he immediately felt shamed for it. His parents hadn't raised him to be unkind. After all, he knew nothing about her.

And a woman like that? He never would.

He parked the buggy in front of the house and led Scout to the water trough. It was a fine house, plain whitewash with a big porch, two stories. Modest flower beds in the front. Just as he made it up the front steps, a tall man opened the screen door.

"Isaac King?" he said in a low voice. He had dark hair and an even darker beard, though there were evident flecks of gray along his temples.

"*Jah.*" Isaac felt momentarily intimidated by the large man with a striking presence. "And you're John Zook."

"Since the day I was born." The man grinned and stuck out his hand for Isaac to shake. The polite gesture made Isaac feel calm again. "Nice *gaul,*" he continued, walking toward Scout. "Arabian?"

"Good eye," Isaac replied.

"Racer?"

"*Jah.*" Isaac followed him to his horse.

"Criminal what they do to them, ain't so?"

"*Jah,*" Isaac repeated, grateful he'd found a kindred spirit in John Zook. Not enough of his Amish friends felt that way. Then he couldn't help thinking of the young woman he'd just met and that stick she insisted on using.

"Well," John Zook said as he gave Scout a friendly stroke, "I'm glad you were able to find the place."

"Oh, it wasn't difficult."

"And I see you met my daughter."

"Daughter?"

"Aye." John Zook pointed toward the woman with the dimple—the one Isaac had just scolded and then insulted to her face.

His stomach hit the ground like a rock.

Available now!

Love may be right around the corner in the heartwarming, sweet, and gentle Pine Creek series from Amity Hope.

Pine Creek COURTSHIP

After the death of her beloved father, Emma Ziegler just wants to keep her family's maple syrup farm afloat and raise her two young siblings. But when her meddling aunt's first choice of a husband for her turns out to be Emma's last choice—Pine Creek's most notorious bachelor—Emma grows desperate. Her aunt won't listen, no matter how much she tries to tell her the man in no way embodies the Amish values of faith or hard work.

Kind and industrious Levi Bontrager has always wanted to protect his best friend Emma, even after a secret from their youth left them growing apart. Which is why he steps in to claim that Emma cannot wed anyone else, as she is currently courting *him*. Yes, the small lie leaves him feeling guilty, but Levi's hope is that if he can win back the beautiful Emma's trust, he can also win over her heart...for real.

But can a courtship that began just for show ever blossom into a true romance that could save both their futures?

an imprint of Entangled Publishing LLC